For all truth-seekers who ask,
"Tell us a story."

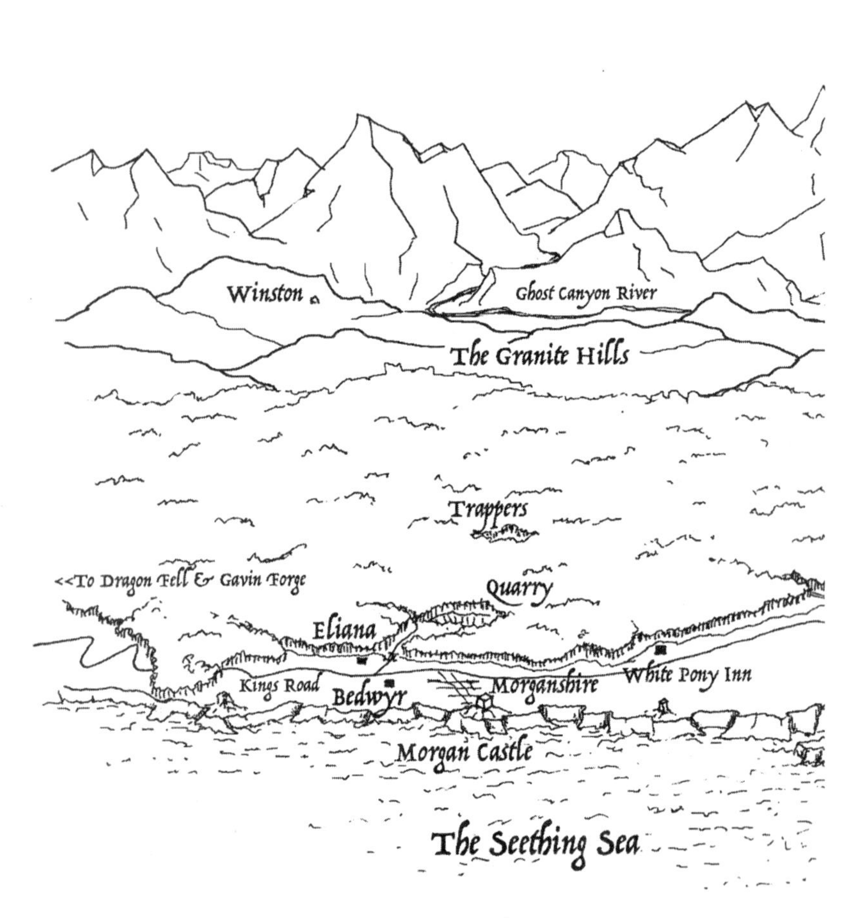
Winston
Ghost Canyon River
The Granite Hills
Trappers
<<To Dragon Fell & Gavin Forge
Quarry
Eliana
Kings Road
Bedwyr
Morganshire
White Pony Inn
Morgan Castle
The Seething Sea

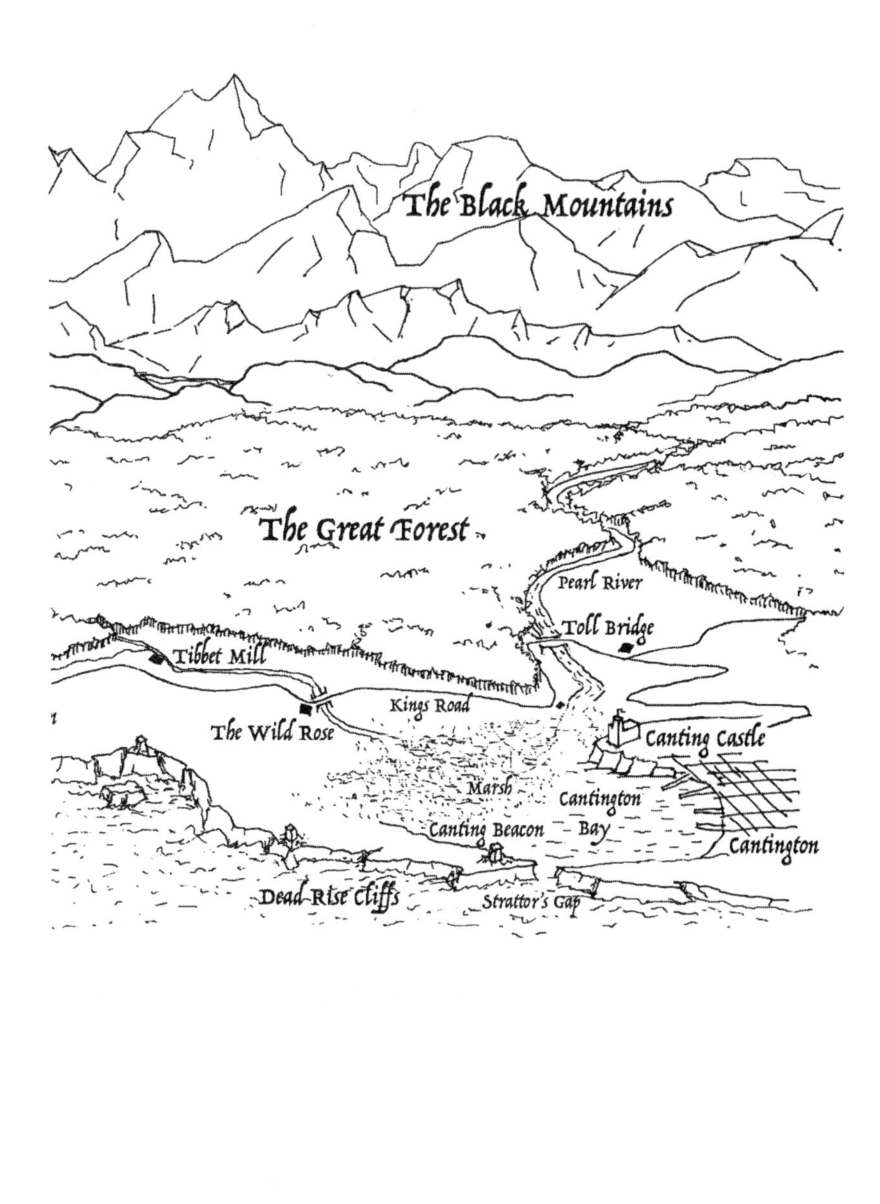
The Black Mountains
The Great Forest
Pearl River
Toll Bridge
Tibbet Mill
Kings Road
The Wild Rose
Canting Castle
Marsh
Cantington Bay
Canting Beacon
Cantington
Dead Rise Cliffs
Strattor's Gap

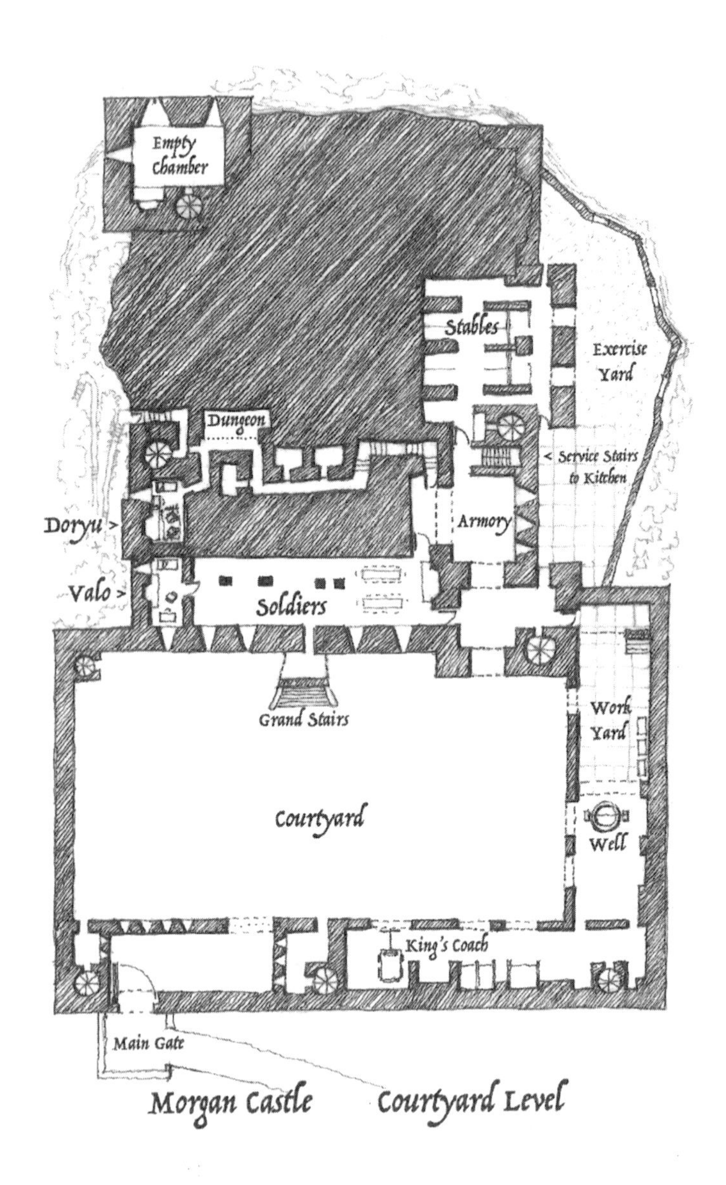
Empty chamber
Stables
Exercise Yard
Dungeon
< Service Stairs to Kitchen
Armory
Doryu >
Valo >
Soldiers
Grand Stairs
Work Yard
Courtyard
Well
King's Coach
Main Gate
Morgan Castle
Courtyard Level

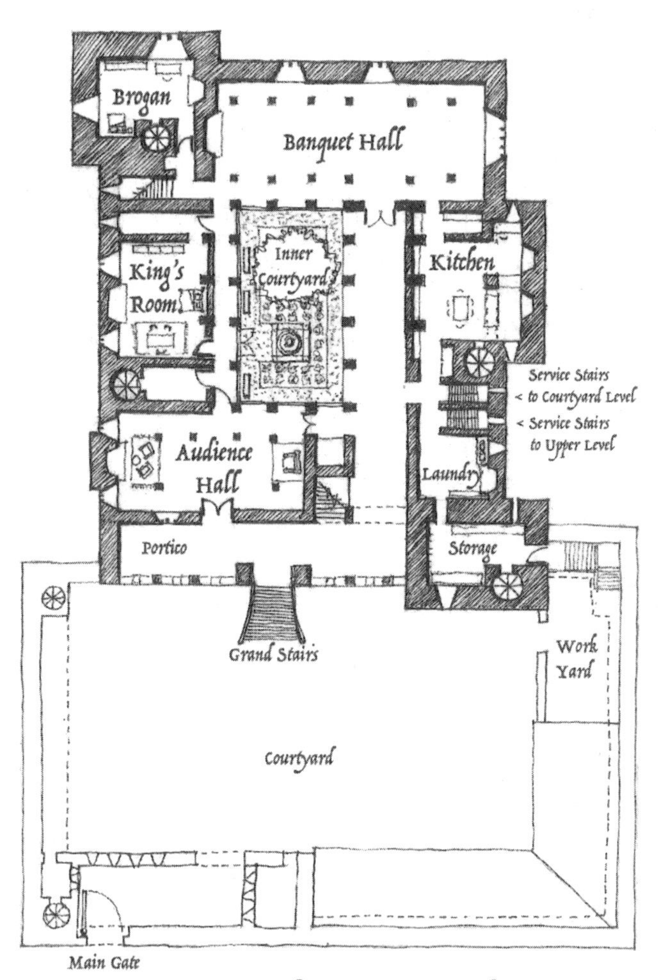

Morgan Castle Main Level

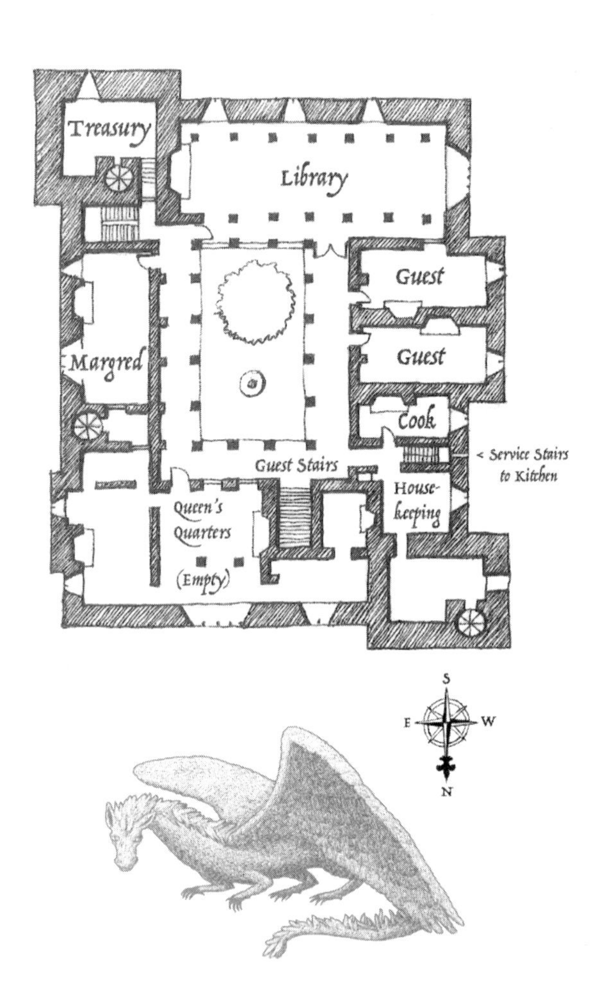

Morgan Castle Upper Level

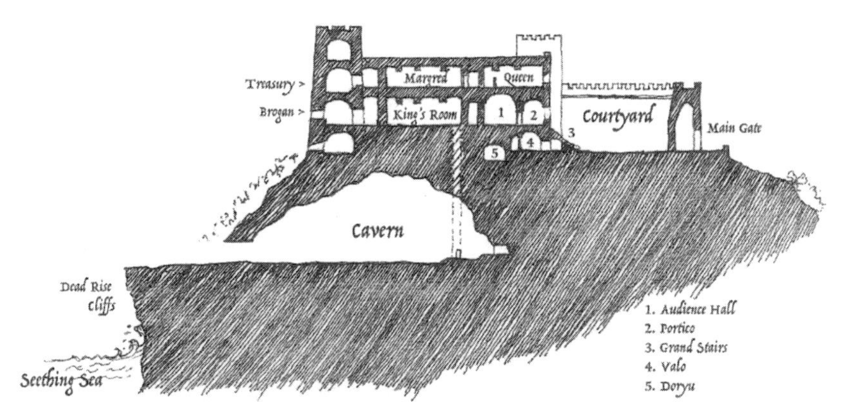

Morgan Castle Section looking West

Prologue: Hidden Things

Untold years ago, volcanoes unleashed their fury on this land. Liquid fire flowed from the north, heading toward the southern seas. Lava cooled into rock, glaciers formed, and winds raged. Mountains were worn down, valleys were carved, and mighty rivers were created by rushing water. Streams filled low plains to become lakes. Fish and frogs and snakes came to swim in the waters; birds opened flight among the trees that spread across the green hills. Red squirrels, owls, deer, wildcats, and badgers made the great oak forests their home.

And of course, dragons flew among the mountain peaks, caring for their young in caves inaccessible to the people who built their townships and villages below. As men grew bolder, having been nursed from childhood on fearful tales of the unknown, they used ropes, spears, and arrows with poisoned tips to hunt the enormous dragons, and finally they declared the terrible creatures wiped from the face of the earth. But sometimes, men declare things they only hope are true. And sometimes, things remain hidden, until they are once again found.

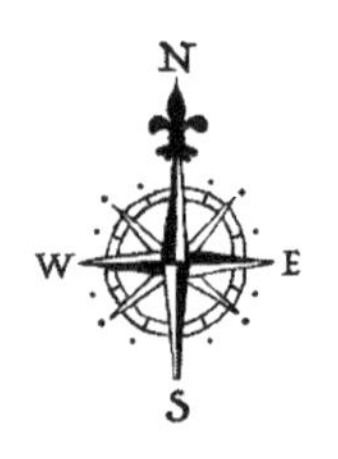

Chapter 1: Eliana

DAY ONE

It was a morning like every other, or so Eliana Fallond would have said had anyone asked. She got up early, her day as predictable as every other day. First this, then that. Always the same, like a song sung too many times.

I wish . . . she thought as she pulled her wool dress over her head, but the thought evaporated before it had a chance to become anything more. She had no idea what to wish for beyond a vague idea of change. She knew only her life of chores, taking care of her younger brothers, and trying once again to get her embroidery stitches to be as perfect as her older sister Alethia's. Too old for playing pretend, too young for an apprenticeship, and now she couldn't even explore the forest by herself.

For the past few months, Eliana and her siblings had

been forbidden to venture into the forest alone. Trappers had reported seeing strange blue torchlight in the woods one night that disappeared when they tried to find the source. Although Eliana's father maintained the trappers must have had too much ale, her mother's caution won out.

Eliana sighed, thinking that nothing exciting ever happened to her, like people often do before something completely unexpected happens.

As usual, her father had left for the stone quarries by the time Eliana tiptoed out of the sleeping room into the kitchen. Her first task was to wash and dry his porcelain teacup. Today, the pale morning light from the window filled the cup so the mysterious blue designs seemed alive, and Eliana smiled to think of her father holding it in his broad, rough hands. It had been his grandfather's, passed down to Cadoc, the lone survivor of his siblings.

After placing the cup on the shelf, Eliana picked up a cloth to clear his breakfast crumbs. Alethia's embroidery project lay on the table where she left it last night. In the middle, surrounded by delicately stitched flowers, were the words, "The best journey leads home." Eliana sniffed as she moved the hoop to Alethia's chair.

"The best journey leads to the *forest*," she whispered.

Egg basket in hand, Eliana opened the heavy, wooden back door and stepped outside. A low mist swirled around the squash vines and sunflowers in her mother's garden. On her way to the chicken coop, Eliana brushed her long, tangled brown hair back from her face and wrapped the ends of her scarf around her neck against the chill of late spring.

Her father, as clever with wood as he was with stone, had crafted the large coop so that it nestled against the hill behind their house in the countryside of Morganshire. Three of the walls were of oak, as smoothly planed as the furniture he built for his own home. The back wall of the coop was the rocky hillside itself, the nooks forming natural nesting places for the hens.

Eliana unlatched the door to the coop and breathed in the warm, grassy smell of the flock. "The girls," as they fondly called the hens, hurried through the door into the yard, a flood of fowl around Eliana's ankles, eager to begin their day of foraging.

"Good morning, sire," said Eliana, with a curtsy.

Henry the Fifth hopped down from his perch, regally strutting, chest held high. He was beautiful, this large gray and white bird, red comb draped dashingly over his head. Although fierce when protecting his flock, he was calm and gentle with Eliana, sometimes allowing her to run her hand along his back while he stood watch.

When her eyes adjusted to the dimness of the coop, she saw Opal still sitting on her nest. The chicken's fluffy white breast covered the eggs she had been sitting on for a week now.

"Opal, I hope you're getting enough to eat and drink."

Opal blinked a stoic reply.

"I'll bring you a treat in a little while," Eliana promised her favorite hen.

Eliana felt around beneath the layers of straw in the rock nooks and found eleven eggs, warm and heavy, with shells varying in color from a light tan to a deep brown. She nestled them in the egg basket and went to put them just outside the back door. Rowan and Sage often got up early too, shattering the early morning quiet, and today she didn't want to risk waking the twins by opening the door to put the eggs inside.

Eliana headed to the garden, which provided much of the family's food and her mother's medicinal plants. Father had built a fence of hip-high tree branches stuck in the ground to keep the chickens out. They loved the tender leaves of basil, oregano, and mint—and a ripe tomato hanging right at their eye level didn't stand a chance.

It was Eliana's job to pull any weeds that had sprung up overnight and to check the tomato plants for worms. As she worked, several of the chickens stood on the other side of the barrier, following her every move, always hopeful for a treat. They were rewarded when she found three squishy tomato worms and tossed them over the fence.

Eliana then filled a wooden bucket with water from the stream that meandered across the back corner of the yard. The rain had been sparse the past few weeks, so today, it took six bucketsful to saturate the garden. Her arms and shoulders ached, and her feet were wet and cold by the time she finished, but Eliana knew that losing any of the garden to weeds, insects, or drought meant less food for her family both now and during the fast-approaching winter months.

After giving Opal a few bites of an overripe tomato,

Eliana took off her scarf and sweater to use as a pillow as she lay down in the grass by the stream.

I'll check the sheep in a little while, after I rest a bit, she thought.

The mist was gone, and the morning sun warmed her face. Every now and then, a chicken came by to check for another tomato worm in her hand, but the chickens were such a part of her everyday life that she hardly noticed.

A slight breeze shifted the branches of the massive oak trees that grew just beyond the stream. The musical rippling of water dancing over rocks in the creek soothed her, and she closed her eyes, drifting somewhere between awake and dreaming about building an Eliana-sized boat to take her wherever the water flowed . . . until she heard a sound that stood apart from the usual morning symphony. Different. A rustling.

She sat up.

There it was again. Coming from the forest—much louder than that of a squirrel. Maybe a deer? No, it wouldn't make that much noise unless wounded.

Eliana scrambled to her feet. No wild cat had been seen in the forests around Morganshire in years. The activities of humans kept them far from the village and outlying private lands. Even so, she looked for the telltale tawny form now, though she felt certain a wild cat wouldn't be so loud. The dense summer canopy of the trees allowed only a diffuse light to drift to the forest floor, and shadows swayed, forming shapes that shifted with the breeze.

Eliana realized then that Henry had herded his flock back into the coop. He stood in the open doorway of the wooden structure, staring into the forest, which now seemed too close. Eliana scanned the dark green world under the trees for the glowing eyes of a wild cat crazy enough to come within a hundred feet of humans.

Wait. There.

A flash of vivid turquoise lit by a sliver of light descending through the trees, gone so fast Eliana was sure she had imagined it. But then there was a flicker of emerald green, so bright that nothing in nature could have produced it unless the King's jewels had mysteriously gone for a stroll in the woods behind her yard. Certainly no forest creature sported such amazing colors, and no torch had ever burned with colors like these.

Eliana took one step forward and then another. Even if the trappers did see strange blue lights, they wouldn't be dangerous, would they? Just a little closer and she would stop. In all her twelve years, the forest had never frightened her; why should it now? Her parents worried too much sometimes . . .

Eliana took another step. The rustling had stopped, but there, just beyond the tree line, she could see glints of turquoise and that amazing emerald green. She barely felt the chill of the stream as she waded through and up onto the wildflowers growing on the slender strip of land outlining the forest. Over the murmur of the stream, she heard her brothers pushing their way through the back door. Before the screeching of the door stopped, Eliana ran the last few yards to the first oak trees, stepped into the cool dimness of the forest, and found herself staring into the large, blue-green eyes of a dragon.

In the cottage, Eliana's mother Glenna finished dressing in the sleeping room and lifted the curtain to the kitchen. Tying her apron strings behind her, she saw that the egg basket wasn't sitting on the kitchen table where Eliana was meant to leave it. Frowning, she stepped out the back door and found the eggs on her gardening table.

Eleven eggs. Perfect. Seven for breakfast with porridge, she thought. *Two for Cadoc's lunch tomorrow, and two for Alethia to take to Bedwyr today.* Cradling the basket in her arms, she said a whispered prayer of thanks for the hens and for the eccentric Cartographer who had apprenticed Alethia for the mere cost of two eggs a day.

Bedwyr, the Cartographer, was slowly losing his eyesight and was convinced two freshly laid eggs a day would prevent further deterioration. He'd left Morgan Castle just last year to find solitude in the countryside while he completed his magnum opus, a grand map of the known world. Alethia helped him mix paints and record compass bearings, and each morning, she prepared his eggs and tea.

Glenna could hear Alethia stirring in the sleeping room and hoped she felt better this morning. Her eldest had developed a cough the past few days that hadn't responded to chamomile tea. Glenna pondered what remedy to try next while she stood at the back door and scanned the yard for the rest of her children. Rowan and Sage ran in figure eights in the middle of the yard, holding sticks aloft like swords and kicking dust that swirled and drifted into the garden.

"Boys, stop kicking! And go wash your feet off in the stream. Breakfast will be ready in a few minutes." Looking for Eliana, Glenna noticed that none of the chickens were out, and Henry the Fifth was standing in the open door of the coop. He stared toward the boys who were now splashing in the stream, soaking their clothes and hair in the process.

Glenna wondered why the rooster would herd his flock into the coop just because the boys were outside. Henry the Fifth and the chickens were well-accustomed to the twins' shenanigans and usually paid them no mind. Glenna set the egg basket back on the gardening table and walked to the coop.

"Eliana?" she called, stooping to peer inside.

Henry cocked his head as she stepped around him but didn't move from his post. The hens were piled on top of each other on the floor of the coop, making *ber ber ber* noises of distress. Opal, still sitting on her nest, nudged an egg farther under her breast. Glenna turned to look for a hawk circling or a fox in the underbrush. The soil in the garden was damp, and the water bucket was back where it belonged.

"Eliana!" she called, before turning back to her sons. "Boys, hush." Glenna took a step toward the stream. She saw

Eliana's sweater and scarf lying on the ground and stooped to grab them.

"Eliana!"

The boys stopped their cavorting and turned to stare at their mother. "What's wrong?" asked Rowan. He reached to take his brother's hand. "Where's Eliana?"

"I don't know," she said. "Go check the sheep pasture. Maybe she went to check on the new lamb." Glenna watched the twins run to do as she'd instructed.

At least the boys are occupied, she thought, turning back to the stream and the wall of trees beyond. She took a step toward the stream. She felt sure Eliana—her daring and sometimes impetuous daughter—had crossed here and gone into the woods despite her strict orders not to go alone.

In the forest, Eliana stood as still as her pounding heart would allow. She was so close to the dragon—for indeed it *was* a dragon—that she could see the slow blink of its eyes as the lids moved up and then down again. Somehow, she was able to take in the fact that the creature was much smaller than the old stories portrayed. Its scaly tail and feathered wings were wrapped around its body so it looked to be only about as big as a draft horse.

In the old stories, the last dragons were said to have been killed before her parents were born. But Eliana could feel this one's warm breath moving rapidly in and out of the tear-shaped nostrils on either side of its blocky snout. They were breathing in unison, she and this impossible dragon.

"You're afraid, too," she whispered.

The creature drew back, crouching lower on its powerful haunches; its shimmery turquoise and green scales and feathered wings quivered as it began to move away from her, deeper into the forest.

"Please don't go," Eliana said, using the soft, cooing voice she used to soothe Opal when the hen was frightened. "I won't hurt you."

The dragon stopped, its pointed ears twitching.

"My name is Eliana. What's your name?"

The sound the dragon made then reminded her of the twins when they tried to talk with their mouths full of porridge.

What was I thinking? she wondered. *Of course it can't understand me.* But something—the way the dragon looked at her so intently—made her try again.

"El-i-ana . . . Eliana. My name is. . ." She placed her hand on her chest. "Eliana."

"Umm-mmm-mm-um," the dragon repeated, sort of.

"You can understand me!" Eliana cried but clamped her hand over her mouth at the sight of the dragon crouching even lower as it seemed to be trying to cover its ears with its front legs.

"You can understand me," she repeated, softer this time.

It nodded its huge head and what looked like a smile curled the corners of its mouth. Eliana tried not to focus on the square, white teeth that were now clearly visible.

"What's your name?" she asked, careful to move her hand slowly as she pointed at the dragon.

"Umm-mmm," it replied, laying a taloned claw on its own chest. Except for the missing syllables, it sounded almost the same as when it had tried to say her name.

She tried again. "What's your name?"

Again, the mumbled reply.

"Soooo, you can understand me . . ."

The dragon nodded vigorously.

"But I can't understand you," said Eliana.

The dragon looked almost as disappointed as she felt.

Eliana sank to sit on the soft, green moss of the forest floor. *A dragon?* She shook her head. Despite what she'd always heard, this beautiful creature was very much alive.

The dragon stretched its neck so its eyes were once again staring into her own. Slender shafts of light fell on the dragon's scales and on its feathered wings pressed against his sides. The colors were like nothing she had ever seen before, seeming to gather sunlight to create shades unknown in nature. Without a thought about what she was doing, she reached out her hand and laid it on the creature's neck.

"Winston. My name is Winston," said the dragon.

Eliana simultaneously gasped and pulled her hand away. Wisps of colors—the same as those of his glittering scales—streamed between her hand and the dragon. Within seconds, the wisps faded and disappeared.

"Your name is Winston?" she breathed.

The sizable head nodded, and the smile returned.

"How . . . ?" Eliana looked at the palm of her hand.

Winston moved slightly so his neck was only inches away. She gently placed her hand on his scales again.

"It's when you touch my neck that you can understand me, Eliana."

Winston was right: when he'd tried to talk before she touched him, she couldn't understand him at all. It reminded her of the time she'd seen a traveler in the village who spoke what her mother had said was a language from another land. The sound of his speech had been fascinating, like music with high notes and low notes woven together. She could *hear* the man but had no idea what he was saying.

Now, with her hand on the dragon, it was as if Eliana had learned another language. Winston's language. And her mind whirled with all the questions she wanted to ask him.

"Eliana!" Glenna's piercing call reached both Eliana and Winston. Eliana's hand jerked back from the dragon, and once again, colorful wisps streaked into the air.

"I have to go," she whispered.

Winston had flattened himself as much as he could, his head and stomach pressed against the moss, and his eyes closed so tightly they almost disappeared.

"Don't worry," said Eliana, as she got to her feet. "I won't tell anyone."

"Eliana!"

Eliana cringed at the frustration mixed with fear she

could hear in her mother's voice. "I'll come back tomorrow," she said to the cowering dragon.

I have to come back tomorrow, she thought. *A dragon. A real live dragon!* But he'd seemed so afraid at first. She had to find out why.

When she burst from between the gigantic forest trees, Eliana saw her mother scanning her from head to toe. She knew Glenna was looking for signs of blood, broken bones, a rabid animal chasing her, burns from a rogue torch. Seeing that she was unscathed, Glenna's hands went to her hips. Eliana splashed across the stream and up into the yard. Her mother's lips were pressed into a thin line, and her brow was as deeply furrowed as a plowed field.

"Mother, I . . ." But Eliana knew she couldn't tell her mother what had happened. She'd promised Winston, and she wanted to keep him to herself, just for now. There was no harm in that, in waiting a day or so, just until she had a chance to learn more about him. She wiped her hands on her skirt and slowly walked to where her mother stood. Eliana stopped a few feet from her and stared down at her wet shoes.

"Eliana." Glenna's voice was tight with exasperation. "What were you . . . *why* were you in the forest? Alone? You *know* what your father and I said."

"I'm sorry, Mother."

Glenna put her hands on her daughter's shoulders and gave them a gentle shake. "You know you aren't supposed to cross the stream alone! Not now. What if the boys had followed you? You could've all been . . ." Her words trailed off, as if she were afraid to say what came next. "What were you thinking?"

"I . . ." Eliana hesitated. "I thought I saw a horse. A horse just there on the other side of those trees." Eliana gestured to a spot several yards from where she thought Winston might still be.

"A horse?" Glenna shook her head. "That's ridiculous! What would a horse be doing loose in the forest?" She paused, staring at her daughter. "Go on inside and heat the porridge."

As her daughter hurried to the back door, Glenna clasped her arms across her chest and stared for several moments at the place in the forest where Eliana had pointed. Nothing but dark green shadows stared back at her. As she turned to go back inside, she vowed to talk to Eliana later. To her knowledge, her daughter had never deliberately deceived her before, but she could feel that what Eliana had told her hadn't been the truth.

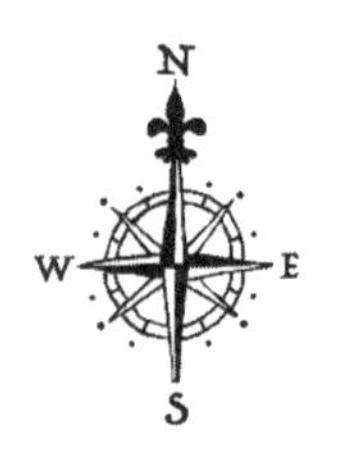

Chapter 2: Winston

DAY ONE

After Eliana ran back across the stream, Winston lay for a long while, pressed against the forest floor, sure he was at least somewhat camouflaged by the velvety moss. Even with his head flat on the ground, he could see between two huge oaks into a treeless clearing. *Eliana's clearing.* He had seen her run to someone who must have been her mother. Winston could tell by the way she pulled Eliana to her and the following sharpness of her words. Warm like a spring rain, then ferocious as a lightning strike.

Maybe humans and dragons weren't so different after all.

Eliana and her mother disappeared into a structure made of stone and tree branches. A gray and white bird stood in Eliana's clearing, staring directly at the place where he lay. Its coloring and its watchfulness reminded Winston of his father. The bird remained motionless for several minutes before finally moving to the other side of the clearing, followed by a flock of other, smaller birds.

Winston watched the flock roam the yard, pecking at insects, grass, and sometimes, each other. He knew if he moved, the alert gray one would sound the alarm once more, and Winston didn't want to frighten them again.

I'll wait here a little while longer, until they move farther away, he thought.

The scales on his neck rippled where Eliana had touched him. Wisps of color from her hand still drifted and sighed in the air. She hadn't been at all dangerous, *and* she'd understood him. Two sparkling miracles that hung in the air along with the wisps. *And* she said she would come back tomorrow. Three miracles!

All the questions Winston wanted to ask Eliana swirled in his mind. A shaft of sunlight fell across his head. The warmth of it was soothing, and soon, his heart rate slowed as he slept in the gloriously soft moss.

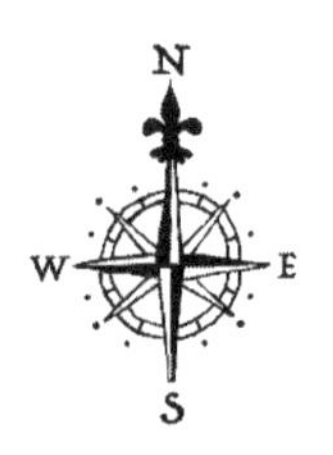

Chapter 3: Eliana

DAY ONE

Eliana stood in front of the huge stone and slate fireplace her father had built, stirring the porridge. The oats had soaked with water overnight, and now she added a ladle of creamy sheep's milk to the pot. Even though there were only glowing embers from last night's fire, the heat generated by her father's clever design kept the porridge bubbling. Rowan and Sage were in their favorite spot under the kitchen table, laughing and kicking at each other. Dust and bits of grass swirled in the sunlight streaming from the front door, which of course the twins had left wide open when they'd come back from the pasture.

Eliana's cheeks burned, both from the steaming porridge and from the shame of lying to her mother. A horse? What had made her say she thought she'd seen a horse? She stared at the palm of her left hand, the one that had touched Winston's smooth, warm scales. The one that had allowed her to understand him and still held fading remnants of his colors. Winston . . . so much smaller than the dragons in the stories she'd been told since she was young. Eliana smiled and put her hand to her cheek.

Behind her, Glenna put the egg basket on the table.

"Eliana, we need to talk about . . ." her mother began but trailed off, distracted.

Uh oh, thought Eliana. She hunched her shoulders and kept stirring, wiping her left hand on her skirt.

"Where's Alethia?" asked Glenna.

At the alarm Eliana heard in her mother's voice, she stopped stirring.

"She should have been up and dressed by now. She's going to be late for her apprenticeship." Glenna pulled back the curtain to the sleeping area.

In the dim light, Eliana could see that Alethia was back in the bed they shared and was almost buried by both her own and Eliana's quilts.

"Oh no," Glenna whispered as she began pulling off the heavy blankets.

Alethia tried to hold them back but was too weak and turned away, curling her long, slender arms, legs, and torso into a tight ball. Glenna leaned to put her cheek on her eldest daughter's forehead.

"She's burning with fever," said Glenna.

Without the covers, Alethia shivered and grabbed for the quilts again.

"No, Alethia. We need to cool you down a little. I'll get you some water." Glenna hurried back to the kitchen.

"Eliana, put water on to boil. Sage and Rowan, get me two sprigs of mint and thyme from the garden."

The twins scrambled from under the table and out the back door. Eliana hung another pot on the bar above the fire and filled it with a pitcher of water.

None of the children questioned their mother; this was Glenna as Healer. Recognized in the region for knowing what remedies to use for which ailments, she was calm and controlled even when someone close to her was injured or sick. Eliana watched her mother take two mugs off the shelf. She filled one with cool water and left the other on the table.

"Eliana, get the mortar and pestle down. When the boys come back with the herbs, wash a few leaves of each for tea."

As Glenna took the water into the sleeping room, Eliana heard her sister coughing. She pulled a chair over to the shelves so she could reach the stone bowl and rounded grinder, which had belonged to her grandfather. After setting them on the table, Eliana climbed back up to get the jar of honey. She knew her mother would want it for the mint and thyme tea she would make for Alethia. By the time she climbed down again, the boys had returned with the herbs.

"Is Alethia going to be all right?" Sage asked the question, but Eliana could see worry in the faces of both brothers.

"She'll be fine. Mother is the best Healer in the region.

And remember, a fever is the body's way of taking care of itself." Eliana rinsed the herbs in a bowl of water and put them on a clean cloth. She smiled at the boys but couldn't help remembering her friend Mary. The girl's father had come late one night, his face etched with worry for his daughter who was ill. Even though Glenna had gathered her remedies and run to the wagon in mere minutes, even though Mary's father had driven the mule to a lather, by the time they got to their house, Mary had died.

"Alethia will be fine," Eliana repeated, as much for herself as for her brothers. "Sit down. The porridge is done, and I'll fry the eggs." She spooned some lard into the skillet and when it began to sizzle, cracked four eggs into the center.

As the egg whites turned opaque, Glenna walked back into the kitchen and rested her hand on Eliana's shoulder before grinding herbs with the mortar and pestle. Stone grated against stone. Sharp scents of mint and thyme swirled around Eliana, and thoughts of Winston were hidden away beneath the weight of Alethia's illness.

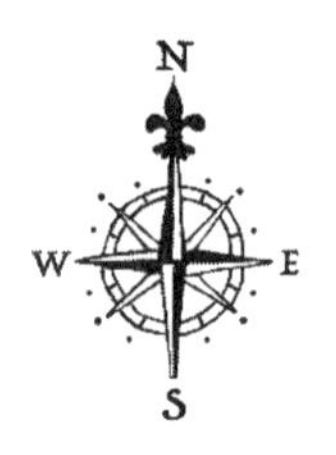

Chapter 4: Winston

DAY ONE

Winston knew there was something about the light . . . the moss in the clearing was so soft and comfortable, and his head was still filled with fuzzy dreams, but there was something about the light. In an instant, his eyelids snapped down, and he was wide awake. The shafts of sunlight that found their way between the heavy foliage of the trees had shifted, and he knew he'd slept too long. Lifting his head slowly, he could still see the gray and white bird and his flock foraging in Eliana's yard. But they had all moved to the far side of the staked garden, seemingly oblivious to the dragon nearby.

Winston backed out of the clearing and into the forest. His muscular haunches swayed side to side as he moved between the trees, using his front legs to brace against the spongy forest floor. His wings lay smoothly along his back so as not to impede his progress. After several minutes of this awkward maneuvering, hampered at times by his tail and the protruding roots of oak trees, Winston managed to get himself deep enough into the forest that the watchful rooster could neither hear nor see him. The sun-filled meadow he found there was just large enough to contain a dragon his size.

Winston pushed himself up on his hind legs and raised his head to its full height. Although seeming to be the size of a horse lying down, when he stood on his back legs, he was much taller than even a red deer reaching for leaves high in a tree. Tilting his head back, he closed his eyes and lifted his wing blades to unfurl the massive wings that had been tucked back for so long. He sighed a warm and happy sigh as he extended them their full span, tip to tip more than three times that of a condor. His turquoise and emerald feathers caught the sunlight and threw it back into the air like jewels whirling around the clearing.

This Winston, this unfurled and stretched out Winston, was how he felt his best. Well, *almost* his best. Bending his back legs as close to the ground as possible, Winston thrust against the forest floor, pushed against the air with his wings, and was aloft. He rose gracefully up and out of the meadow and, with both wonder and apprehension, flew across the treetops toward home.

Flying just above the forest meant it took Winston longer to get home than if he had been able to catch the warm updrafts and ride high above the trees. But that was dangerous—he might be seen—so it took him until the sun was well on its way to the west to cover the distance to the craggy mountain range on the far side of the forest. Heart pounding now with more than exertion alone, he glided down to land beside his mother on the smooth ledge of rock in front of their cave. Of course she was there, likely scanning the skies for him.

"Winston! Where have you *been*?"

Her eyes—deep amethyst flecked with sapphire—were just as Winston had feared: filled with worry and frustration. Worry because of his long absence, frustration because of how he'd worried her. Yet here he was, safe and sound. It certainly didn't feel like the right time to tell her about Eliana.

"I stopped . . . to take a rest, and . . . I fell asleep. The sun was so warm and . . ." Winston stopped as Nerys shook her head. Wisps of steam swam from her nostrils, heating the air around them.

"Come here, Winston."

He went to her, and she laid her head across his neck, pulling him closer until he was against her chest. The sound of her giant heart beating filled his head. He closed his eyes and whispered, "I'm so sorry, Mother. I didn't think . . ."

"I know, son. But you *must* think. We can't afford for you to be young and carefree anymore. It is time for you to grow up, to learn . . . " She paused and took a deep breath. "Even this far from humans, we must always be on guard,

Winston. Always! Especially now, with your father gone."

Winston pulled back and stared up at her. *Gone.* She'd said gone. "But you said he would come back. You promised . . ."

Winston's father, Raiden, had been missing since the last full moon. Winston remembered waking early one morning, cold and shivering on the huge bed of moss he shared with his parents. The chill of winter had lingered even in mid-spring. His mother, who usually kept him close and warm at night, stood at the mouth of the cave, the pale gray sky surrounding her silhouette. Still half-asleep, Winston saw her turning her immense head from side to side, searching the skies.

"Mother . . ." he said, confused. He was accustomed to waking sometimes to see his father standing just where she was standing, doing just what she was doing. But that day, the light in the cave was enough to show him the bed was empty. His father wasn't there, either.

"Mother!" he said, loud enough that she heard him.

"Go back to sleep, Winston. It's early. Everything's fine." But she stayed by the mouth of the cave, and Winston grew colder still, with both the chill of the cave and worry.

In all thirty springs of his young life, he'd awakened to his mother's warmth and his father's rumbling snores. He loved those moments just as the sky began to lighten. He'd lie, unmoving, and think about the day ahead. He'd imagine the dives and twirls he might perform in the vast canyon on the other side of their hills or the cool streams they might find. Before he knew it, he would wake again to bright sunlight outside the mouth of the cave and his parents softly talking together in the vaulted cavern just inside.

But that day, there was no warmth, no snoring, and nothing was fine. After a full day and another night of watching, Nerys left the mouth of the cave to return where Winston lay awake, confused and hungry.

She lay down and curled herself around him. "Your father left late in the night, the night before last. He heard something in the forest, a sound he'd only heard once before. He went to the mouth of the cave and saw, down in the forest at the foot of the mountain, lights. Strange lights. He woke me to say he was going to glide down, while it was still dark, to see what they were. He said with the cloud covering the full moon, he wouldn't be seen. He said he'd be back in a few minutes . . ."

Winston trembled, and Nerys pulled him closer. "Your father is so powerful, Winston, both in strength and knowledge of the world. He knows how to remain unseen, how to fly mere feet above the ground or so high that the eagles can't see him. He can find water when no one else can, and he can survive on the most meager of sustenance. But the most important thing . . ." Nerys paused to nuzzle Winston's head. "The most important thing is that he loves us. He loves us so much, he *will* come back to us. He will find a way."

But still, many days later, Raiden had not returned. Nerys spent most of every day on their ledge, her enormous tail twitching occasionally so Winston had to be on alert to avoid getting knocked onto the hillside below. She left only to gather benesaunus from the ancient metamorphic mountains on the far side of the canyon behind their home.

The greenish-gray substance—a delicious cross between fungus and vegetable—kept their muscles strong, their eyes bright, and their feathers gleaming. Winston especially loved it gently steamed for a few minutes by one of his parents. Now, he just ate it dry from the supply in the far reaches of the cave, not bothering to steam it for himself.

Nerys only let him fly for short periods at a time, watching from her perch on the ledge. As spacious as it was, the cave only allowed him the space to stretch his wings and turn in circles, his feet shuffling on the smooth floor. He had begun to sleep more, even during the day, dreaming of soaring through the air with his father.

But then, that very morning, just as Eliana had been drying her father's unusual teacup, Winston's mother had awakened him with what looked amazingly like a smile.

"Get up, Winston! The sun is rising, and there is a wonderful cloud cover and a nice cool breeze. It's a good morning for a flyout!"

Winston was up in a flash of green and turquoise. "A flyout? Really? I can go?"

"Yes, a *short* flyout."

A flyout was what Winston and his parents called

Winston's solo forays over the forest. From their ledge, the tops of the giant oak trees stretched as far as they could see, to the west, east, and south. Birch, holly, and hazel trees were interspersed here and there, but the oaks dwarfed them all in size and number. From the age of twenty trips around the sun, Winston had been allowed flyouts, time to skim above the trees on his own. As it was essential that he remain unseen, his parents had always chosen days when the sun wouldn't cast a dragon's shadow across the treetops.

As he'd gotten older, Winston had ventured farther and farther from the cave. Although he loved flying with his parents in the vast river canyon behind their hills, he reveled in the freedom during flyouts. They made him feel strong and grown up, both physically and mentally. Without his parents hovering nearby, he could decide when to do a long, slow turn to the east, when to drop and skim the tops of the trees, and when to head back to the ledge.

Before his father disappeared, Winston had been allowed longer and longer flyouts. These had stopped since then, adding to Winston's misery. But that morning his mother said he could go!

Nerys insisted he eat a quick breakfast, during which she reminded him of the flyout rules, which he knew by heart:

1. Don't fly too far above the trees; someone in the hills might see you.
2. Don't fly between the sun and the trees; someone might see your shadow on a branch or even on the ground in a clearing.

Winston knew the "someone" was a human. She meant

a *human* might see him. And humans were to be avoided at all costs.

"And," Nerys added, "don't be gone long."

Winston promised, then scrambled out of the cave and onto the ledge as fast as his powerful back legs would take him, and, with an exuberant unfurling of wings, he plummeted off the ledge, dropping, dropping, pulling up in a smooth arc just above the beautiful green treetops.

He really had meant to be gone only a little while. He'd promised. But after all the weeks confined to the cave, the air moving over and through his feathers was like a cool stream on a scorching day. He felt the power in his wings as he turned in looping circles above the forest. Swooping lower, he startled flocks of black birds, which erupted from the treetops, scolding him with their *chacker chacker chacker* call.

Flying farther south, the thin scales of Winston's underbelly skimmed warmer pockets of air. The farther south he flew, the warmer the air became, as if the sun were beneath him. He flew on, soaring on increasingly warmer currents until, between one wingbeat and the next, he realized he'd almost reached the southernmost edges of the forest, farther than he'd ever been before and near the border between the forest and the beginning of human habitation. Making matters worse, a shadow formed beneath him, a gray replica of himself that came and went as the cloud cover thinned.

Terrified he might be seen, Winston drew his wings back against his body and dropped into a cramped space, not even quite a clearing, his fall only somewhat muffled by the dark green moss on which he landed. He pulled his back and front legs under him, wrapped his tail around himself, and tried to be as inconspicuous as possible.

Opening his eyes just a crack, Winston saw between two tree trunks: wildflowers growing beside a stream, a strange cave-like thing against a hill, a clearing with plants growing in the middle with sticks all around them, and another cave-like structure—this one much larger—at the far side of the clearing. He saw unusual birds strutting around, one that reminded him in a strange way of his father.

Winston raised his head to get a better look and, to his horror, saw something rise up just beyond the stream. Larger than the birds, with curly brown fur on its head, thin front legs, no wings. It rose up even more, slowly standing on long, spindly back legs, and the young dragon's panic-stricken mind finally caught up with the fact that it must be a human. A human who then splashed across the stream, ran through the wildflowers, and moved between the trees. He had just a brief moment to think the human was much smaller than he'd ever imagined, before he found himself looking directly into its startled brown eyes.

After meeting Eliana (and discovering she was not at all how he'd always heard humans could be), after sleeping way too long in the warm softness of the moss on the forest floor, after flying back to the cave, and after seeing the fear and disappointment in his mother's eyes and hearing her say "gone" in reference to his father, Winston crept to the back of the cave. He knew he should have told his mother about Eliana, but he didn't want to worry her more than he already had. How could he explain to his mother about the human who had put her delicate hand on his neck and had somehow been able to understand him? And that he could understand her when she spoke aloud? Would she believe him that humans weren't dangerous after all?

Winston wrapped his tail around his body, closed his eyes, and fell into a deep sleep. He dreamed about flying around and around in circles above an endless forest lit from beneath with glowing balls of fire that disappeared as soon as he drew close.

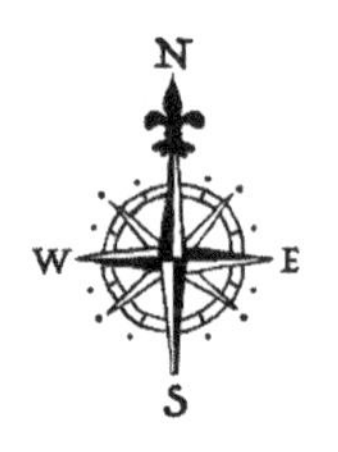

Chapter 5: Eliana

DAY ONE

It was Sage who remembered the Cartographer's eggs. As Eliana was wiping out the skillet and rinsing the porridge bowls, her brother appeared beside her, holding two brown eggs.

"What about Bedwyr's eggs?" Sage's pale face was sprinkled with dozens of freckles and smudged with dirt from the yard, his forehead creased with concern. "He needs his eggs so he can see."

Eliana reached down to gently massage the wrinkles between his eyes with her thumb. Although ready to follow his twin in whatever escapades Rowan concocted, Sage was the one who noticed when their sword fights were bothering Henry the Fifth, when their yelling and exuberant laughter were giving their mother a headache, when their father was more tired than usual and less apt to put up with their antics. Lately, Eliana had noticed that the worry lines on her brother's face were becoming more prominent, too deep for a seven-year-old boy.

"You're right, Sage," Eliana said. "Let's pack up his basket. We can take it to Bedwyr."

"What about Rowan? Can he come, too?"

"Of course! Go tell him . . . and wash your faces!"

She tiptoed into the sleeping room, where her mother was laying a damp cloth on Alethia's forehead. The water and tea mugs were sitting empty on the floor, and the severity of Alethia's cough had lessened.

"More tea?" whispered Eliana.

"Not just yet," said Glenna. "She's gone back to sleep."

"The boys and I will take Bedwyr's basket to him," Eliana said.

Glenna nodded absently.

Back in the kitchen, Eliana put a clean cloth in the bottom of the round, woven basket they all thought of as Bedwyr's. Sage gently laid the two eggs in the bottom and tucked the edges of the cloth around them.

These were, to their family, the most valuable of eggs. Apprenticeships were rare and costly. Families paid dearly to afford their children the opportunity to learn a skilled craft from a master. Although their father's work and their land and animals provided enough to sustain their family, there was little left over that could translate into coin. Even when their mother provided remedies for neighbors, they were only able to pay in trade—a few yards of cloth, a quart of milk, oil for the lamps. When Alethia had turned fourteen in February, no one had even discussed the possibility of an apprenticeship.

When Bedwyr moved into the abandoned farmstead just up the road—with his sculpted, silver beard and trunks of miniature bowls, brushes, rolled-up charts, and musty books—families in the area with children of apprentice age began to assess their resources. Even this far out in the countryside, people knew of Bedwyr the Cartographer. They knew of his mysterious arrival in Morganshire (some said from beyond the Black Mountains), his work for King Halwyn, and the maps Bedwyr had painted to guide the expeditions of soldiers and merchants. Word of his magnum opus—his current grand project—spread, as did knowledge of his failing eyesight.

One evening, shortly after Bedwyr's arrival to the countryside, a pounding on the Fallonds' front door startled the family. When Eliana's father flung open the still-vibrating door, they were all stunned to see the bear-sized Cartographer standing on the doorstep.

"Sorry to disturb! Sorry to disturb!" he said, his voice reverberating like a clap of thunder.

Cadoc stepped aside to invite him in, while Glenna hurried to hang the kettle over the fire.

"You have a child of apprenticeship age," Bedwyr said, gesturing with his walking stick toward Alethia. "And you have the best chickens in the countryside." His massive mustache covered most of his mouth, but his deep brown eyes crinkled with pleasure at his pronouncements. He nodded to the family.

They nodded back because it was the polite thing to do, not because they had any idea what Alethia and eggs had to do with each other. Fortunately, at that moment, the water began to boil. As they all sat around the table sipping herbal tea, Bedwyr explained about his eyesight, the failure of glass spectacles or the King's healers to help, and his own research on the benefits of eggs, which had led him to their door.

"Everyone speaks highly of your daughter, Alethia. She would be of great assistance to me in my work, and I can teach her as much as I can before I go completely blind. I just need two of your magnificent eggs every day."

For several moments, no one spoke. Eliana watched the puzzlement on her parents' faces turn from incredulity to joy. Father stood and reached his hand across the table to shake the Cartographer's gigantic hand.

And so the agreement had been reached, and Alethia started her apprenticeship the very next week. She told Eliana that at first, she'd been intimidated by Bedwyr. He seemed to fill his workshop with his powerful sloping shoulders, his deep voice, and his massive hands. But she soon grew accustomed to his bulk and could move deftly around him as he called for more azure blue or the little pot of jet-black ink. She said his true nature could be seen in the way he gently unrolled a parchment, muddled delicate flower petals in his mortar, and held the tiny brushes in his broad hand.

He was kind and patient as he taught her about his craft, how to estimate distances on the land to depict them accurately on paper. She spoke in amazement about how Bedwyr was translating their southern world onto a corner of his grand map—land and sea created from the perspective of the clouds.

During dinnertime, Eliana would smile to see her sister sitting, unused spoon in her hand, staring up at the corner of the rafters. When Cadoc would gently interrupt her reverie with a question about her work, she would wave her spoon around, droplets of soup flying everywhere, and talk about the wondrous colors she and Bedwyr had concocted that day to designate water, land, and mountains.

Even now, as her mother placed yet another cool cloth on her fevered forehead, Alethia murmured about the vast map Bedwyr was creating one beautiful inch at a time, amazing colors flowing across creamy paper.

With Sage carrying Bedwyr's basket, Eliana and her brothers headed down the pathway in front of the house. Their father had laid pieces of rough slate in a zigzag pattern along the path, which helped to keep their boots dry when the rains made muddy streams in the front yard. Now, hardy spring wildflowers grew in the dry dirt between the stones, colorful and happy in the slight breeze. Rowan ran ahead, leaping from stone to stone, while Eliana and Sage followed behind, mindful of the fragile eggs.

"Bedwyr must be worried about Alethia and his eggs," said Sage.

Eliana silently agreed as she saw how high the sun was in its arching path from east to west across the southern sky. Bedwyr was accustomed to having his eggs for breakfast, but now it was nearer to noon.

"We can fix them for his lunch today. With extra butter as a special treat," said Eliana, as she squeezed her brother's hand.

To their left, the family's sheep grazed beyond a rough wooden fence, woolen coats short after their late spring shearing the week before. They barely lifted their heads as the children passed, used to their scents and sounds. The new lamb—still teetering on spindly legs—peered at them from between her mother's legs. Owen the mule brayed a brief hello but went right back to rubbing his head against a stunted apple tree.

A few minutes later, Eliana and Sage caught up to Rowan, who was waiting for them at Kings Road. Eliana grabbed Rowan's hand as they turned east toward Bedwyr's house. Glancing over her shoulder, Eliana could see the road winding its way to the west, toward Gavon Forge. Beyond that, farther to the west, were Dragon Downs and Dragon Fell. Did Winston live in the fell? High on a rocky hill? She'd never been as far as the forge, but her father had promised he would take her the next time he went. *When would that be? Not soon enough*, she thought.

"Eliana, why are we stopping?" Rowan tugged on her

hand, bringing her back to their present task.

"I'm sorry, Rowan. I was just... thinking," she said, turning to walk east once again.

Although grand in name, Kings Road was composed of packed dirt with stones scattered here and there. The occasional wagons had worn deep ruts during the winter rains, and a child could twist an ankle in one if he were careless. Eliana kept the trio off to the far, less-rutted side of the road where it bordered the length of the Fallonds' five acres.

The precious land had belonged to their mother's father, who'd been a doctor in Morganshire when Glenna was a child. He'd been granted the land, a long and narrow parcel between the forest and the road, as payment for saving the life of a wealthy merchant. When Glenna's father died, he gave the land to her. With a stream that meandered the length of the parcel, fertile soil for their garden, land for the chickens and sheep, as well as Cadoc's job as a slate thacker in the quarry, the family was blessed with plenty.

The sun on Eliana's head was warm, and a slight breeze lifted curly strands of hair off her shoulders. Rowan had stopped pulling on her hand as they walked along the road. No wagons, horses, or mules passed by. Bees buzzed in the wildflowers and lavender on the side of the road. Eliana broke off a few sprigs of rosemary growing among the rocks that marked the eastern corner of their land. Its clean, green smell filled the air; a few snips would go well with Bedwyr's eggs. They passed Quarry Road on the left, narrow and cool under the shade of overhanging oaks.

Eliana drew a quick breath as the dark green tunnel of trees brought back the memory of finding Winston in the forest clearing. Sage glanced up at her, but she shook her head and smiled at him.

"Almost there!" she sang out, although they still had almost a mile to go.

Sage went back to watching his feet and Bedwyr's basket.

Winston. The unreal colors of his feathers and scales, like she imagined jewels to be. Her mind tumbled with what she knew now—that the last dragons hadn't been killed before her parents were born, that at least one had survived and wasn't a terrible, bloodthirsty creature after all, that touching him somehow allowed her to understand him, that she already knew they would be dear friends.

Her happy reverie was clouded then by the problems lying before her. She'd promised her new friend she would be back to see him tomorrow. Tomorrow? How could she, with Alethia sick and Bedwyr needing his eggs? And worst of all, she'd lied to her mother about Winston. How many times had her parents talked with her and her siblings about the importance of truth? That lies on top of lies create quicksand that grabs and won't let go? Eliana was cold despite the sun, and there was an ache in her chest that had been there ever since she had lied to her mother.

That night, Eliana lay squeezed between Sage and Rowan, who had only grumbled a little at having to share their bed with her. She listened to her sister struggling to breathe without coughing, wheezing filling the sleeping room. Her mother moved from her own bed to Alethia's, back and forth, giving her water with various remedies mixed in, changing the cloth on her forehead, trying to sleep in between.

Eliana told herself not to worry. How many times had she heard her mother say that the fever is the cure? That fever is how their bodies fight infection? Alethia would be feeling better soon, and then Eliana could tell her sister about Winston. Of course she would tell her. Alethia loved all creatures and would love Winston, too.

And Eliana would tell her parents as well. Soon, she would tell them.

Eliana knew she couldn't go into the forest to see Winston the next day; she needed to get her chores done and take Bedwyr his eggs for breakfast. He'd been only a little grumpy when she and the boys had shown up that afternoon with what turned out to be his lunch.

"Tell Alethia I hope she feels better soon," he'd called as they left.

As Eliana had pulled his front door closed behind her, she glanced back to see the Cartographer standing in the middle of the room, a somber loneliness in his eyes.

Eliana drifted to sleep that night, trying to figure out

how to let Winston know that she'd really meant to go to the clearing that morning. She dreamed of writing on a torn piece of paper and leaving it in the clearing where she'd found him before. But the note blew away, was stolen by a raven, disintegrated in a sudden rain, was lost forever in quicksand, and she never saw the dragon again.

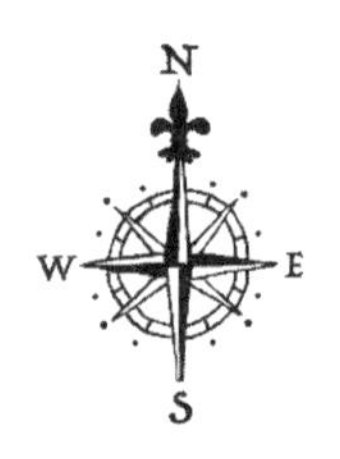

Chapter 6: Winston

DAY ONE

That same night, in the dark cave far across the forest, Winston turned circles in the sleeping nest. He'd slept the entire day after returning from his flyout, and now that it was nighttime, he was wide awake, his mind filled with jumbled thoughts. Faced with the truth that his mother wasn't sure if his father would ever come back, he'd almost forgotten the joy of meeting Eliana.

Eliana. Her name was like a little song, one that a small brown bird sings when its eggs hatch in early spring. His thoughts flowed like two streams weaving back and forth across each other. Thoughts of dread at what might have happened to Raiden, thoughts of happiness at being able to talk to Eliana, thoughts of how he—only a young dragon—could possibly find his father.

His mother went from their sleeping nest to the front of the cave and back again. Back and forth. Winston knew he'd frightened her that morning when he was gone so long. He knew her fear was compounded by the fact that Raiden was gone, and she had no idea where he was or if he were coming back. So now she checked on Winston over and over, in between scanning the night sky for Raiden from the mouth of the cave.

Winston pretended to sleep, curled in a ball to keep warm. He decided it still wasn't the right time to tell Nerys he'd flown to the southern reaches of the vast forest, let a human touch him, and had even spoken to her. And he knew he wouldn't be allowed to do a flyout again anytime soon. How would he see his new friend again?

Sadness upon sadness. Winston tucked away in his heart the small but bright happiness that was Eliana and finally slept.

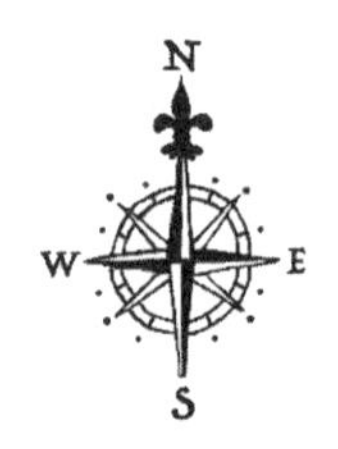

Chapter 7: King Halwyn

DAY ONE

Four miles away from the Fallonds' home as the hawk flies, in a castle perched on a hill on the southern side of Morganshire, King Halwyn paced back and forth in his Audience Hall, hands clasped behind his back. What had once been a fine burgundy velvet robe dragged on the castle's dusty stone floor behind him. Now and then, the frayed hem—a dirty brown now—caught on a chipped stone, causing him to stumble, curse under his breath, and yank until it came free.

The King had a round belly that preceded his arrival wherever he went, upon which rested the Royal Pendant, symbol of his sovereignty over this small and mostly insignificant kingdom. He was shorter than the average man, but his hair sprang up around his head like a white aura, lending him a somewhat regal look, especially when he sat upon his elevated throne and issued decrees. Tonight, he merely looked overwrought and pitiful as he shuffled from one end of the Audience Hall to the other.

Even though it was late May, his chambers—especially his bedchamber—were colder than usual. He had begun sleeping in front of the fireplace in the Audience Hall more and more because of the cold and—if he had to admit it—because of the Trouble. The nightmares plaguing him these days were fewer here in the glow of the fire, especially with food and drink close at hand.

Following the advice of his Royal Counselor, Margred, he'd ordered that fires be kept blazing in his chambers at all times to fight off the cold. But now, to his consternation, he noticed his ale cup was empty and only crumbs were left of his evening snack.

The King crept out into the corridor and cracked open the heavy wooden door to the Banquet Hall. Lit by only a few torches, the voluminous room was draped in shadows that fell across the huge dining tables and benches. A fine layer of dust had settled where goblets of wine and platters of meats and cheeses had been presented in glorious splendor in better times. A heavy silence had replaced the dance music. The King had stopped entertaining mayors, generals, merchants, and lovely widows over a month ago, proclaiming he was much too busy to engage in such frivolous diversions.

"Brogan . . ." he called into the echoey room. His voice was a raspy whisper from lack of use and all the smoke in his chambers. He cleared his throat and called again a bit louder this time.

"Brogan!" The King started to step into the Banquet Hall but stopped himself before his slippered toe crossed the threshold. He'd forgotten once again that his Head Steward was gone, was . . . where? Tibbet Mill? Should he go look for . . . what was her name? Linette?

"Better not," he mumbled to himself, making his way back into the Audience Hall. "It's much too cold out there."

The King had been avoiding any and all "out theres" for the past several days. He kept solely to his private chambers, allowing only his Counselor Margred to enter. Margred had suggested that a period of complete seclusion would give him the time and quiet he needed to consider the best way to deal with the Trouble. That's what she called it: The Trouble. In Halwyn's mind, it was always spoken with a capital T. And indeed it was a trouble deserving of capitalization for, inexplicably, the kingdom was almost penniless. His storeroom where modest piles of gold and silver once stood, was empty, except for dust and rat droppings. The massive wooden chest, once filled with the kingdom's jewels, was barren except for one ruby the size of a single drop of blood. The annual tribute to the Overking of Canting Castle was due in two weeks, and none who served in Morgan Castle had been paid since the treasure had gone missing.

The Trouble had started a little over two months ago. At the end of March, a few days after the Spring Equinox Banquet, the King's Finance Minister had come to the Audience Hall, scroll in hand, to report that some of the royal gold and silver was missing. Halwyn, busy with a land dispute, had distractedly waved his hand and told him to find it. The Finance Minister had bowed and scurried from the King's audience room with worry on his brow.

Three weeks went by, then—on a dreary gray day in mid-April—the Finance Minister had come once again, the scroll shaking in his hands, to tell the King that not only had the missing gold and silver not been found, but also, there was much less left in the storeroom and that someone—or something—had pried open the brass lock on the jewel chest.

"The level of jewels has diminished, Your Highness," said the Finance Minister, quaking in his woolen booties.

"What? The jewels . . . *what*?" shouted Halwyn, heaving himself to his feet.

The Finance Minister scuttled behind as the King strode as fast as his short legs would stride to the storeroom. Indeed, it was plain to anyone who looked that the kingdom's wealth—jewels, gold, and silver—was not just diminished, it was gone. Except for the one, blood-red ruby.

"Someone's stealing from you, your most Royal Highness." The King's Counselor Margred seemingly came from nowhere to stand behind him in the doorway of the storeroom. Her long, pale hand emerged with a sigh from her silken midnight blue robes and swept like a white moth in an arc before her.

"You perhaps should consider calling in the Guard to investigate." Her voice—as always—like a whispery, tuneless song.

And so, King Halwyn decided to mount a search. Valo, his Captain of the Guard, investigated; for two days, he and his men searched every nook and cranny of the castle and hillside around the castle. Nothing was found but dust and rat droppings. Over the next two weeks, they searched all of Morganshire, the village that lay at the foot of the castle.

"Well?" demanded the King when Captain Valo came late one evening to report his findings.

"Nothing, Your Highness. Nothing but dust and rat droppings," said Valo. "We really need to do something about the rats," he muttered to himself.

"Rats? Rats? The kingdom has been robbed, and you want to talk about *rats*?" The King was both angry and terrified. Valo was a diligent and intelligent man who should have been able to find the missing wealth if anyone could.

Halwyn climbed onto his throne and started massaging his temples. The Tribute Banquet at Canting Castle was—as always—on June the sixth, just little over five weeks from that day. What if the treasure were gone for good? The Overking of Cantington wouldn't hesitate to replace Halwyn if the annual tribute weren't paid on time. King Denross's feckless nephew was a young adult now, and Halwyn had heard that Denross was looking for a minor castle for him.

A dethroned minor king had no options other than to beg for cups of gruel in the village square.

Halwyn wrung his chapped hands. If only he'd married years ago and had an heir or two. Denross would be less apt to replace him if his lineage were assured. He'd just not thought it pressing; he'd only turned fifty a few months ago. And he'd never found just the right woman to be his queen, one who would enjoy sumptuous banquets, dancing, and overflowing goblets of wine.

At that moment, his Counselor Margred appeared—again as if by magic—from the shadows. She stood wraithlike beside the extremely tall Captain of the Guard whose dark skin—it reminded the King of the sweet chestnuts his father used to bring home from the forests to the east—glowed in the torchlight of the Audience Hall. Margred's skin was white as alabaster and seemed to absorb light like heavy paper absorbs spilled water.

"Yes, yes . . . what is it?" Halwyn asked her.

"Perhaps you might want to consider a more . . . drastic action, Your Highness."

"Drastic?" The King's bushy eyebrows drew down to hang over his narrowed eyes.

"Yes, *drastic* is perhaps best for Trouble like this." As she spoke, Margred glided into the center of the Audience Hall as if sliding on ice. "We'll need to enlist the assistance of . . ." she paused and then finished with a sweep of her hand. "A *dragon*."

Valo's hand went to the sword at his side, and Brogan

nearly dropped the platter of dried fruit and cheeses he was holding. The King—trying to maintain his composure—leaned forward on his throne and put his broad, hairy hands on his slightly-shaking knees.

"What are you talking about, woman! Explain yourself!" he commanded, in what he felt was his most regal and authoritarian voice.

With an ever-so-slight nod, Margred continued, "Contrary to what most commoners say, dragons still exist. They were never completely destroyed as the tales would have you believe, Your Excellence. A few still cower in caves beyond the Great Forest. And in this case, it is a good thing. A good thing indeed." She smiled, her lips forming a thin upward-turning gash in her porcelain face. Her violet eyes seemed to be lit from within. "You see, from vast heights, dragons are able to see what men can't. And they possess a special talent—the ability to find gold and jewels no matter where they are hidden."

"Did they . . . Are *they* the ones . . .? Did they take . . .?" asked Halwyn.

"No, Your Highness. They wouldn't dare come near a fortress such as ours. They no longer have the courage or strength to attack seasoned soldiers." She glanced at Valo, who held her gaze and kept his hand on the hilt of his sword.

Margred moved slightly closer to the King and continued, "Not only do dragons lack the courage, but they're few in number and don't interact with humans anymore."

"Then how will we *enlist assistance* from one?" Valo was the one to ask the obvious question. His leather boots creaked as he too stepped to stand closer to the King.

"I'm glad you asked, valiant Valo," Margred said. "King Halwyn will need you and your loyal men to find one and convince it to help us. You'll need to venture deep into the northernmost forest, close to the Granite Hills. I'll provide special torches that you'll light in the darkest hours of the night. These torches will attract the dragons to you. Simple."

She smiled her slivered smile again and ran her fingers in and out of the folds in her silken robes.

"And just how do I convince one of these dragons to help us? Merely wave these special torches and ask politely?"

Margred's eyes narrowed at the sarcasm in Valo's question. "You will take Doryu with you. He will *convince* the dragon."

"Doryu?" The King rubbed his hands on his knees. "Doryu?" He had a vague memory of a man with that name.

Margred stepped even closer to the King but still out of reach of Valo's sword, which was now pulled halfway from its scabbard. "Doryu is the only remaining Dragon Speaker in the kingdom, Your Excellence. He still lives in your castle."

"Explain yourself, woman! Why am I only now hearing about dragons and men who can speak to them?" The King's words bounced off the damp gray stones of the Audience Hall, and even Margred took a step back.

"Forgive me, sire. I had not thought to bother you . . ."

"Bother me? It is your *job* to bother me! It is *my* job to be bothered! Now, you will tell me all there is to know about dragons and Dragon Speakers and how to recover the missing wealth of my kingdom!"

The King asked Brogan to call for ale and more logs for the fire. He hadn't noticed the cold before, but now he could see his breath huffing from his mouth. The winds blowing off the sea to the south whipped around the castle, spitting needles of late spring sleet at the heavily curtained windows. King Halwyn pulled his robe snug around his girth and gestured for Margred to continue.

And so she told them there was a time, over a hundred years ago, during Halwyn's great-great-grandfather's reign, when a few shrewd rulers—Morganshire's king among them—realized giant creatures that could fly from the sea to the farthest mountain range in less than a day might be useful. Dragons could see armies being amassed in lands far to the east, pirate ships approaching the Dead Rise Cliffs, and stolen treasure carried by wagon along obscure roads. Somehow, they were even able to find gold and jewels that had been buried or hidden in abandoned mines.

By artfully gathering information and sifting truth from fancy—calling on the skills of trusted Counselors and Captains of the Guard—the kings had learned there were those who could communicate with dragons, who could understand their speech. These Dragon Speakers became valued members of kings' counsels and were given opulent chambers, fine clothes, and the best food and drink. For their part, the dragons were provided with a portion of the jewels they found, along with a promise that they could live in peace.

"However," Margred continued, "After a time, ignorant men broke that promise and began to hunt and kill dragons, driving them deep into the Granite Hills. At some point, even the best of kings forgot about using dragons for the good of their people, forgot about Dragon Speakers, forgot that dragons even existed."

"And Doryu? He is a Dragon Speaker?" asked Halwyn.

"Yes," said Margred.

"And he's here, in the castle?"

"Yes, sire."

"Brogan, bring him to me at once!" the King commanded his Steward.

Brogan, still holding the platter of forgotten cheeses, bowed and hurried from the room.

Bringing the Dragon Speaker to the King "at once" turned out to be impossible, for he could not—at first—be found. Brogan searched all the guest chambers, as well as the bright, yet freezing, turret apartments. He even checked the servants' quarters, the stables, the sheepherders' huts in the fields, and—to be thorough—the village tavern.

Finally returning to the kitchen to get the King's breakfast (for he'd spent the entire night searching for the Dragon Speaker), Brogan happened to mention the frustrating wild goose chase to the head cook. She turned from the huge pot hanging on one of the massive fireplace rods and said, "Doryu? You're looking for Doryu? He's in the dungeon."

"In the *dungeon*? Why? What has he done?"

Cook turned from her pot-stirring task, shrugging. She handed Brogan a hot bun wrapped in a cloth and said, "Nothing. He likes it down there. Here, take him his breakfast, will you?"

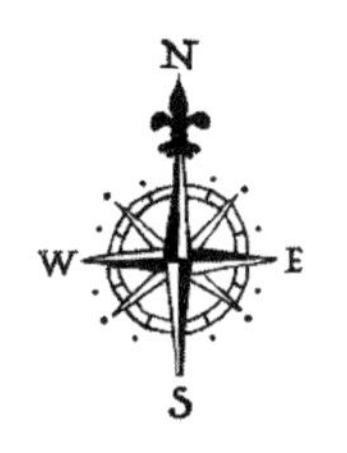

Chapter 8: Doryu

A MONTH AGO

And so it was that a month before Eliana met Winston, King Halwyn's Steward Brogan made his way down the service stairs to find the Old Dragon Speaker.

Doryu, was just finishing his first cup of tea of the day. At seventy-five years of age, he wasn't surprised by much anymore, so when the King's Head Steward appeared without warning at the open door to his cozy cell, he merely rose from his reading chair and thanked him for his morning bun. The old man smiled at the bafflement on Brogan's face and gestured for him to sit in the guest chair beside the small cast iron stove.

"Tea?" Doryu asked as Brogan ducked his head and entered what was surely the warmest room in the castle. In the orange and gold light emanating from the stove, the

Steward gaped at the brightly woven blankets on a cot in the corner, a patterned rug on the floor, a colorful tapestry hanging on the stone wall, a well-used broom hanging from a hook, and a book with an ornate green cover lying open on a rustic wooden table by the stove.

Brogan shook his head. He folded his long legs and lowered himself onto the burgundy velvet cushion adorning the beautifully made, stick-back chair.

Doryu set his bun on the table and retrieved two porcelain teacups from the shelf above his bed. Light from the narrow, barred window high on the cell wall fell into the cups so that the intricate blue designs seemed to dance and swirl. Doryu was pleased to see that, although gnarled and veined with age, his hands were steady as he set the cups beside the bun.

Doryu placed tea leaves in each cup, glancing up to see Brogan's shoulders start to relax. Doryu poured hot water from a tea kettle over the leaves, and the Head Steward crossed his legs and took a deep breath of the fragrant steam. And when Doryu handed him one of the cups and half the bun, Brogan returned the Dragon Speaker's gentle smile.

"Now, tell me why I have the pleasure of breaking my fast with the King's Head Steward. . .Brogan, I believe?" said Doryu, after lowering himself into his own chair.

"Yes," said Brogan. "But how did you know . . ." He stopped and looked around the comfortable haven Doryu had created in the dungeon of the old, dank castle. "I guess after seeing all this, I shouldn't be surprised you know who

I am." He took a sip of tea. "The King has need of a Dragon Speaker. I was sent to find you and take you to him."

Ah, thought Doryu. *The day of reckoning has finally come.*

He took a sip of his tea and a nibble of the bun. A few crumbs fell on his soft gray robe as he studied the man seated opposite him. So young, carrying an almost visible burden of responsibility. A strong face, yet pale. Serious dark eyes that slanted upward at the outer edges. Straight black hair. Even with his diminishing eyesight, Doryu could see a few strands of silver among the black.

"What do you know about Dragon Speakers?" Doryu asked.

"Almost nothing. I didn't even know dragons still existed until yesterday."

"Do you have time for a story?" asked Doryu.

Brogan nodded and settled back in the comfortable cushions of the guest chair.

The Dragon Speaker continued, "I was born only a few years before Halwyn's father Chares. Although we were contemporaries, Chares was heir to the throne of our kingdom, and I was the third son of a trapper. The prince lived in this castle; I lived in a cottage in a clearing in the Great Forest. Other trappers lived nearby, so my brothers, sisters, and I had other children with whom to climb, forage, and fish. Chares was an only child, knowing only the companionship of his tutors and his Steward."

Brogan shifted in his seat at the mention of a steward,

perhaps remembering why he was there to begin with.

"You will forgive the length of my story once you hear how Chares and I finally met, what happened after we did, and why I am still here," said Doryu.

Brogan nodded and motioned for him to continue.

"Chares's father, the King, loved to hunt. He would ride out with his soldiers, often staying for days in the forest, hunting wild boar, deer, and even wild cats, though these were only for sport, not dinner. Chares would beg to go along, but his father only laughed and told him he was too young. 'When I am twelve?' 'Yes, when you are twelve,' the King would promise.

"Each time the hunting party left, Chares would wait on the parapet high on the wall of the castle that faced the forest. He would drag blankets and food there, and at times sleep under the stars. If he waited long enough, he could sometimes spot the hunting party returning from afar, see them carrying their kill slung on a long pole, hear their bawdy songs.

"When Chares was ten, in the spring of that year, he saw glimpses of the hunting party returning only a day after they'd left. As they came closer, Chares couldn't hear singing. Even the birds were silent in the trees. Growing alarmed, the boy ran down the stairs to the courtyard and made his way through the goats and servants and wagons to the front gates, which were open to the road. He ran down the road toward the horsemen, stopping abruptly when he realized that the lead horseman was not his father but the Captain of the Guard.

The Captain saw the boy and pulled his horse to a stop.

"It was at that moment that Chares realized the Captain was holding the reins of the King's black stallion and that, slung over the stallion's back was a man, hands and feet tied beneath the horse to keep him from sliding off. Chares's screams brought the entire castle to the road, brought the queen to her dead husband's side, brought the entire castle to their knees before the new, ten-year-old King."

After a slight pause, Doryu continued. "That same day, I had been playing hide-and-seek with my siblings and friends. I was twelve that year, full of confidence and bravado. I ran deeper into the forest than ever before, well beyond the fallen oak that marked the boundary of my permitted range. I ran not because of the game but for the sheer delight of running. The day was bright, sunlight creating shifting patterns on the forest floor. Deeper and deeper into the forest I ran, knowing no one would find me.

"Then I heard a sound I sometimes hear even now as I am drifting off to sleep. It was a cry of anguish and heartbreak. A high sound of pain and sorrow. Yet as terrifying as it was, there was something in the cry that pulled me. Instead of running away, I ran to the clearing that was filled with . . ."

Doryu paused again and took a sip of tea. "It was a dragon. Orange and blue, like the setting sun in an evening sky. Huge. I couldn't even see all of him spread out on the ground, but what I could see was horrifying. In his shoulder, where his wing met his body, was a sword embedded so far that only the grip was visible. On the end of that grip was a round pommel covered with jewels. The blood running from the wound and down the dragon's wing was a red I'd never seen before, neither human nor animal. The smell of the blood, the swirling colors of the dragon, and the jewels on the sword . . . all of it was awful. But worst of all was the sound of the dragon dying there in the clearing."

Brogan leaned forward, his own tea abandoned on the table before him. Doryu took yet another sip of tea and cleared his throat.

"At least at that moment I thought the terrible sound was the worst thing. Until the dragon's head fell to the ground at my feet, his eyes reflecting my face like a clouded mirror. I knew he saw me, that he saw me see myself there in his eyes just before he died with a gush of bloody steam emerging from his mouth.

"Then I saw a flash of silver just under the blood-covered orange and blue feathers. The tip of a much smaller wing under the wing of the dead dragon. Something was moving, struggling, buried under the weight of the larger wing. I ran to lift what I could of the dead dragon's wing, while what was beneath it used incredible strength to help me free it. I suppose you'll guess by now this was the child of the slain dragon. The one he'd died to protect from a hunting party. When the dragon child emerged from under his father's wing, he was dazed, swinging his head from side to side.

"Please don't suppose this young dragon was small. Yes,

he was small compared to the monstrous size of his father, but he was still much larger than I. I was afraid and began to back into the forest, thinking I'd completed the task the dying father had wanted. But then, the dragon child fell to the ground and began to cry out. Realizing his father was dead, he convulsed with what looked like sorrow there in the bloody, trampled wildflowers.

"I took a few steps toward him and then a few more. He finally saw me and pulled back in terror, breathing rapidly and closing his eyes. I must've looked like a member of the hunting party. Without thinking, I reached toward him and spoke in a soft and soothing voice as I would to an injured puppy. He was making a mumbling sound—*mm . . . mmm . . . mm*—like he was trying to communicate with me, so I kept talking. After a few moments, his eyelids lowered, and his breathing slowed. I took a few more steps, and still without a thought for my own safety, put my hand on his neck.

"What happened next was a miracle. I could understand him. 'My father, my father,' he said. I heard and understood the words as plainly as I can hear and understand you. It was because of this I knew he was trying to make sense of what had happened. I asked him if he was hurt. I didn't know what to say about his father.

"'Sticks, sharp sticks. They threw sharp sticks at me.' He lifted his wing and there in the silver, black, and white scales of his underbelly was an arrow, feathered in purple, the color of royalty. I could see the arrow wasn't deeply embedded and told the creature I could remove it.

"'Yes. Yes, please,' he told me.

"When I moved my hand from his neck to get a good purchase on the arrow, I saw strands of silver, black, and white flow like wisps of cloud from my palm. The wisps disappeared so quickly I thought I'd imagined them. I bent to the task of removing the arrow, and as it pulled free with a sickening, sucking sound, I realized the dragon was mumbling again. He was staring in horror at the bright blood coming from his wound. I again reached out to comfort him, and when my hand touched the cool scales on his neck, I could hear him clearly once more." Doryu sighed, wonder mixed with sadness.

Brogan shook his head. "So you could understand this dragon? By touching him? A man just has to touch a dragon to communicate with him?"

"No, not any man. A Dragon Speaker. It was on that day sixty-three years ago that I learned I was a Dragon Speaker. I didn't know what it was called or that it was a rare and troubling gift. But I knew that by placing my hand on this distraught young dragon, I could understand him.

"His name was Raiden. He was thirty years old that day—in dragon years, about the maturity level of a ten-year-old, the same age as the King's son. We sat in the clearing for almost an hour until his wound stopped bleeding. He told me what I already suspected: a hunting party—I knew from the sword and arrow it was the King's—had spotted him flying just above the tops of the trees. An arrow had brought Raiden crashing into the clearing. Just as the King had raised his sword to kill the young dragon, a giant orange and blue fury had descended from the sky. Raiden's father and the King had battled, one with a jeweled sword, the other with razor-sharp talons.

"You know the result. Raiden's father died, leaving Raiden to learn to live in hiding from what came next. And Chares's father died as well, leaving a ten-year-old to become King. The boy's deep sorrow turned to rage, and Chares issued his first decree: All dragons were to be hunted and destroyed. And I, the twelve-year-old son of a trapper, became the Royal Dragon Speaker . . ."

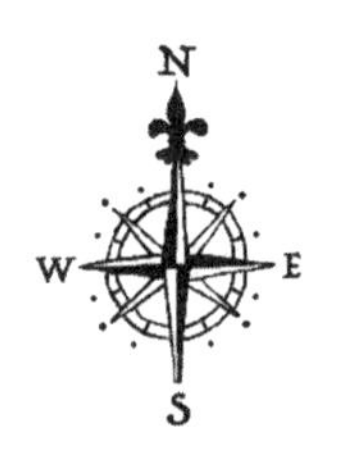

Chapter 9: Eliana

DAY TWO

The morning after Eliana met Winston, she was awakened by her father's gentle hand on her shoulder. She could barely make out his reddish mustache and blue eyes in the darkened sleeping room.

"Shhhhh," he whispered. "Your mother and Alethia are both still asleep. You'll need to take Bedwyr his eggs again this morning, but I want to talk to you first."

Eliana scooted from the boys' bed, careful not to bump either one, and wrapped a blanket around her shoulders. Cadoc held the corner of the curtain that divided the sleeping room from the kitchen so she could duck under. He followed her, then turned to be sure the curtain was completely closed again.

The only light in the kitchen was the soft glow

emanating from the embers in the stove. Even though the days were getting warmer, the early mornings were still cold, and Eliana was glad for the warmth of the stove. Sitting down at the kitchen table, she smelled thyme already steeping, peppery and minty, in her father's teacup. Her father sat beside her with a slab of brown bread and butter, which he put between them.

"Have some," he said, putting both hands carefully around the blue and white teacup.

Eliana could see scars and a few newer cuts on the backs of his freckled hands. She knew there were more on his palms, all from his work splitting slate at the quarry.

Cadoc leaned over to breathe in the steam wafting up from the surface of the tea. When he lifted the cup to take a sip, the red stone tied into the plaits of his leather bracelet reflected the light from the stove. One of Eliana's earliest memories was of sitting on her father's lap, trying to pluck the stone from its bounds. She'd asked many times where he'd gotten the bracelet, but he would only smile and shake his head in response.

Eliana broke off a piece of bread and took a bite, realizing how hungry she was. She hadn't eaten much the night before. Her father took a sip of the hot tea and set the cup on the table.

"Eliana, your mother told me you went into the forest by yourself yesterday." He broke off a piece of bread but didn't put it in his mouth.

Eliana stared at her father's hand with the bite of bread

in it hovering there above the table. Her heart pounded. Suddenly, she wasn't at all hungry anymore.

"Yes, Father. I thought I saw . . ." She stopped herself before telling the lie again.

"Eliana, it doesn't matter what you thought you saw. Your mother and I told you that you weren't to go into the forest by yourself. Not now. Not until . . . things are safe. And we will be the ones to determine when things are safe. Do you understand?"

"Yes, Father." Still unable to meet his eyes, she stared instead at the delicate blue design on his teacup.

"I know you love the forest, and I understand the desire to explore it. I was like you when I was young."

Eliana glanced up and saw that he was looking over her head as if seeing something amazing there. His eyes lowered to meet hers.

"Eliana, I appreciate that you are adventurous, but what you did was disobedient and dangerous." Cadoc sighed, then continued, "Your consequences will be to do your own chores, Alethia's chores until she is well, and some of your mother's chores also. There's wash to be done when you get back from Bedwyr's today. Take the boys with you when you go."

Eliana nodded. She tried to swallow the lump in her throat.

Cadoc finally lifted the bread to his mouth, chewed, and drank the rest of his tea. He stood, opened his arms, and said, "Daughter, I love you."

"I love you, too, Father," said Eliana, rising to bury her

face in his worn shirt. “I’m sorry.” And she was sorry. Sorry to have broken the trust her parents had in her. Sorry to have lied to her mother. She knew she should tell her father about the dragon in the forest. He’d want her to tell him.

But as she was trying to find the words to begin, Cadoc stepped back and said, “I forgive you.”

And at that moment, she didn’t want to risk losing his forgiveness and the gentle smile that came with it. Later. She’d tell him later. She managed to smile back and was glad the light in the kitchen was dim enough to hide the slight shake of her hand as she reached for his teacup.

Her father took his jacket off its hook by the door. “Take good care of that,” he said.

“I will.”

“I know,” said Cadoc, as he slipped quietly out the back door.

By the time Eliana dressed, made breakfast for the boys, and took her mother and sister some freshly brewed tea, the sky was just turning the yellowish-blue of sunrise to the east. She hurried to open the chicken coop and checked for eggs as Henry the Fifth herded the flock into the yard. Only nine eggs today.

On the way back to the house, she reached over the garden fence to poke a finger into the dirt. Still damp. She’d weed when she and the boys got back from Bedwyr’s. She could do the wash after that.

Sage was at the back door, holding Bedwyr's basket, with his hair standing all over his head like reddish shocks of wheat. Eliana handed him the two largest eggs and smoothed his hair down as she went into the house. Rowan still sat at the table, dozing with his head on his arms.

"Rowan, we need to leave soon."

"I'm so tired," came his muffled reply. "I couldn't sleep last night at all with you in our bed, Alethia coughing . . ." He coughed, just a tiny cough, but enough to bring Eliana to his side. She leaned to put her cheek against his forehead. It was cool, but when he coughed again, she told him to go back to bed.

"Sage and I will take the eggs to Bedwyr. Go back to sleep, but if you wake up, stay in the house until we get back." Eliana pulled the back door closed. "And be quiet!" She lifted the dividing curtain and watched him crawl back into his bed without arguing or taking off his clothes. He pulled the blanket up over his head and lay still. Both her mother and Alethia had gone back to sleep.

Eliana dropped the edge of the curtain and turned to find Sage standing just outside the open front door, basket in hand, a green scarf wound around his neck. The sun had crested the hills to the east and lit her brother's eyes—the same color as the scarf—and his pale, freckled face. He smiled at her, and Eliana could see a glimpse of the handsome man he would someday become. She put her arm around his slender shoulder and gently pulled the front door so that it latched behind them without a sound. Today, they'd be on time, and Bedwyr could have his eggs for breakfast.

Walking along Kings Road on the way to the Cartographer's cottage, Sage stopped, handed Eliana the basket, and made his way through rocks and creeping thistle to the wooden fence that bordered their sheep pasture. He began picking the bright yellow blooms of the corn marigolds growing just out of reach of the sheep.

"Sage . . ." she called to him.

"I'm getting these for Bedwyr! He can make paint from them. Yellow paint!" He made his way back to where Eliana waited on the side of the road.

Eliana laughed to see yellow pollen adorning his nose and three bumblebees lazily following behind him. *Paint from flowers?* Obviously, Sage had been paying more attention to the details of Alethia's apprenticeship than she had.

It wasn't until they were passing Quarry Road that Eliana thought again of Winston. Meeting him was starting to feel like a dream already. And seeing the tree-lined road her father took every day to work filled her with the resolve to do as he had told her, to stay out of the forest. Not to go alone.

Alone. That's what her parents had said. So, if she went with Alethia, she wouldn't be *alone* . . . Shaking her head, she thrust the thought aside. Now was definitely not the time to be planning how to see Winston again. She hoped he wasn't waiting for her at the edge of the forest, wondering where she was. She took her brother's hand again, and the two hurried the last mile to the path on the right that led to Bedwyr's cottage.

Eliana followed her brother as the path—mostly dirt and pea-sized rocks—wound through tall grasses and wild-flowers that quivered with hundreds of butterflies. An apple tree growing close to the path was festooned with pale pink blossoms. As Eliana reached toward one of the sweet-smelling blooms, she ran into Sage, who'd stopped abruptly in front of her.

"Sage?"

"Hello, Tal," said Sage.

"Greetings, Sage."

Now Eliana could see a boy—a young man?—it was hard to tell how old he was because he was nearly as tall as her father. But his face was youthful, and he had dark, short-cropped hair and black eyes that tilted up and almost closed when he smiled at them. Eliana thought his smile was the best thing about his handsome face, friendly and open. She felt herself flush and nudged her brother with her knee.

"We're taking Bedwyr his breakfast and some flowers to make yellow paint." Sage held the marigolds up for Tal's inspection.

"He'll like those, Sage." Tal stepped from the path into the meadow, sweeping his arm to gesture for them to pass.

"Sage. Miss," he said, smiling at Eliana.

"Thank you," said Sage, continuing past Tal on the path. "Her name is Eliana," he called over his shoulder.

"Nice to meet you, Eliana."

"Nice to meet you, too," mumbled Eliana, following Sage. When she glanced back, she saw Tal heading back toward the road, swinging his long arms. The tune he was whistling sounded like a birdsong she'd heard before but couldn't place.

"Sage!" she called to her brother, now several paces ahead of her. He stopped. "Who was that?" she asked him. "How do you know him?"

"That was Tal. He's fifteen years old. He's apprenticed to the clockmaker in town. Oh, and he's the King's Head Steward's son."

"And how . . ."

"He comes to the house sometimes to get remedies for his family. I like him. He's nice."

When had he come to their house? *And where was I?* thought Eliana.

Sage turned to run along the path that curved one last time before opening onto a wide, neatly swept yard.

The Cartographer's home was long and low, its gray slate roof looking like a knitted cap pulled down to its owner's eyes. Attached to the left side of the cottage, there was a barn, which was currently inhabited by a black and white cat and her three kittens. The cat—which Alethia had said Bedwyr called "Cow"—sat by the open barn door, licking her paw and watching the children walk to the front door of the cottage. Her kittens tumbled in a pile of fur and little tails in the wildflowers that grew profusely in the yard. When Eliana knocked on Bedwyr's door, the mother cat ran to stand beside them.

"Coming!" called Bedwyr. "Coming!"

The door opened with a bang as it hit a chair just inside. A highly polished leather boot emerged to block the cat from entering.

"Cow, you know you aren't allowed inside!"

The cat flicked her tail and turned to walk back down the path. Partway, she plopped down in a shaft of sunlight, closed her golden eyes, and feigned nonchalance. Only the occasional twitch of her left ear revealed her irritation at being blocked from where, it seemed, she had been many times before.

"Come in, Eliana! Come in, Sage!" boomed Bedwyr.

Eliana was surprised he knew it was Sage; most people couldn't tell the twins apart. Sage smiled and walked up to Bedwyr, thrusting the slightly drooping marigolds into the mapmaker's hands.

"For paint. For yellow paint!" said Sage.

"For yellow paint indeed! And you shall help me make it."

Eliana watched the two—one towering and one barely up to the other's waist—make their way to the benches in the back of the room, which was brightly lit by windows opened to the backyard. In front of the benches were stools, and on the benches were dozens of glass bottles, bowls, spoons, paintbrushes, and mortars and pestles in varying sizes.

Bedwyr swept a space clear, put the marigolds on the bench, and turned to lift Sage onto a stool. Eliana could barely hear Bedwyr now as he leaned his head close to his red-haired assistant and murmured instructions. They both pulled bright yellow petals from the marigolds, placing them into a mortar.

By the time Eliana had cooked Bedwyr's eggs, adding salt and the rest of the rosemary she'd brought the day before, Sage and the mapmaker had put the yellow pulp from the flower petals in a jar with some vinegar and water. As Bedwyr ate, a giant cloth tucked under his well-kept beard, he explained that the petals would have to mellow for a while in the jar before the substance could be used as paint. "Watercolor" he called it.

Sage stood quietly beside the Cartographer while he ate, but his eyes danced around the whole of the room like hummingbirds flitting from one side of a garden to the other.

"Go ahead; take a look around," said Bedwyr.

Sage looked up at Eliana, who smiled and nodded at her brother. She knew he'd be careful.

Sage went back to the bench and scanned the rows of jars on the far end. Green, purple, red, orange, pink, and three jars of varying blues. Eliana caught her breath as he picked up the jar they'd just filled with yellow. She glanced at Bedwyr, who continued to eat, seemingly unconcerned. Sage held the jar up to the light for a moment and then set it back down beside the other jars.

"There's an orange paw print here," said Sage, gesturing to the floor under a stool.

"Oh, that's old. Been there a long time," said Bedwyr.

Sage nodded as he made his way to a huge table on the left side of the room. On it was an immense piece of cream-colored paper, spread almost to the edges of the table. One corner of the paper was blooming with the same colors found in Bedwyr's jars, along with thin black lines that crawled across the watercolors. Sage, hands clasped behind his back, walked slowly around the table, stopping here and there before moving on again.

"This is your map. The one Alethia said you call your magnum opal," he said.

"Yes," said Bedwyr, chuckling and dabbing at his beard with his makeshift napkin. "It is indeed my magnum opus."

"What is a magnum opus? Why do you call it that?"

"It's my last grand project. My great creation."

"And what's this?" Sage pointed to a corner of the map.

"That's a compass rose."

"I never heard of a place called Compass Rose," said Sage, with that little furrow between his eyes.

"It's not a place. It's a . . . let me show you," said Bedwyr, standing to take a rolled parchment off a high shelf. He unrolled it and laid it on a blank section of the giant map. Eliana came closer and saw that it too was a map but much smaller.

"Do you see these blue areas here and here? These are water. Most cartographers color the water blue." He looked at Sage, a twinkle in his eye.

"That makes sense," said Sage, nodding solemnly.

"These purple areas here depict mountains, green for

vegetation. These notes down here tell us what the different colors mean. It's called a map key."

Sage nodded again.

"But," continued Bedwyr, "what if we wanted to find places shown on this map? Like this town, which is merely a black dot? If we know where these mountains are, and if we know how far the town is and in what direction it is from the mountains, we can find the town." He pointed then to a gray and white bar at the bottom of the map.

"This bar shows the scale of the map. Look. This tiny bit—less than the width of your fingertip—is a mile. That means this town is approximately fifteen miles from the base of these mountains, as the crow flies." Bedwyr traced this out with his massive finger.

"But look up in this corner. You probably already found it! A compass rose." He pointed to a small drawing on the old map that did indeed look like a rose, at least if a rose had pointed petals. "Here at the top of the rose is a *fleur-de-lys*, French for 'flower of the lily.' We mapmakers use this beautiful little symbol to represent north. See? And here are the other three cardinal directions: east, south, and west. Now that we know this way is north, we can see that this town is south of the mountains."

"Fifteen miles south of the mountains," said Sage.

Bedwyr nodded and continued. "Now, all you need to know is how to orient the map, how to turn it so that the place you are standing and north on the map are aligned. For that, we need an actual compass. And Tal brought me a new one right before you came! One with larger markings so I can read it.

The mapmaker took a drawstring bag from one of his capacious pockets, opened it, and brought out a round object that just fit in the palm of his huge hand. It was made of a polished metal that encased a piece of clear glass. Beneath the glass was . . .

"Ohhh, a compass rose," whispered Sage.

"Yes," said Bedwyr.

"And it has a *fleur-de-lys!* That's north, right?"

"Yes, indeed. And see this needle? It's mounted on a pin so it can spin. It's magnetized. We hold the compass still and wait for the needle to settle. When it does, it will show us which way is north."

"How does it know?" asked Sage.

"It's being attracted by the earth's own magnetism."

"So we can always find north by using your compass?"

"We can always find *due* north, but not *true* north, which is the actual north pole. Earth's magnetism changes and will lead us off course if we aren't careful."

"Oh, dear . . ." said Sage.

"Not to worry, boy! Unless we are on a miles-long trek or on a ship, due north will be accurate enough. Let's go outside and try out this beautiful new compass, shall we?"

As Eliana cleaned up the skillet and dishes from Bedwyr's breakfast, Sage and Bedwyr first hurried outside, then a few minutes later returned for a different map, one smaller than his grand project but newer than the one they'd been examining before. They traced routes on the newer map, held the compass, and turned around in circles. Occasionally, bits of their conversation reached her. South by east, south-southeast, south by west.

Eliana put the last dish on the shelf, her mind filled with thoughts of little black lines that were actually roads. Roads that went other places, places with people she'd never met. Would she ever get to travel beyond Morganshire? See Dragon Fell, Cantington, the Pearl River? Do something besides the same chores every day? Find her own *true* north? Inside her chest, it felt like a stone was tied to her heart.

Thinking of chores reminded Eliana they needed to get home. "Sage, we need to go."

As he turned to her, Sage's eyes seemed to be lit from within with swirling watercolors.

"Please tell Alethia I hope she feels better soon," said Bedwyr, standing in his doorway as they headed back up the path toward Kings Road. He was still blocking Cow from entering the cottage with his giant foot.

"We will," called Sage. He ran back to the Cartographer and looked up at him. "Your compass rose is the most beautiful of all compass roses. It suits your magnum opal well!"

Eliana could still hear Bedwyr's thundering laugh even when she was several yards down the path. She looked at Sage to see if his feelings were hurt by Bedwyr's laughter.

A contented smile played across his freckled face. "I think Bedwyr needs two apprentices," he said.

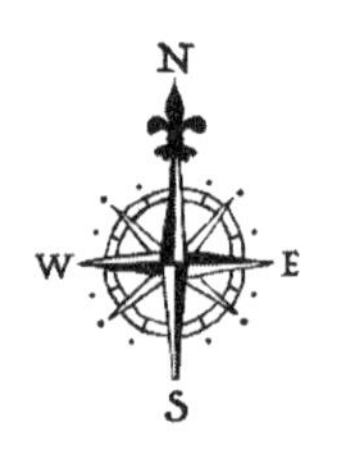

Chapter 10: King Halwyn

DAY TWO

That night, shortly after Sage asked his mother for a few glass jars to start his own watercolor collection, King Halwyn shivered in the Audience Hall, sitting as close as he dared to the huge fireplace. He had dragged a blanket from his bed and wrapped it around his frayed robe and his substantial stomach, but it did little to warm him. He held a corner of the blanket between his thumb and forefinger and rubbed it gently on his dry lips. It soothed him.

His Counselor, Margred, brought his dinner, instead of the young woman who'd been filling in for his Head Steward.

"Where's Brogan's assistant? Linette. Where is she?" he asked. He felt like a petulant child, but he couldn't help it.

"I discerned that you're still in need of complete solitude, Your Highness," Margred said. "All the better to decide your next course of action." She put his tray on the table beside the fire.

As she turned away, Halwyn thought he saw her sprinkle something on the fire, causing it to brighten with blue and white. But when he looked at his Counselor again, her hands were tucked into the folds of her robes. The fire, when he looked back, was burning as it always did; reds, yellows, and oranges danced as they consumed the logs. He started to feel quite sleepy on top of the general exhaustion of the past weeks.

"You may go, Margred," he said, his hand waving weakly in the direction of the door.

"Thank you, Your Excellence," she said, pulling the door closed behind her.

Alone once more, the King barely managed a few sips of soup before he dropped the spoon onto the tray. The fire, though leaping like crazed court jesters, did nothing to warm him.

Why am I so sleepy? he wondered. *It seems all I do is sleep!* And with that thought, he was asleep once again, dreaming of the silver, black, and white Problem in the lower dungeon. A Problem he couldn't quite see or understand. A Problem that sounded like a high-pitched cry he couldn't stop hearing.

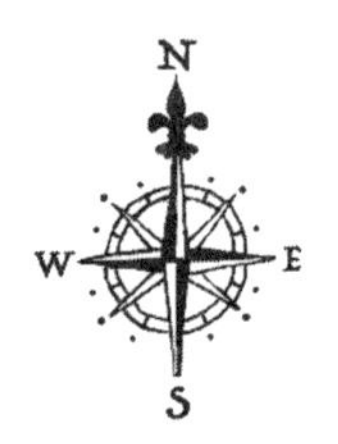

Chapter 11: Winston

DAY TWO

As Eliana sat to eat breakfast with her father, Winston's mother woke him in the cave in the Granite Hills by blowing a gentle stream of warm air into his ear. He moaned and tucked his head under his wing. His head was heavy and achy, filled with the remnants of nightmares.

"Winston, I need you to get up and come with me . . ." Nerys blew a little more steam across what she could see of his head. "To gather benesaunus."

"Benesaunus? With you?" Winston lifted his wing and peered at his mother.

Although he'd flown with his parents in the boulder-strewn canyon to the north of their home many times, he'd never been allowed to go clear to the Black Mountains beyond. He'd always stayed in the cave while either Nerys or

Raiden flew against the formidable updrafts—back and forth—to gather their food.

His father had told him his parents and their parents before them had gathered benesaunus there to sustain their families. It grew under the cool outcroppings of the mountains, the same mountains which had birthed the slate deposits that lay buried beneath the fertile soils of the forests and flatlands.

"Yes, Winston. With me." His mother smiled and nudged a clump of steaming benesaunus temptingly close to him.

He was wide awake now; the smell of the warm food was accompanied by a rumble in his empty stomach. As he ate the last of his breakfast and Nerys moved to the front of the cave to wait for him, he saw how little benesaunus remained behind the sleeping nest. He felt a tickle of worry, understanding why they needed to go to the Black Mountains today. Dragons could eat some of the vegetation that grew sparsely in pockets of the Granite Hills, but it didn't nourish them like benesaunus did, and it tasted awful.

As Nerys and Winston lifted off the ledge that jutted from their cave, he wondered why his mother was allowing him to come today. After yesterday's extended flyout, he'd expected to be confined to the cave for at least a few days. But here he was, flying just behind his mother's glorious gold and amethyst right wing. Staying close to her this way allowed him to be lifted by the updraft created by the movement of air up and over her massive wings.

At first, they rode the cool air traveling from the south, across the vast forest and upward as it met the barrier formed by their rough-hewn hills. Approaching the downwind side of the hills, Nerys glanced back at him, silently warning him of the gusts of swirling turbulence they would encounter as the winds rushed down into the boulder-strewn canyon far below. Winston had flown in those dancing winds before, flaring his wingtips to balance, dipping a wing to turn. But today, he knew they'd both have to conserve their energy for the gathering and transporting of benesaunus.

Winston followed Nerys as they crested the northernmost edge of their ancient hills, and with a few powerful wing beats, they rose high above the canyon where calmer winds led to the towering, snow-peaked mountains. He felt the rising air currents created by the sun warming jagged rocks far below. Three mountain goats with heavy wing-shaped horns sprouting from their heads stood on a rocky outcrop as if standing guard over the rushing river. One was gray and white and reminded Winston of his father. And of the bird in Eliana's yard . . .

"Winston, stay with me!" called his mother.

With a start, he realized he'd fallen behind and had dropped much lower. He could feel the capricious downdraft pulling at his wings. With a burst of energy, he pushed against the tumbling wave of air and flew back into the calmer current where his mother waited, circling.

"Stay close," she called, turning back toward the Black Mountains looming on the other side of the canyon.

Winston had never come this far north before. What had, in the distance, looked like a cloud-draped version of their Granite Hills was revealed to be one mammoth ridge after another of massive, jagged rock. Within moments, they were so close that Winston saw there were no caves, no ledges on which to land, only a few stunted trees, which had somehow managed to obtain a toehold in the nearly vertical side of the mountain. His parents had described the process of gathering benesaunus before, but he could only summon a vague memory now. Sensing his confusion, Nerys slowed so he could come alongside her. She was smiling.

"Just watch what I do. Then try it." With a powerful downward push of her wings, she caught the smooth updraft of the wind as it flowed up the sides of the towering mountains. He followed, happy to have the wind's assistance as they climbed to the upper reaches of a cliff face. Without warning, and to his horror, his mother flew directly toward a rocky outcropping. Surely, she would crash into it and be hurled to the rocks far below!

But with a brilliant flash of gold and amethyst, Nerys pulled her wing blades in, then back again to open her wings as far as they would go. With this motion and with the assistance of the updraft, she was able to hover just for the briefest of moments and extend her back legs in front of her. Winston could see the flare of the undersides of her flight feathers as she reached forward and snatched a huge growth of a greenish-gray substance from the side of the mountain. *Benesaunus!* His mother dropped several feet, clutching the bundle with her back claws. With a few powerful wing beats, she rose to Winston's side.

"You try it," she said. "Just do as I did."

Winston heard her heartrate increase as she fought against the pull of gravity on her heavy load. He knew he had to grab some benesaunus quickly so they would have enough strength to fly home.

His first try was a disaster. Now that he knew just how the benesaunus looked clinging to the rocky edges of the mountain, he could see clumps of it here and there, camouflaged by the dark, rocky mountain face. He flew toward a particularly large bunch but stopped too far from the mountainside. His claws closed on empty air, and he plummeted out of control almost a third of the way down the mountain side.

"Updraft!" called Nerys.

Winston curved his wings, caught the updraft, and was soon ready for his second attempt. This time, he flew directly at the benesaunus, his heart thudding, hoping he could imitate the graceful hovering movement his mother had made. But before he could grab the benesaunus, he was carried up beyond the growth, and his claws scraped along stone instead.

"Once more, Winston! Last try!" called Nerys.

This time, it was perfect. The flight straight at the mountain, the wing blade dip, the flare, the last second grab. And Winston felt the sudden pull of the weight of his prize against his wings.

"Good job, son!" And with a swooping turn, Nerys led them back, flying high above the canyon to avoid the downdraft of the Granite Hills. When they landed on their own ledge once more, Winston released the benesaunus he'd gathered and collapsed with a groan. How his mother had the energy to take her huge cache of food into the cave, he didn't know. He was more exhausted than he'd ever been in his life.

With a deep sigh, Winston realized his mouth was dry; he could feel tiny cracks in the delicate skin around his nostrils, and his tongue felt as if he'd been eating dirt. He pushed himself to his hind legs and—still groaning—made his way to the stream that trickled down the side of the hill by their cave. Tipping his head back, he stood for several moments with the stream diverted into his wide-open mouth. When he turned to get the benesaunus he'd dropped, he and Nerys both laughed to hear the water sloshing in his stomach.

"Go on inside," said his mother. "I will bring your benesaunus in."

Winston felt a burst of happiness to hear her say "*your* benesaunus." He'd done it! He'd flown to the northern side of the canyon, faced the massive Black Mountains, snatched the benesaunus from their grip, and flown back home again.

Father will be so proud . . . would be . . .

Winston collapsed in the moss bed and slept until the sounds of his mother dragging another load of the gray-green food to the back of the cave finally penetrated his dreams. His eyelids lowered halfway, enough to see that Nerys must've made more than one additional trip to the Black Mountains. Benesaunus now filled the back of the cave, like it did before . . . before Raiden had disappeared.

"You're awake, Winston. Good!" Nerys nudged another mound of steamed benesaunus so close that the smell of it filled his nostrils and cleared away the last remnants of dark dreams.

"More benesaunus? Is it morning already?" He looked toward the front of the cave, attempting to judge from the light if he had indeed slept most of the day and entire night.

"No, it's midday. But gathering benesaunus is hard work. You need to eat again. And when you're done, come outside." Nerys turned and made her way to their ledge.

As Winston ate, the midsummer sky framed Nerys's silhouette. As usual now, her head moved in an arch, up and around, always searching. Winston wondered why she'd asked him to join her this time. He realized he was eating in gulps but made himself slow; he now had a much better idea of what it took to build their supplies of benesaunus.

It took benesaunus to build the strength needed to gather benesaunus. How many times had he heard his father say those words? Now he understood and chewed thoughtfully and slowly to help his body absorb every bit of the energy it provided.

When he was done, he swept the moss from the sleeping nest back into place, using his tail as he'd seen his mother do. As he walked the length of the cave toward the opening to the ledge, he felt larger somehow, more grown up. He would be thirty-one autumns soon. Most certainly not a baby dragon any longer.

Winston emerged from the cave into the warm sunlight and stood beside Nerys. Even though she smiled when she looked down at him, sadness had joined the worry he'd seen in her eyes these past weeks.

"I was proud of you today, son," she said as she resumed scanning the sky. "It only took you three tries to get your first benesaunus. It took me two trips and five tries when I was your age."

Winston lifted his head to stand taller and searched the sky along with his mother. He knew she was looking for Raiden. He knew she'd never given up hope. He wouldn't give up hope either, even though he was starting to forget the sound of his father's voice.

"Winston, I need you to stay by yourself for a few days."

"What? Why?" All at once, Winston didn't feel so grown up anymore.

Nerys lifted her gigantic wing and pulled him against the warmth of her body.

"I have to search for your father," she said. "There's something preventing him from coming back. A broken leg or wing blade. It's been too long. Whatever happened, he'll be greatly weakened if he can't get benesaunus. I have to find him, help him, take benesaunus to him . . ."

She paused, and from under her wing, Winston saw her shake her head slowly. She took a deep breath and pulled him even closer.

"I'll be fine, Mother," Winston said. "There's plenty of benesaunus, and I'll keep the cave clean and stay inside and . . ."

Nerys laughed. "You can sun yourself on the ledge and go on short flyouts. *Short* flyouts. And I know you'll be fine." She paused, then continued, "Watching you today . . . you have grown so much. In fact, I'd take you with me to look for your father, but I need you to stay here in case he makes his way back while I am gone."

Winston nodded. "When are you leaving?"

"Now. There are still many hours left in the day. And if I don't find him before dark, maybe I can find the lights he saw the night he disappeared."

"Don't you need to eat first?" Winston asked, his heart starting to pound.

"I ate while you were sleeping. And drank plenty of water. Two days, Winston. Three at the most. But if it's longer . . . if you run low on benesaunus, you know how to gather it now."

"But Mother . . ."

"I'll be back as soon as I can. And maybe your father will be with me."

She dropped off the ledge, was out of sight for a wingbeat or two, and then rose up and up, her massive wings lifting her high into the air currents. Winston watched long past when he couldn't see her anymore, watched the sky like he had seen her watch. Watched until he was as exhausted as he'd been after flying to the Black Mountains. Even though he could still hear songbirds calling in the forest treetops far below, he turned, his tail following in a sad curve, and went back to the sleeping nest.

He realized how accustomed he was to hearing two heartbeats, to feeling his mother's warm breath. He thought about how Nerys had said he knew how to gather benesaunus if the stores in the back of the cave ran low. He stared for a few minutes at the huge mounds of food piled there, enough for three dragons for half a moon. Did she think she'd be gone for more than two or three days? What if she too disappeared? He covered his head with a wing, blocking out the light from the mouth of the cave, and fell asleep once more.

Winston slept until twilight. He crept out onto the ledge, where the air was cool. The sun was round and rosy-red, edging toward the horizon. Spreading to the left and right of it, were layers of magenta and orange, which lit the evening clouds from below, so it looked like they were on fire. One cloud, dark on top and almost purple underneath, looked like a dragon chasing the sun as it made its way to the far west.

Winston could hear the whirring of the strange ground-dwelling creatures and an occasional hoot of the tree-dwelling birds of prey. A breeze brought the familiar smells of moss, mushrooms, and other forest vegetation.

Winston had always loved these long, summer evenings when the night was pushed back by the long days. He'd never flown on a summer evening, not even with his father, but now he was filled with a longing to fly, one so strong that, without stopping to think, he ran to the edge of the ledge and out into the balmy air beyond. His wings unfurled and reached farther than they ever had before. A cool updraft tickled his flight feathers, and he began to swoop and soar in great loops over the forest. His eyes adjusted to the dimmer light, and he could see for miles across the treetops.

Winston dropped down to fly, faster and faster, just above the trees, heading south. All the exhaustion he'd felt after gathering benesaunus was forgotten. The strength in his wings and lungs told him he could easily get to the far southern edge of the forest, see if Eliana were there, and still get back to the cave before true nightfall. Surely the darkening sky and the gathering clouds would camouflage him, would make it impossible for anyone to see him. In all the days and nights of scanning the skies, his mother hadn't seen anything. Not Raiden, not strange lights, nor anything else except the usual inhabitants of the forest and hills.

Faster and faster he flew through damp, heavy air. Then he was there, approaching the far southern edge of the forest. He circled once, skimming the thinning trees, before he spotted the meadow from which he'd taken off before. He tilted slightly backward, lowered his tail, and raised the tips of his wings. He dropped into the meadow, extending his strong back legs to cushion his landing. Without the sound of the air flowing under and over his wings, the silence of the meadow was like feathers over his ears. Tucking his wings close to his body, he made his way back to where he'd met Eliana, his moss-muffled footsteps seeming far too loud in the deep quiet of the forest.

There they were—the same trees, the same cushions of moss. Joy flowed through him, the joy that was Eliana. He didn't really think she would be there; it was far too late. She had probably come that morning, as he was gathering benesaunus with his mother. His mother . . . His heart thudded twice, three times. She'd wanted him to stay at the cave in case his father returned. He'd have to hurry—to be cautious, yes—but hurry.

He waited until the sky grew darker by just a few shades of blue. At the far side of the clearing where Eliana lived, golden light shone through openings in what he knew must be her home.

Eliana is there, he thought. So close. She wouldn't even know he'd come back. He sighed and began the ungainly backward shuffle that would take him out of the confines of the clearing, but then he stopped. Turning, he used his teeth to pull one minor feather from his right wing and stuck it in a thick mound of moss by one of the trees.

Flying back to the cave in the deep dark blue of the late summer evening, he hoped Eliana would find the feather, would know he'd come back. He knew he would come back again and again until he saw her.

Eliana.

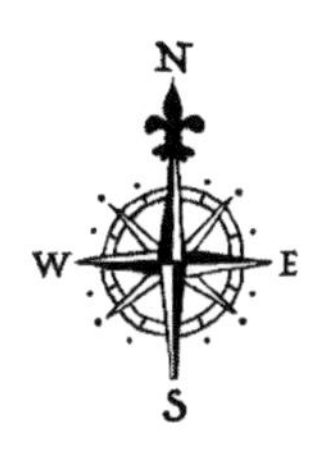

Chapter 12: Doryu

A MONTH EARLIER

Before Brogan the Head Steward could escort Doryu from his snug dungeon cell to the King's Audience Hall, the old Dragon Speaker insisted on cleaning the blue and white teacups they'd used. He placed them back on the shelf above his bed and took a heavy cloak from a hook just to the left of his cell door.

"It will be cold up there," Doryu said with a wink.

They made their way past a half-dozen empty cells, none of which had been used in years. At the foot of the service stairs, Brogan offered Doryu his arm.

"The stairs are steep and a little damp today, sir."

"Please, call me Doryu, dear Brogan. Remember, I am just the third son of a trapper."

The two climbed to emerge in a dim, narrow corridor.

In the kitchen to their right, they could see Cook chopping vegetables with what looked like a woodcutter's hatchet. Enticing smells wafted from the giant pot hanging over the fire, reminding Doryu that he'd had only half a bun some time ago.

Approaching the Audience Hall, Doryu shivered. It was always frigid in the drafty, aged castle in May; winds from across the Seething Sea bred freezing rains and sometimes even snow. But this year, the cold seemed alive, reaching to grab at hands and feet.

A tremendous fire blazed with furious futility in the fireplace beside which sat the King. When Brogan saw his king was sound asleep, head propped on his hand, with a little drool running down his beard, he asked Doryu to wait by the door.

"Sire, the Dragon Speaker is here," the Steward whispered to Halwyn.

"What? What? Dragon Speaker?" The King sputtered and wiped the drool from his beard.

"Yes, I finally found him, Your Highness." Brogan gestured for Doryu to approach.

"Ah, you look like your father," said Doryu to the King, giving a slight bow of his head as Halwyn sat up and pulled his cloak around his stomach.

"My *father*? Why is no one making any sense these days?" shouted the King.

"I was twelve and Chares was ten when he became King, and I became the Royal Dragon Speaker."

Doryu and Brogan waited while the King stood, walked around the chair in which he had been sitting, strode to his throne, sat upon it for a moment, and went back to sit once again in his chair by the fire.

"I think I remember you," Halwyn said at last, squinting at the old man standing before him. "You were with my father, here in this very room. He was angry; you were angry. Neither of you even realized I was there."

"I knew you were there, sire," said the old Dragon Speaker. "I was just too angry to stop myself even though you were only five or six and far too young to be privy to our argument."

"He wanted you to help him kill dragons. I remember now. He wanted you to . . ." Halwyn looked back at the fire, shaking his head.

"Yes," said Doryu. "He couldn't forget what happened to his father, your grandfather. Chares saw his father's body slung over his stallion, and something broke inside him. He was sad, of course, but it was anger and hatred that consumed him. Chares's first decree the night of his father's death was that all dragons were to be hunted and slain."

"So that's when it happened," said Halwyn.

"That's when it *began*. During the first few days, the new King's guardsmen were unable to find any dragons to kill. Chares grew more furious and commanded that all the region's hunters and trappers join the hunt. They were more successful . . . unfortunately."

"Unfortunately? Why?"

"Because I knew that your grandfather was killed because he was trying to slay a dragon *child*. I knew because I'd found both dragons, father and son, as well as the King's sword. And the young dragon told me what had happened."

At that, Halwyn rose to his feet and commanded Brogan to find a stool for Doryu, to summon Valo and Margred, and to bring food, wine, and ale.

When all were gathered, the King said, "We'll hear the whole story now, Dragon Speaker. Brogan, you will stay as well."

And so Doryu told them about the bloody scene in the forest that day, the cries, the last breath of the dragon, the freeing of his injured son, the discovery that he could hear the child speak by touching his scaled skin.

"His name was Raiden."

"What? This, this . . . *creature* had a name?" sputtered the King.

Valo had his hand on his sword again. Margred's mouth was a thin downward slash upon her pale face.

"Yes, he told me," said Doryu.

More sputtering from the King.

Doryu continued, "When I returned home that dreadful day, dragging the King's heavy jewel-laden sword, news of the King's death had already spread. My father yelled at me for going so far into the forest, for approaching a dragon, and for bringing the bloody sword back to our home. He was sure we'd be blamed for what happened to the King.

"But when I told him about the colors streaming from

my hand and that I'd been able to understand the dragon, he grew very still. He stared into the fire for a long time, then called me to him. Instead of yelling, he put his arm around me and told me about Dragon Speakers. He told me that in certain families, once every few generations or so, someone is born who can do what I'd done in the forest. That kings would provide handsomely for this service, for someone who could communicate with dragons. That a Dragon Speaker would live royally and perhaps help his family out as well.

"Well, you can imagine my mother's reaction when my father wanted to take me—and the dead King's sword—to the castle. After two days and nights of weeping and discussion, it was decided that I should go to the new King, tell him what I'd seen, and offer my services as a Dragon Speaker.

"I was terrified, even more afraid than I'd been in the forest with the dragons. When the King saw I had his father's sword, would he order my immediate execution? And even if he were willing to listen to my tale, how could I explain my ability to communicate with dragons when I didn't fully understand it myself?"

Doryu paused and cleared his throat. Brogan poured water into a brass goblet and handed it to the old man. The King continued to stare at Doryu as if trying to connect what he remembered of him with what he was hearing. Valo shook his head, shifting from one foot to the other. Margred's eyes were closed, her bloodless face icy and still.

Doryu continued, "One of the other trappers had a cart and a mule. He agreed to take me and my father to within a stone's throw of the castle gate. I can still see my mother standing by our cottage door, holding my baby sister Jade in her arms. I knew then I'd never see either of them again." Doryu's hands shook, and his light gray eyes shimmered in the firelight.

"It was so long ago. So very long ago," he said.

Doryu waved to his mother and sister for as long as he could see them while the mule-drawn cart bumped along the road running beside the trappers' cabins. It was more a dirt path where nothing grew than a road, and Doryu—facing backward—clung to the wooden sides of the cart to keep from being flung into the trees. His father and the cart's owner sat on a board set across the front of the cart. When Doryu turned his head, all he could see was his father's broad back, stiff and resolute. The King's sword lay beside the boy, tied with a length of frayed rope to the rough floorboards. The dragon's blood had dried to a dull reddish-brown, and its bitter-sweet scent smelled like death.

At twelve, Doryu was used to seeing blood. He and his two older brothers worked alongside their father to skin and tan the hides of the animals he trapped. Their family depended on the meat of the animals for food, and the hides were used for clothing, household items, and in trade for supplies they needed. But now Doryu shifted as far as he could to the other side of the cart, distancing himself from the blood on the sword. He rubbed at a spot of blood on the cloth bag his mother had thrust into his hands before he left.

The fabric will need a good soaking soon, he thought. He tried to stop thinking about the blood by looking at the golden sunlight filtering through the tree branches overhead. But his eyes kept returning to the hilt of the sword, to the gleaming red stone flashing in the morning sun.

Just when Doryu began to think he couldn't hold on to the sides of the cart any longer and he'd be flung into the forest—along with the sword—never to be seen again, the path emerged from the deep forest. It smoothed and widened as it crossed the west edge of the quarry. Here, many of the trees had been cleared but no stone thacking had begun. To his left, Doryu could see the immensity of the quarry, the far east side a blue-gray mountain rushing up to meet the sky. In the middle of the quarry, huge chunks of dark gray and black slate had been hacked away until it looked like a giant staircase to another land.

The path continued across the quarry floor until it finally met up with Quarry Road. They turned south and wound their way through a meadow bordered by younger oaks. Being on a road with an actual name meant they were that much closer to the castle, and cold fear shot through Doryu's spine. Glancing again at the sword, it seemed he could actually taste the blood. Would his blood be added to it before the day was done?

"Father?" he said.

But his father either didn't hear or chose not to answer.

All too soon, the cart emerged from the forest onto a much wider dirt road, enough for at least four of the trapper's carts to travel side by side. Doryu realized this must be Kings Road. The trapper pulled the mule's reins to turn it to the left, and the cart followed, heading east. Doryu could hear the deep voices of the soldiers who were stationed here and there along the side of the road but could only catch an occasional word or phrase. *Dragons, King Chares, reward.* Were they looking for him? Doryu's father turned and laid his cloak over the sword, tucking the edges under, smothering the light spun by the red jewel.

The sun was much brighter on the road, but despite its warmth, Doryu's hands on the sides of the cart began to shake. His pale blond hair and his face seemed to be on fire, but he felt as if water from a cold mountain stream filled his lungs and belly. By the time the cart turned on the road that wove through Morganshire, he could hardly breathe.

The cart lurched to a stop. They'd passed through the village proper, and Doryu saw only fields on either side of the road. He heard the buzzing of flies, the huffing of the mule, the creaking of its leather traces, the scuffling of his father's feet. There was another buzzing inside Doryu's head, one that grew until it was all he could hear. He saw his father's hand held out to help him down from the cart, he saw his father remove the cloak that covered the sword, he felt the weight of the sword in his hands. He felt his father's hand on his shoulder, saw his mouth moving, telling him something, but Doryu could only shake his head, trying to stop the horrible buzzing.

His father turned him to face the steep hill leading to Morgan Castle. The gates to the courtyard were open. On the front of the castle, a square tower—composed of huge, shaped stones—rose into the cloudless sky. Black pennants hung lifeless on their poles. Just outside the courtyard, there were more soldiers, goats and chickens, farmers pushing wheelbarrows of limp vegetables, and a massive black horse galloping toward him. On the horse was a boy draped in a purple robe that kept slipping off his thin shoulders. The buzzing in Doryu's head was abruptly replaced with the sound of his heart throbbing in time with the dull thunder of the stallion's hooves as they carried the angry young King ever closer.

Just when Doryu was sure that Chares meant to run him over with his horse, the new King leaned back and pulled hard on the reins, bringing the stallion to a skidding stop in a cloud of brown dust. Chares dropped the reins, slid off his mount, and fell to his knees in front of Doryu. For a brief, ridiculous moment, Doryu thought the King was kneeling before *him*, but then Chares reached for the sword—his father's sword—that Doryu held by its jeweled hilt.

"Why do you have his sword? Explain yourself!" Chares stood and grabbed the hilt of the sword, wrenching it from Doryu's hand. The new King's face throbbed with anger, and the authority in his voice made him seem older than his mere ten years. Just before Doryu dropped to his knees, he saw tears making rivulets in the dust on Chares's face.

"Sire . . . Your Highness . . . please. I can explain," said Doryu.

Chares stared at him, doubtless seeing him for what he was: a boy not much older than himself, dressed in tattered clothing, the lowly son of a trapper. The new King's gaze shifted to Doryu's upturned hand and the thin line of blood where the sword's ruby had cut his palm. Chares's eyes turned back to his, blazing with anger layered over sorrow. The King leaned so his face was only inches from Doryu's as he shouted to his guardsmen.

"Take this boy to my Audience Hall. I'll listen to what he has to say. It's what my father would have done. And if execution is called for, then execution it will be."

Now, sitting before Chares's son so many years later, Doryu paused and ran one gnarled finger across the scar on the palm of his right hand. Perched on the low wooden stool, the old man's legs shook beneath the thin fabric of his trousers. The fire seemed to be fighting a losing battle of adding even a little warmth to the great stone room. His mother . . . his sister, Jade . . . Even all these years later, his brothers and sister might still be alive. Why had he hidden away in the dungeon instead of trying to find them, to at least be sure they were well? But then he would have had to tell them what he had done.

That the great Dragon Speaker helped to slaughter dragons.

Doryu looked up at Brogan whose face held only compassion. "Might I get a little wine?" the old man asked the Steward.

King Halwyn, the son of Chares (who had died of a fever at the age of fifty-one) said, "Brogan, you may as well pour everyone a goblet. And get this old man a plate of food."

As Doryu ate and sipped some wine, the King sat, rubbing his hands on his knees, his bushy eyebrows lowered until only the bottom half of his eyes were visible. His lower lip pushed in and out, in and out.

Doryu saw the King's Counselor's mouth turn up at one corner in what may or may not have been a smile. When she saw him looking at her, Margred held his eyes and nodded slightly, just enough that her long, silky black hair shifted on her shoulders. Outside, the wind-blown snow found the chinks in the castle walls.

Whatever this is about, I need to figure out Margred's part in it, Doryu thought.

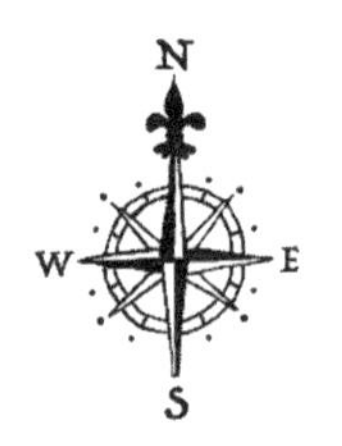

Chapter 13: Eliana

DAY TWO

When Eliana and Sage got home from Bedwyr's, they heard their mother talking in the sleeping room. The curtain was pulled back, and bright May sunlight pooled on the stone floor just inside the room. Eliana smiled with relief to see Alethia propped up against a mound of pillows on their bed, sipping broth from their father's special cup. She'd brushed her hair so that it lay straight and smooth on her slim shoulders. It was the color of corn silk. Her sky-blue eyes were bright and clear. Glenna sat beside her, one hand on her elder daughter's leg. Rowan and Sage's bed was a tangle of empty, rumpled blankets.

"I'm going to be a cartographer when I grow up!" said Sage as he ran to find his brother.

Glenna smiled and patted the bed beside her. "Come sit, Eliana."

"How's Bedwyr?" asked Alethia. "Thank you for taking his eggs to him. Was he upset?"

"He was worried about you," said Eliana. "He told me to tell you to feel better soon. It's a good thing Sage is only seven, or he just might take your apprenticeship," she teased with a grin. "He and Bedwyr made a jar of paint out of flowers Sage picked on the way to his house today. The two of them spent a long time talking about maps and compass roses."

Alethia swirled the liquid in the teacup and took another sip of broth. "Well, it's a good thing I'll be well enough to resume my duties tomorrow." She stared down into the blue and white teacup. Then she smiled and added, "Can you imagine Bedwyr being able to get anything done with Sage's constant questions?"

Eliana laughed to see her sister's sense of humor back again. "I'm so glad you're feeling better, Alethia," she said.

"I'm going to make some tea," said Glenna. "Eliana, keep your sister company for a little while."

As soon as their mother left the sleeping room, Eliana leaned forward to whisper to Alethia. "I need your help with something, but it's a secret. You have to promise you won't say anything to anyone."

Alethia's blue eyes opened wide. "A secret?"

"*Shhhhhh*. Yes. I promised him I wouldn't tell anyone. He was so afraid . . ."

"*Who* was afraid?"

"The dragon."

"What?" Alethia sat straight up in bed and almost

dropped their father's cup on the floor.

"Shhhhhh! You have to whisper!" said Eliana, taking the cup into the safety of her own lap. "He's beautiful. Green and turquoise. He's not big like the old stories. I mean, he's big, but not that big. And he's nice and sweet. His name is Winston."

Alethia sat, shaking her head, her lips pressed together. Finally she said, "So, you found a dragon and named it Winston? Eliana, you are far too old to have a make-believe friend. Winston? What kind of name is that anyway?"

"It's *his* name. He told me. And he's not make-believe! I saw him, I touched him, and he told me his name is Winston." Eliana grabbed her sister's hand. "Please, Alethia! I need your help. I promised him I'd come back, but I can't go into the forest alone again. I promised Father. But if you come with me, it'll be all right. And you can meet him, too!"

"Eliana . . ."

"Please, Alethia!"

Alethia sighed, "All right, I'll go with you tomorrow morning . . ."

Eliana kissed her sister's hand, squeezing so hard that Alethia pulled it away.

"Ow! That hurt! I'll go with you, but it'll have to be early, before I leave for Bedwyr's. You can show me what you found that you thought was a dragon."

"Thank you, Alethia!" Eliana started to grab Alethia's hand again, but Alethia quickly thrust it under her quilt to protect it from her sister's overly enthusiastic grasp.

"Eliana!" Glenna called from the kitchen. "Go see what the boys are up to. It's way too quiet outside!"

As Eliana stood to leave the sleeping room, she smiled at her sister who continued to shake her head. Alethia was muttering to herself under her breath but loud enough that Eliana could still hear a few words.

"Winston? Really? A dragon . . .?"

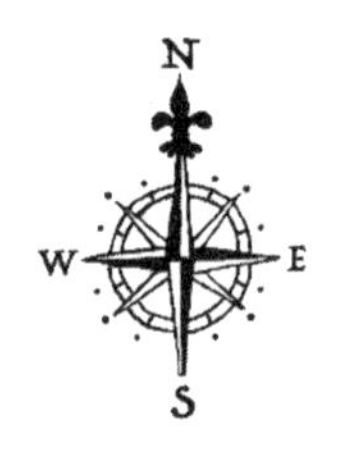

Chapter 14: King Halwyn

ONE MONTH BEFORE

While the old Dragon Speaker refreshed himself with wine and food, King Halwyn sat in his chair by the fire, contemplating the many things he'd heard so far: that his grandfather had been killed by a dragon, that supposedly the old man in front of him could talk with dragons, that his father Chares had tried to kill every last dragon, and that maybe there were still dragons hidden away that could help find his kingdom's treasure.

As he sipped wine from his royal goblet, Halwyn stared into the flames blazing beside him. He remembered more now about the terrific argument between Chares and Doryu. He'd been, as Doryu had said, just six years old. He remembered because he'd gotten a child-sized sword—more like a large, blunt knife—for his birthday, and he'd been jabbing it in the air in the corner of the Audience Hall when his father summoned Doryu.

"You wanted to see me, Your Highness?" Doryu bowed his head to Chares, who was sitting by the same fireplace as Halwyn was now.

"It is well past moonrise, and you still haven't reported to me about today's hunt." Chares gripped the arms of his chair, his knuckles white. His face, partly covered by his sparse beard, was ashen as well. Although only thirty at the time, he looked much older. He'd spent the previous twenty years consumed by only one aim—to destroy all dragons in the kingdom—and his health had suffered from the hatred that burned inside him.

His Dragon Speaker had played a key role in the slaughtering. Chares had commanded that any dragon cornered be roped and held until the Dragon Speaker could be brought to speak to it. Doryu was to promise the dragon that its life would be spared if it would reveal where to find other dragons, whose lives would be spared as well. Most of the time, the dragon wouldn't believe the lie, would refuse to cooperate and be summarily killed, spears and swords slashing and stabbing until all that could be seen was bright red blood. But sometimes, young dragons, terrified and trusting, could be convinced to give up the location of other dragons, and then, just like the others, they were killed.

"Well? Today's hunt?" commanded Chares again, as his son pretended to hunt dragons in the corner.

"The dragon captured today wouldn't tell me anything, sire."

"Liar!" Chares burst from his chair, hand on his dagger. "I *know* it told you something. One of the guardsmen told me the pathetic creature was shaking all over like a baby bird flung from its nest. The guardsman told me you spent a long time with your hand on his neck, that you were whispering so no one could hear what you were saying. That when you removed your hand and told the soldiers that it had told you nothing, it went crazy, flinging its head around and making horrible noises. I know the ones who refuse to talk go silently to their deaths. This was not one of those."

The two men stood only a few feet apart, glaring at each other. In the corner, the boy—Prince Halwyn—stopped stabbing the air and stood staring at his father and the Dragon Speaker.

"Chares . . ." began Doryu.

"*King* Chares," said Chares. "You will call me King!"

"The dragon told me nothing, *King* Chares!" Doryu yelled, too, spittle from his mouth, landing on Chares's face.

"He told you something! Something you decided to hide from the soldiers. And from me!" Chares wiped the spittle from his face and closed his eyes.

Doryu, jaw clenched, glared at him in silence.

"Get out of my sight, Doryu." The King was shaking and a vein in his neck pulsed, but he stopped shouting.

And Doryu left, turning without a bow, striding to the

door, past a scared little boy holding a useless sword in his hand.

Now, still staring into the fire, King Halwyn could clearly remember his sixth birthday, the amazing gift of the child-sized sword, playing with it in the corner while he waited for his father to show him how to use it. He remembered his father calling for the Dragon Speaker and the horrible argument that followed. He hadn't understood what the argument was about, only that he'd never seen Doryu again.

Thinking back, Halwyn realized that after that night, Chares had ceased proudly announcing, during dinners with dignitaries, how many dragons had been killed that day. In fact, Chares had entertained less and less and seemed to shrink in size. He could frequently be found slumped in this very chair, sipping goblet after goblet of red wine, looking as if he'd lost his best friend. Which, it seemed to Halwyn now, that he had.

"It would seem you lied to my father about the green dragon, about what he did or didn't tell you that day," Halwyn said to the old Dragon Speaker. "Is that correct?"

"Yes," said Doryu. He took one last sip of wine.

"Why?"

"Because the young dragon told me where to find Raiden, the dragon I'd helped save when I was a boy. The young dragon they'd captured that day was doomed either way. At that moment, I knew I couldn't continue to help

Chares kill dragons. I knew they weren't the evil monsters Chares thought they were. Raiden's father only fought with the King that day to save his son. I knew dragons didn't kill for any other reason; they don't even eat meat. All those times I laid my hand on a captured dragon's neck, I could hear everything he said. I learned many things about them, none of them bad. I just couldn't do it anymore, regardless of the cost."

"So that's why you were in the dungeon? My father threw you down there?" asked Halwyn.

"No, no," Doryu waved his hand, shook his head, and smiled sadly. "He just never summoned me again. Although, he continued to send supplies and coin to my family. I stayed in case Chares . . . in case he summoned me again. In case we could somehow repair our friendship. And after he died, it had been too long; this castle was my home.

"For several years, I lived in the quarters I had been granted in one of the Guest Towers. But there were too many stairs to climb, and it was far too cold. I moved myself, with help from Cook, down to the dungeon, where my little stove doesn't have to compete with the drafts."

Halwyn—who had forgotten that anyone else was there besides the old man—saw a dark movement to his left. Margred glided forward, eyes fixed on Doryu, who turned on his stool to face her. Halwyn opened his mouth to speak, but Margred spoke first.

"And now, old man, you will earn the past forty years of your keep. You will help your King find his missing treasure."

"Mind your place, woman," said Valo. With two strides, the massive Captain of the Guard stood between Margred and Doryu.

Halwyn saw what looked like flames in Margred's eyes before her glance slid down and away.

"Valo," said the King. "Let's hear Margred's plan. That's why I summoned this . . . Dragon Speaker."

Valo bowed and stepped back, but Halwyn saw the man's jaw muscles flexing and even heard the grinding of his teeth. He wondered, not for the first time, why Valo and Margred seemed to dislike each other so intensely.

Margred bowed to Halwyn, her eyes once again a cool violet, and said, "Your Highness, now is the time to enlist a dragon to help you recover the missing treasure. Valo and his soldiers will go beyond the northern edge of the forest, taking Doryu with them. They will use the torches I give them to call the dragon from its cave."

Doryu started to rise from his stool, shaking his head, but Margred held up her hand. "Don't worry, Dragon Speaker, no one will harm this dragon. You will merely use your special skills to convince it to find the missing treasure."

"Why would a dragon help us?" asked Doryu. "They live well over a hundred years. Do you think he won't remember, or at least have heard of, the murders of his kind under Chares's rule?"

"Because the dragon we seek owes you a debt," said Margred, tilting her head to the side, smiling at Doryu. "You saved his life when you were twelve years old."

"Raiden . . ." said Doryu, the name a slow exhale of breath.

"Yes. Raiden," said Margred.

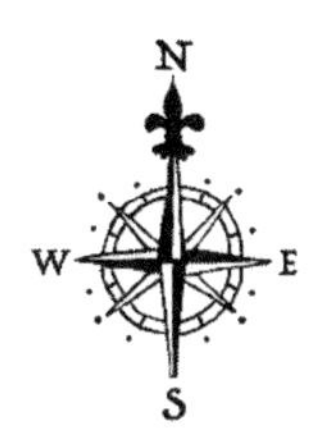

Chapter 15: Doryu

Doryu sat, his hands shaking on his knees, his heart beating without rhythm in his chest. *I will refuse,* he thought. *What can they do to me? I've lived a long life . . . and . . .*

"Doryu," said Margred, "You're looking unwell. Are you feverish?" The King's Counselor bent to place her hand on Doryu's forehead, leaning toward him in what—to others—might look like concern. Her lips brushed his ear, her ebony hair shielding her actions from everyone else.

"Do you remember your sister?" she whispered. "She's a mother now, a grandmother! Living comfortably in the same cottage where you both were born. It would be a shame if an accident cut her life short, wouldn't it?"

His sister, just a baby when he'd last seen her, wisps of hair so pale she'd looked like a dandelion. Like a puff of wind could blow her away. Jade. So long ago, but he remembered how she always grabbed onto his thumb when he held her. She was still alive. At least there's that to be thankful for. But how did the King's Counselor know about her?

Margred stood and smiled down at him. "No, no fever. I'm sure all this has been almost too much for you, dear Doryu. I'll get you a cup of tea to revive your spirits. You'll leave tonight to guide Valo to Raiden."

She turned to speak to Valo, her thin smile in contrast to the Captain's scowl. "I'll prepare the special torches after dinner. The storm's dying down. It'll clear soon. You'll leave at moonrise."

Valo, eyebrows raised in doubt, turned to King Halwyn who nodded. Doryu could see that the King looked as exhausted as he himself felt. When the King finally spoke, he stared down at the dusty stone floor.

"Valo, ready your guardsmen. Take twenty tonight in case of any trouble in the forest."

All that happened next seemed to Doryu a hazy dream in which people moved slowly yet inexorably toward certain disaster. The tea Margred brought did seem to revive him somewhat physically, but his thoughts were muddled, and he felt incapable of clear speech. Someone brought him more food and warm boots to replace the tattered slippers he'd worn for so many years. Brogan? Yes, Brogan. The Head Steward. A kind young man. He kept patting Doryu on his shoulder, but Doryu couldn't make out what he was saying.

He dozed for a while on a bench in the corridor outside the King's Audience Hall and was awakened at moonrise by the same kind young man. *Was his name Brogan?* Doryu stood on steady legs, surprised by how strong they were compared to his befuddled mind. Surprised by how good the boots felt on his feet, he followed Valo, and what seemed an entire army of soldiers, through a long corridor, down a stairway, and out into the inner courtyard of the castle.

It was a glorious night, clear and bright. The moonlight reflected off the drifts of melting snow heaped against the courtyard's inner walls. April was finally pushing back the fiercer cold of March. Doryu breathed in the crisp, clean air, happy to be going . . . *where*? Valo, his second-in-command Angus, and the rest of the soldiers mounted horses that seemed to materialize out of nowhere. Doryu tried to remember where they were going but had only a hazy thought of a baby girl in the arms of . . . someone. Without warning, he was being pulled into the air. He looked at his arm and saw Valo's gloved hand around it. Valo lifted him as if he weighed nothing and swung him around to sit behind him, high on a massive gray horse.

The journey along Kings Road seemed to take only minutes. When Valo turned north on a smaller road, Doryu saw a fenced pasture on the left with a flock of sheep standing beside some gnarled trees. Moonlight reflected in the eyes of the few sheep that were awake, standing watch against predators.

Doryu was beginning to feel less hazy now and found his voice to ask, "Where are we going? I seem to have forgotten."

"To the Granite Hills, old man." Then a few moments later . . . "That witch put something in your tea."

Witch? Ah, yes, the woman in the dark blue robes. Her breath on his ear had felt like air blown across an ice-covered pond. Was she a witch? Doryu had heard stories about people who could cast spells, but he assumed they merely had extensive knowledge and skill in the use of herbs. It did seem the tea had both strengthened him physically and confused his mind, which could've been from a combination of herbs. He had a vague recollection of telling Valo they needed to go to the Granite Hills, but he wasn't sure until Valo said it: *To the Granite Hills.*

Doryu listened to the rhythmic *clop clop* of hooves on the frozen road and the occasional soft nicker of a horse. A lattice of shadows lay on remnants of snow where moonlight found its way through the oak branches.

Doryu's mind grew clearer, and he noticed the oblong leather pouch slung behind him. It lay against the horse's right flank, and protruding from it were torches made of birch bark, rolled and tied with leather thongs. Mixed with the usual tinder of dried and fresh grasses were lumps of something shiny and midnight blue that burned his nose when he bent over to sniff them.

"Leave those alone, old man," said Valo. "Margred made them, and they're probably poisonous. She claims the light from them will call the dragon to us." He snorted.

At some unseen signal from Valo, the horse veered off the road and began climbing upward through the thickening trees, following a mere suggestion of a path. Looking back, Doryu could see the other horses and riders following, leaving the road one by one. To his left, there were glimpses of the stone quarry, tremendous slabs of slate jutting out of the ground, black and gray and white.

Like Raiden.

Gagging, Doryu let go of Valo, fell to the ground, and staggered to the side of the path. His vomit was watery and green and smelled like the tea Margred had given him. How could he do this? How could he lead them to Raiden? The dragon he'd saved twice before, once from beneath his dead father's wing and again when he'd lied to Chares about knowing where Raiden was.

But Margred knew about Jade, had threatened to kill her. Even though Doryu knew Jade was an old woman now, he still thought of her as the baby he'd last seen in his mother's arms. Once again, he wondered how the King's Counselor knew about his sister. How did she know about the family she has now? Her grandchildren? He exhaled in frustration. It didn't matter how she knew; the threat had been clear.

Maybe Margred had been telling the truth, that the King just needed Raiden's help to find the missing gold and jewels. Surely King Halwyn would honor the promise not to harm the dragon. It had been Chares who was set on killing all dragons, and he'd been dead for twenty years. But why should Raiden assist them? He could hardly be expected to know that Doryu had been the boy who'd helped him that horrible day in the forest. And Raiden would have no way of knowing Doryu had lied to protect him from Chares years later.

"We need to ride on now," said Valo.

Doryu stood, fighting new waves of nausea. Valo's horse's nostrils flared and blew warm, grassy air across Doryu's face, which amazingly calmed his stomach. He reached up his hand to Valo, who once again effortlessly lifted him to the horse's back.

"Her name is Destre, my horse," said Valo. "She likes you."

The wonder of this immense horse liking him and the lingering warmth of her soothing breath on his face helped settle Doryu's mind and stomach, and he began to think through all the problems at hand with more clarity. How likely was it that Raiden would still be in the same cave over forty-five years later? And if not, where might he be now? And even if they could find him, how would he be able to convince him to help the King? Would an old Dragon Speaker be able to work with Raiden to find the missing treasure? How could he protect both Jade and Raiden? And lastly, how could they all avoid further interactions with Margred?

As Destre carried them deeper into the forest, climbing

steadily upward, the air grew colder and Doryu was glad for the warm boots. He decided he would face one challenge at a time, the first being to find Raiden. Although it was so long ago, he clearly remembered the conversation he'd had with the doomed younger dragon before Chares's men had killed him. In his attempt to save his own life, the dragon had told him where Raiden lived with his brother in a cave in the Granite Hills, a half day's flight west of the river that flowed to the sea.

Doryu knew that a young dragon like the green one could fly over a hundred and fifty miles in a day. He assumed the river was the Pearl River that left the foot of the Black Mountains almost forty miles north and twenty miles west of Cantington Bay. So, if Doryu's calculations were correct, Raiden's cave (at least the one he'd lived in before) was about twenty-five miles northwest by north of the quarry they'd passed before.

"Valo, I think this path is taking us too far west. We need to be almost due north of the quarry."

"The forest is too dense to head due north," said Valo. "We'll stay on this path—such as it is—until we get to the foot of the Granite Hills. Then we can make our way back east."

"Do we have climbing tools? Rope? The Granite Hills are jagged and layered in higher and higher rows of rock. We'll need . . ."

"The dragon will come to us," said Valo. "Margred said that these torches will call him." He patted the side of the leather pouch. "Although the way they smell, they might just drive him away."

They continued to climb, northwest by north, Destre picking her way on the narrow path. Overhead, clouds formed, covering and uncovering the moon like a dark cloak flapping in the wind. The forest grew denser, closing in on the line of horses and riders; even when the clouds stepped aside for a moment or two, it was so dark that only the trunk of a tree a few feet away could be seen from time to time. Despite his fears, Doryu could not keep his eyes open, and he leaned his cheek against Valo's back . . . just for a moment, just for a few minutes . . .

Doryu jerked awake when Destre's smooth rocking movement stopped all together. All the riders were gathered in a clearing in the forest, beyond which were glimpses of the base of the Granite Hills. Doryu wondered yet again who had named this range of mountains "hills," for they rose steeply and massively, row after row of jagged rock, bare, save for a few stunted bushes in shallow pockets of rocky soil.

He must've slept for longer than a few minutes, for now the clouds were a nearly solid mass of moisture, and it was only because Valo lit one of the malodorous torches that anyone could see anything at all. The light it shed was not the oranges, reds, and yellows of fire, but burned blue with streaks of white. Only Destre remained steady; the other horses tossed their heads and rolled their eyes, nostrils flaring.

"We'll ride out in two lines, just there within the edge of the tree line." Valo gestured with the torch to the area where the forest ended, right where the rocky foothills began. "We want him to see the torches but not us or the horses. Angus, you take your men east. The rest of you will come with me to the west."

"But . . ." said Doryu.

"Don't worry, Dragon Speaker, we've already made our way back east to make up for the westward heading of the path. We are as close to due north of the quarry as we can be." Valo reached back and patted Doryu on the knee.

It was as one of Angus's men was lighting a foul-smelling torch that his horse began to scream and jump stiff-legged to the side. The soldier slid to the ground, handed the torch to another rider, and grabbed his own horse's reins. Speaking softly to him and walking away from the torches, the soldier was finally able to calm the horse, but the damage had already been done.

Cursing under his breath, Valo shook his head. "Let's just hope the dragon didn't hear that," he said, turning Destre to follow the tree line to the west.

The torches' strange blue light seemed to float on the air, while the soldiers and horses looked like gray shadows moving below them. Even when the clouds shifted and the moonlight briefly lit the Granite Hills, Doryu noticed that the horses and soldiers were still shrouded, almost as if the torchlight were somehow hiding them.

Just as Valo abruptly raised his closed fist to call for frozen silence, the torchlight went out completely, allowing them to remain hidden from a group of trappers who had come to investigate. When the trappers moved back to the south and could no longer be heard, the torchlights began to glow again until they were once again fully lit. A few of the men exchanged looks of confusion and what looked like fear, but at a nod from Valo, they once again began following him, moving west. Closer to where Raiden might be.

Raiden. A full-grown dragon now. Remembering the immensity of Raiden's father who'd died to protect his son, Doryu felt small and old and weak.

I wish . . . he thought. *For time. More time.* To make amends for the wrongs he'd done. To see his sister again. To have one more cup of tea beside his stove and finish the book about ancient cities he'd been reading.

Doryu closed his eyes and tightened his grip on Valo. The Captain of the Guard once again reached to pat his knee. The old Dragon Speaker was grateful that the darkness hid the tears he couldn't hold back any longer.

Chapter 16: Winston

THE EVENING OF DAY TWO

After leaving one of his feathers in the clearing for Eliana, Winston flew back to the Granite Hills in what was now full dark. Stars paraded across the sky, and the winds were warmer than they'd been in many moons. As he skimmed across the treetops, the leaves whispered, and an occasional nocturnal creature scrabbled along on the forest floor. He was larger than any other animal living here in these woods, so Winston had no fear of them. But since the night a month ago, when Raiden disappeared after going to investigate strange lights in the forest, Winston had been afraid of the night. His mother's cautious watch and the faster beating of her heart—especially at night—signaled fear.

But now, on this night, Winston's powerful wings pushed and lifted again and again; he could feel the soft air moving under and over them, and he knew he had never flown faster. Along with the glorious speed, his breath began to settle into a new rhythm. It was the same rhythm he'd heard when he flew with his father. In and out, slow and steady. His father, who wasn't afraid of anything.

Winston realized he wasn't afraid anymore even though Nerys had left to look for Raiden. He knew he must be cautious, to be on the lookout for danger, but now he knew that not all humans were to be feared. That one of them had been able to understand him with a touch of her hand.

By the time Winston landed on the ledge outside the cave, he'd decided he should help his mother find Raiden. If Raiden hadn't come back to the cave yet, there was a reason. His mother had said he might be injured or . . . Winston knew he was strong enough to fly more miles in a day than he'd ever flown before, and he could carry benesaunus to his father when they found him. But the most important decision he made that night was that he would tell Eliana about his father. Would tell her about the glowing lights, would enlist her help. She could ask other humans if they'd seen a giant gray and white dragon. And Eliana would tell him what she learned from them. Together they could find Raiden.

Winston knew he should have told Nerys about the human he'd met. That Eliana was kind and could understand him when she touched his scales. But surely she would forgive him when Eliana helped find Raiden.

As Winston curled up in the sleeping moss, the

decisions he'd made filled him with a calm he hadn't felt since his father disappeared. He felt the slowing of his heart and his breathing, the state of a dragon at peace.

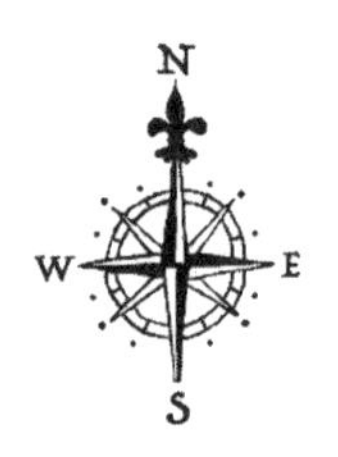

Chapter 17: Eliana

THE NIGHT OF DAY TWO / DAY THREE

As Winston flew back over the moonlit forest, Eliana could only sleep in bits and pieces, waking and dreaming all blending together, flinging the covers off and pulling them back on as she grew too hot, then too cold. Awake, asleep. Hot, cold. She was awake when her father slid almost silently out of his bed, pulled on his clothes, and pushed past the curtain to the kitchen. He put the kettle on the stove, and a spoon clinked against the edge of the teacup. When her father opened the front door to leave, it was only a whisper across the stone floor.

Wide awake now, Eliana waited for several minutes to be sure her father hadn't forgotten anything. Had she heard him take his lunch basket off the shelf? She didn't want him to come back and find her up and dressed, or worse yet, leaving out the back door before the sun began to rise.

As Eliana waited, she thought about how her father's hands had looked the morning before, holding his teacup as gently as he would a newborn chick. She remembered her promise to not go into the forest alone. Her mouth was dry, and she shook her head at the thought that he probably didn't want her going with Alethia, either. But he hadn't said that, really; just not to go *alone*. And she had to go. She'd promised Winston that she would come back. And in that moment, she thrust aside the promise she'd made to her father in order to keep the one she'd made to Winston.

Please be there, Winston. Please be there, she thought. She'd told the dragon she'd be back the next morning. Now it had been two days. Would he come? Would he be so afraid of Alethia that he'd hide? She smiled, remembering how ineffectively Winston had hidden when she'd met him. *No, if he is close by, we'll be able to see him,* she thought.

Sure now that Cadoc wouldn't be coming back to the house, Eliana gently nudged her sister's shoulder. Alethia groaned and pulled the quilt up.

"Alethia," Eliana whispered in her sister's ear. "Get up!"

The girls weren't as quiet as their father had been as they got up, dressed, and tiptoed out of the sleeping area, but Glenna and the twins were so deep in slumber they didn't even stir.

Eliana made sure the dividing curtain was completely closed and made her way toward the back door, feeling in the dark for the chairs. She didn't want to bump one and wake her mother. She could feel Alethia shuffling behind her. Eliana was well-practiced in lifting the back door so it didn't scrape on the stone floor. She waited until Alethia stepped past her to lift and pull it closed.

The backyard was still dark—the garden, fruit trees, and chicken coop darker still. The sky was black overhead, strewn with stars, fading to midnight blue in the east. The stars they could see were fewer there, disappearing altogether in the pale lavenders and soft pinks of sunrise just beginning. The chickens were still asleep; it was still too dark for them to see. Not even Henry the Fifth made a sound as the sisters crossed the yard and waded through the stream to stand on the strip of land that bordered the forest. A slight breeze moved like a whisper through the tops of the trees.

"Eliana, let's go back to bed. It's cold and there's nothing here," said Alethia, her voice soft. "I know you thought you saw something, but . . ."

Eliana reached for Alethia's hand; her sister's long, slender fingers were cold, and Eliana tried not to think about how sick her sister had been just a day and a half ago. "Wait. Just a few more minutes. It's still too early. When I saw him before, it was after I did my chores."

"Then why did we come so early today?"

"Because you said you wanted to come before you went to Bedwyr's. And because I wanted to be sure no one saw us come over here. Just wait a few more minutes. Please."

Alethia sighed but didn't pull away. They waited there by the edge of the forest, while overhead, the sky lightened until only a few of the brightest stars could be seen far to the west. Behind them in the yard, Henry the Fifth's raspy-sounding crow called the flock to hop from their perches.

Light began to sift down through the leaves above, revealing glimpses of damp moss between the massive tree trunks. Eliana could make out the small clearing just inside the forest where she'd first seen the brilliant green and turquoise flashes that turned out to be a dragon. Today, the clearing was dragonless; Winston wasn't there.

As disappointed as she was, Eliana wasn't surprised. Why would he be here, two days later? He probably had come yesterday when she'd promised to be there. Promises. She shook her head, then told herself once again that because she and Alethia were together, she wasn't breaking her promise to her father. She pulled on her sister's hand and stepped into the shadows of the forest. Other than the faint sound of the uppermost treetops shivering in the breeze high above, the forest was silent. As they stood on the edge of the clearing, Eliana smelled the pungent mushrooms that grew in gaps of the tree bark. An acorn fell and landed on the cushioned forest floor.

Stepping into the clearing, Eliana put her finger to her lips. She was still hoping Winston was nearby and didn't want to scare him.

"What's this?" asked Alethia, breaking the silence with her whisper.

Eliana whirled at the wonder she heard in her sister's voice. It was just light enough to see the rich greens and blues of the enormous feather Alethia held up in front of them.

"It was sticking straight up in the moss over there, almost like it was left there on purpose. I've never seen a feather like this." Holding it by the sturdy quill, Alethia turned the feather back and forth; faint early morning sunlight bounced turquoise and green light around the clearing.

"It's amazing," said Alethia. "And so long . . ."

Eliana reached over to run her fingers along what was obviously one of Winston's feathers. The edges were soft but strong. They'd have to be, she thought, to lift Winston in the air. She could almost picture him high above the trees although she hadn't seen him fly. Even tucked closely to his sides, Eliana had seen the powerful wing blades and wings that covered his whole body. Had he lost this feather when they'd met? Had it been here all this time? Or, she wondered, had he come back yesterday morning? Would he ever come back again? Would he ever come back again? She blinked back hot tears.

Alethia handed the feather to her sister. "Well, you saw something here for sure. And it was obviously something big. A bird?"

Eliana could only shake her head. Would she have believed she'd come face to face with a dragon if she hadn't done so herself?

"We need to get back," said Alethia, as she began to wind her way back to the edge of the forest. "I have to get ready to go to Bedwyr's."

Eliana started to follow but stopped, took off her scarf, and put it on the ground where they'd found the feather. She laid her hand on it, just like she had on Winston's neck.

"I was here, Winston. I found your feather. I'll come back tomorrow. I promise."

Another promise. Another promise that tiptoed around the one to her father. Waving that thought aside as she would a cloud of gnats, she hurried to follow Alethia back to the stream and across into the yard. The chickens walked to and fro, bumping into each other and clucking at her from inside the coop. Eliana tucked the feather inside her sweater and let them out into the yard.

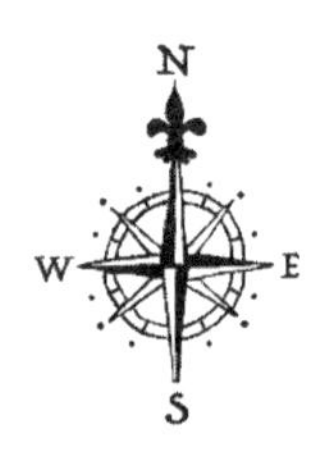

Chapter 18: King Halwyn

A MONTH AGO

After Valo left with his guardsmen and the Dragon Speaker to attempt to capture a dragon, King Halwyn paced the length of his Audience Hall, from the heavy oaken doors to the fire and back again. Outside, the April wind had finally settled into a frigid stillness. It was quiet in the hall except for the *slap-slap-slap* of his slippers and the *pop-snap* of a log in the fireplace. He looked at his hands clasped together on his rounded stomach. The hair sprouting on his fingers was grayer than he remembered.

"Ten years ago, I would have gone with them," he muttered. "I'm getting old."

"I beg your pardon, sire?" said Brogan. His Head Steward had slipped in through the side door and stood holding an etched metal flagon. Halwyn just shook his head and plopped down by the fire. Brogan refreshed the wine in his goblet; the King took a sip, then one more.

"What are we going to do with the dragon, Brogan? If they catch it, if they bring it back here? It's much too big to even bring through the courtyard gates . . . if Doryu is to be believed. We can't very well just tie him to a tree outside."

Brogan stood, staring into the flames.

"Well?" said Halwyn.

"I don't know, Your Highness. I was wondering the same thing."

"Margred seems to know a lot about dragons. She's the one who said it'll help us find the missing treasure. Perhaps she has a plan regarding where to keep it. Summon her."

"Yes, sire," said Brogan.

As his Steward hurried to do as asked, Halwyn strode across the room once again, this time counting.

"One. Two. Three. Four. Five." He glanced back to his chair, fifteen feet away. "Bigger than that? The dragon is bigger than that? Six. Seven . . ."

As the King paced, Brogan searched for Margred. First, he went to her quarters off the southeast corridor, just down from the empty treasury. He knocked on the heavy oak door; when there was no reply, he pounded with his fist.

"Counselor! The King has summoned you!" Still nothing. He tried the latch, but it wouldn't budge.

After waiting another minute, Brogan made his way to

the library where Margred often sat with a musty book in her lap. There was a fire in the fireplace on the wall to the left, but the chair beside it was unoccupied.

Turning to continue his search elsewhere, Brogan saw, tucked under the edge of the chair, a book facedown on the floor. The cover was black leather with the title stamped in gold leaf. The lettering was ornate and spelled out words in a language he'd never seen before. Bending to pick it up, he saw that the pages to which the book had been opened were written in what looked like the same language, indecipherable, but accompanied by intricate drawings of leaves.

The book was warm—almost hot—in his hands, and a sudden wave of dizziness made him sway. Brogan started to put the book back where he'd found it, but instead, he turned to one of the bookshelves flanking the fireplace. He moved some of the books on the top shelf, set the black book at the back, and concealed it with the ones he'd removed. He nodded, smiling grimly.

Continuing his search for Margred, Brogan made his way into and out of dusty unused rooms, some of which were so dark he had to take a torch from one of the metal sconces in the corridor to light his way. He was sure the Counselor would be somewhere much more comfortable than these drafty places, but he wanted to be thorough.

Growing tired and hungry, he headed down to the kitchen. He kept thinking about the locked door to Margred's quarters. If it were locked from the inside, it meant she was in there, didn't it? Why hadn't she answered?

"It is very brazen indeed for her to willfully ignore the King's summons," he said to himself.

"What?" asked Cook. "Who?" Even at this late hour, she stood before the massive soup pot, stirring and stirring with a wooden spoon the size of an oar. Strands of frizzy gray hair had escaped her kerchief, framing her round, red face.

Brogan hadn't realized he'd been talking aloud.

"Margred," he said, reaching for a bun on the oak table that ran the length of the kitchen. "The King asked me to summon her, but I can't find her."

"She's down there," said Cook, gesturing to a wooden rack of pots and pans hanging on the stone wall to the right of the fireplace. Seeing the confusion on his face, she added, "Pull on the left side."

Brogan went to the rack, hoping she wasn't trying to trick him into helping with a cooking chore. He peered around the left side of the panel and saw a dark gap, a perfect fit for his fingers. At his touch, the entire rack of heavy pots and pans swung open without a sound; behind it was an opening, gusting with cold, dank air. The light from Cook's fire revealed a set of stone steps curving downward to the left in a steep spiral.

With a glance at Cook, who was still stirring, Brogan grabbed a torch from the kitchen torch basket, and thrust it in the fire under the soup pot to light it.

"How is it you seem to know where everyone is?" he asked.

"All paths lead through the kitchen," she said. "You should know that by now, Brogan."

Holding the torch well in front of him, Brogan stepped past the door rack and down onto the first step of the twisting stairway. Another step, then another. A whisper of air and then, above him, the door to the passage closed. The stone walls of the stairway were cold and damp and seemed to close in on him tighter and tighter.

A bigger man would have trouble making his way, he thought. The steps were slippery, and the smell of mold surrounded him. He kept expecting the steps to come to an end, to emerge in the soldiers' quarters. But the steps continued downward, and the air grew colder still.

Just as Brogan contemplated turning around and declaring a lost cause, the torch flame fluttered and a draft of freezing but fresh air brushed across his face. The steps came to an abrupt end at a rough wooden door. He gave the surface a tentative push. It opened soundlessly into a black emptiness that smelled briny and tasted like oysters plucked fresh from the sea.

Stepping tentatively through the door, he could tell the floor was stone like in the soldiers' quarters, but here Brogan could hear a roaring sound, like distant waves crashing against cliffs. Moving the torch in an arch in front of him, he could see only a few feet beyond, but it was enough to see he wasn't in the soldiers' quarters. Beyond those few feet, the darkness swallowed up the meager light of his torch. Reaching to his left, his hand found a wall of rock, even colder than the walls of the secret staircase. For that is what he was sure it was. He had heard the castle had hidden passages, built for escape or seclusion. And now, Cook had—with a mere gesture—revealed a secret staircase. Leading to . . . where?

Brogan continued to move along the wall, holding his torch as high as he could. Moving this way for several moments, he encountered only more wall. By now, he'd determined the stones here, both on the floor and on the wall, were massive. Much larger than those in the castle above. He could tell the wall curved just slightly, indicating a circular space of gigantic proportions. He was afraid to step away from the wall into the space itself. How would he ever find his way back to the door if he did?

The reason he was here came back to his mind in a rush. Margred. Cook had said Margred was "down there." Did she mean the Counselor was here in this frigid darkness? And if so, why?

"Margred!" he shouted as loudly as he could. His voice sounded like a whisper caught up in a spider's web. "Margred!"

Just as before, when he'd been pounding on the door of her quarters, there was no reply.

Well, he thought. *All paths may lead through the kitchen, but Margred isn't down here. Cook was wrong about that.* And with that thought, his torch guttered and went out, leaving Brogan in a darkness so profound it felt like a shroud.

He was glad he had stayed by the wall; he began moving back the way he'd come, feeling his way stone by stone. He'd have a few words for Cook, friend or not, when he got back to the kitchen. Just then, Brogan became aware that his eyes were adjusting to the darkness. He could see his right hand on the wall beside him, and looking down, he could see a gray blur that was his left foot. Turning, he looked out into the gargantuan space and saw, at least a hundred yards away, a vast arched opening in the curved wall. And beyond the opening, Brogan could see the deep blue night sky, scattered with stars that gleamed like diamonds.

He took one step toward the opening but stopped when torchlight flared just outside. One, two, three torches, much larger than the one he'd carried down the spiral stairs. The torches began moving into the cavern; he could see now it was a cavern: a gigantic circular stone space. As his eyes adjusted further, he could see that carrying the torches were two very tall soldiers—one a man, the other a woman—dressed in dark cloaks and high boots. Coming behind them was a slender figure dressed in flowing, midnight blue.

Margred.

Silently apologizing for doubting Cook, Brogan strode across the stone floor. His King had sent him to summon this woman and summon her he would.

"Margred!"

The three figures stopped abruptly, now close enough that Brogan could tell he'd never before seen the soldiers accompanying the Counselor. They were definitely not the King's. Margred began to glide toward him, holding her torch aloft as if it weighed nothing.

"Brogan. What a surprise." She came to a stop several feet away.

"The King has sent for you, Margred. Some time ago," said Brogan.

"Well, you've done your job exceedingly well, dear Steward. You've found me all the way down here. How unfortunate for you."

"Unfortunate? For me?" he asked.

But then the two soldiers separated and circled around Margred to flank him on the left and on the right.

By the time he realized the danger, the two stepped forward and grabbed him by the arms. In the light of the torches they carried, he could see, with horror, that their eyes were completely black and their faces slack as though asleep. They were both exceedingly strong. Margred's violet eyes shone in the torchlight, and she tilted her head as she looked at him.

"Yes, most unfortunate, Brogan. Put him in the third cell," she said, gesturing to the far left of the cavern.

The soldiers easily lifted and carried him, dangling like a gutted hog, to an opening in the stone wall. Tossing him onto the floor of a cell, one of the soldiers closed a door of rusty iron bars with a clang that echoed in Brogan's ears.

Bruised and in shock, the Head Steward reached to grasp the bars. He was both terrified and shaking with anger. Angry that Margred had dared to defy the King, and terrified by the two soldiers, the look on Margred's face, and the huge iron chain he'd seen as he'd been dragged across the floor. The chain was attached to a massive iron ring embedded in the stone. At the other end of the chain was an iron collar, monstrous enough to encircle the neck of a dragon.

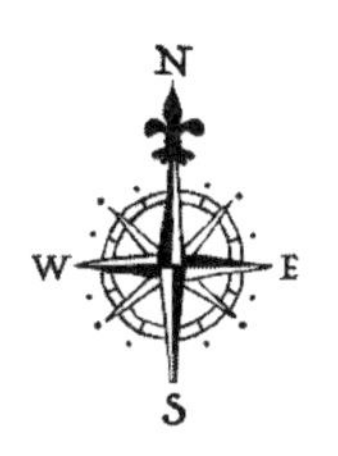

Chapter 19: Doryu

As the King paced and Brogan gripped the bars of a dank cell, Margred's plan to procure a dragon was underway. Far from the castle, at the edge of the forest, Valo's horse Destre wove between the trees, carrying her master and Doryu closer to the Granite Hills. As they moved farther west, the torches never seemed to dim, even though they'd been burning for an hour or more. Behind Destre, the other horses with their riders were quiet now. All Doryu could hear was the muffled footfalls of the horses and the occasional cough of a guardsman who'd breathed in too much of the torch smoke.

How are these torches supposed to call Raiden to us? Doryu wondered. He trembled at the thought that Valo and all these men were out here on a freezing mid-spring night because he, Doryu, supposedly knew where Raiden was. And that he was somehow going to be able to convince Raiden to go with them. Go where? Back to the castle? Did no one realize how big a fully grown dragon was? Did Valo think he and his men were going to be able to rope him and drag him back through the forest to Kings Road?

Doryu shook his head. The only way to get Raiden back to the castle was to somehow convince him to fly there, to willingly put himself at the mercy of Margred. Now that his mind had completely cleared of the tea-induced fog, Doryu knew with certainty that Margred was behind everything, even manipulating the King himself. To what end, he had no idea, but he was sure it was nothing good.

Caught in his spiraling thoughts, it took Doryu a moment to realize they were no longer moving. Destre stood completely still; Valo's hand moved slowly, slowly toward the hilt of the sword hanging in its leather scabbard. And overhead, a darkness filled the sky above the sparse trees where they stood, above the rocky ground at the foot of the hills. A darkness filled with the beat of massive wings. A darkness that flew closer until Doryu could see the light of the torches reflecting off onyx, silver, and white scales. *Raiden.*

Doryu wanted at that moment to call out to him, to warn him, but Valo reached back with his left hand and gripped the old man's knee. After that, things happened so quickly that Doryu could only watch—helpless—as Raiden hovered over the torches. His wing beats slowed until he crashed through the trees just beyond where Destre stood.

The dragon fell, one wing caught up in tree branches, the other on the rocky scree at the base of the Granite hills. He was struggling to keep his head up, nostrils flaring, eyelids covering and uncovering his black and silver eyes.

Valo lifted his left hand, two fingers raised, and pointed to the dragon. Two of the guardsmen handed their torches off and uncoiled lengths of rope.

"Old man, stay here," said Valo, grabbing Doryu's arm to lower him to the ground.

The Dragon Speaker watched as Valo rode Destre directly at Raiden while the two men with ropes moved to either side of the dragon.

Doryu saw the sword in Valo's hand, the ropes flying through the air, the confusion in Raiden's eyes.

Before he could think about what he was doing, Doryu was on his feet, running. He ran past Destre, ducked under the rope held by the guardsman on the left, and reached his gnarled, shaking hand toward the dragon. Doryu could barely hear Valo's shouts of warning, could only hear Raiden's cries, and then he was there, his hand touching Raiden's neck.

"Raiden, Raiden, it's me. Doryu." There was a long pause. Would the dragon remember him?

"Why have you done this?" Raiden's head was lying on the ground, his breathing labored. "You saved me before."

"I won't let them hurt you. They promised me they wouldn't. We . . . I need your help."

"This is how you ask for help, Doryu? By poisoning me with those lights? By putting ropes around my neck?"

"No. Yes. I'm sorry. This wasn't my idea. But my sister . . . the King's Counselor will kill my sister. We just need to help Margred find the kingdom's missing treasure."

"The King!" Raiden raised his head only to have it fall back to the ground.

"Yes. King Halwyn. Chares, his father, is long dead. Halwyn won't hurt you. He didn't even know dragons still existed."

"No thanks to Chares. Or you . . ."

"Raiden . . ."

"You may have saved me, Doryu, but you helped Chares kill scores of my kind. How can I trust you?"

Doryu closed his eyes, his hand still on the great dragon's neck. He thought of his baby sister, Jade, with her bright eyes and sweet smile. He thought of the dragons he'd helped Chares kill. He thought of the argument he'd had with Chares, his final refusal to help with the slaughter. He thought of Margred and her evil smile. Tears streamed down his wrinkled face, and he started to pull his hand away.

"Wait," said Raiden. "I'll help you, Doryu."

"But why? After everything . . ." asked Doryu.

"I could see . . . and hear . . . your thoughts. Just now. Your sadness. The weight you bear for your part in the killings. Your bravery in defying Chares by saving me a second time. Your sister. And the witch's threats."

Doryu stared at Raiden. In all the years since he first put his hand on a dragon, it had only given him the ability to understand them, to hear what they were saying. And now

Raiden was telling him that Doryu's very thoughts were communicated to him through his touch. How was this possible?

Under his hand, Raiden spoke again, "I'll help you, Doryu. But you must extinguish those torches. And remove the ropes. I'll help, but I won't be a prisoner. And these men must never come back to this place again."

It took Doryu several minutes to convince Valo that Raiden had agreed to help them and that the men needed to do away with the torches and ropes. By then, Angus and his men had joined the others, and it took all of them some time to pile enough dirt and rocks on the malodorous torches to smother them. Afterwards, everyone—man, horse, and dragon—breathed more easily.

Valo helped Doryu remove the ropes from around Raiden's neck but then moved well back from the gigantic creature. The Captain of the Guard stood with Destre under the branches of an oak, his hand never far from the grip of his sword. Doryu sat with his hand on Raiden's neck while the dragon dozed, still under the effects of Margred's poison. The sky was moving from black to deep blue by the time Raiden was finally able to stand and stretch his head up and up to a height more than four times that of Valo.

Doryu called up to him, "The castle is . . ."

Raiden gave one great nod of his head and began to spread his wings. Crouching down, he gave a tremendous push with his hind legs and flung himself into the early morning sky.

Valo's eyes followed the dragon as a rush of air and a whirlwind of dust and leaves surrounded them. Doryu saw the man's face soften with what looked like awe. The old Dragon Speaker knew the feeling—to witness the splendor of a dragon in flight. Then Valo shouted an order, pulled Doryu to his now customary place behind him on Destre, and turned her to head back down the forest trail.

Looking up, Doryu could make out the shape of Raiden as he circled above them, staying low so that he skimmed the top of the Great Forest. Valo handed the Dragon Speaker a sheep bladder waterskin, and the old man drank deeply. Valo took the bag and finished the rest of the water.

"I'll take you to the water trough as soon as we get back, Destre," he whispered.

His horse softly whickered her reply and walked on as morning broke over the forest and Doryu fell into a deep sleep.

In the cavern, Brogan was startled from a restless sleep by the harsh sound of metal banging on the bars of his cell. A hand reached in and set a cup on the floor. Brogan recognized one of his captors from the night before.

"Who are you? Why . . ." Brogan began, but the woman walked away without answering, disappearing into the gloom.

There was enough light coming through the arched opening to the cavern that the Steward could tell it was early morning. His whole body ached, not just from the bruises, but from the icy cold of the cell floor. He was huddled in one corner, holding in as much body warmth as he could with his legs and arms. He was afraid to move, but his mouth was so dry, his tongue was stuck to the roof of his mouth. Water. Was that what was in the cup? He crawled to the cup. Gruel. Some sort of rough grain mixed with water.

Brogan ate what little there was in the cup, using his fingers to scoop the mush past his lips. He tipped the remaining liquid into his mouth until there was nothing left. By then, more light had found its way into the vast cavern. He could clearly see the chain with its massive collar. His eyes searched for and found, on the far side of the cavernous space, the battered wooden door leading to the spiral staircase. There was no sign of Margred or the soldiers who'd been with her the night before.

He grasped the bars of his cell and shook them. Though they left his hands reddish-brown with rust, underneath the iron was whole and strong. Brogan crawled back to the corner of his cell and curled up once again. It was clear Margred intended to keep him here, but for how long? Was she planning to use the chain and collar to imprison the dragon? Why? How could it help them find the missing treasure with the horrible shackle around its neck?

Brogan could only hope that someone would think to ask Cook where he was. And that she would tell that person,

"Down there." *Down there . . .* Brogan felt himself drifting back to sleep, the words *down there* going round and round in his mind.

Chapter 20: Eliana

DAY THREE

After Alethia hurried back to the house to get ready to leave for Bedwyr's, Eliana let Henry the Fifth and the rest of the flock out of the coop and tiptoed over to check on Opal. Before the silkie shifted to cover it with her breast feathers, Eliana saw the fuzzy, pale gray head of a newborn chick. On the floor of the coop were several pieces of tan shell.

"Opal," whispered Eliana to the small, fluffy hen. "Your babies hatched! Father will be so happy."

Cadoc loved the chickens as much as Eliana did. He often stopped to see them after a long day at the quarry, and the downy newborn chicks would be a delight to him. Eliana ran to the garden, picked a ripe tomato, and went back to the coop to feed bites to the new mother.

"Good job, little one," said Eliana. On her way to get the

egg basket, she fed the last bite of the tomato to Henry the Fifth, who was—as always—standing guard over the flock. Under her sweater, Winston's feather tickled her armpit, and she smiled to think of her new friend. Yes, she decided. That is what he is: my friend.

Eliana found ten eggs in the other nesting crannies and carried them into the kitchen where Alethia took two and tucked them into Bedwyr's basket along with sprigs of thyme.

"I'll use this to brew some tea for him," she whispered. "His hands have been aching more and more."

Both girls were doing their best to be quiet, as their mother was still asleep.

"Alethia, thank you for coming with me to the forest," said Eliana, putting her hand on her sister's slender arm.

Alethia smiled at her younger sister. "Well, that's what sisters do," she said. "We're there for each other even when it seems crazy . . . not that you're crazy, Eliana," she hurried to add, when Eliana started to protest. "I know you saw *something* in the forest. We'll just have to figure out what it was . . . together. But now I need to—"

A soft rapping at the front door startled them. Eliana dropped the wooden spoon she'd just picked up.

"Who could that be so early?" said Alethia.

"Who's here?" called Glenna from the sleeping room.

Two heads of tousled red hair appeared at the edge of the curtain.

"We're not dressed yet," called Rowan.

"Boys, put on your clothes. Girls, tell whoever it is I'll be right there."

Eliana went to the door, sure that whoever it was had clearly heard all of the discussion but nonetheless said, "Please wait. My mother will be right there."

"No problem," answered a voice on the other side of the wooden door planks.

Young, thought Eliana. Where had she heard that voice before?

Glenna emerged from the sleeping room, tying her hair back with a strip of red cloth. Behind her, the twins were rolling around on their bed, laughing and punching each other.

"Boys, get dressed this instant!" said Glenna, as she walked to the door.

Eliana thought that whoever had been there must've given up by now, but when her mother opened the door, there stood the boy they'd met on the Cartographer's path, the tall one with the smiling, tilted eyes.

"Tal!" said Glenna. "Is everything all right? Is it your mother? Come in, come in."

Tal—yes, that was his name, Eliana remembered now—stepped through the doorway, carrying an earthen jar in one hand.

He smiled and said, "Yes, Mrs. Fallond, everything's fine. My mother's well. She wanted me to bring you this. Milk from our cow. Fresh this morning. Hello, Eliana. Hello, Alethia."

Eliana was surprised he remembered her name but was

even more surprised he knew her sister's name. Glancing at Alethia, she saw her sister's cheeks were bright pink and she was smiling a very large, odd-looking smile.

"Thank you so much, Tal," said Glenna. "And please thank your mother for me. I'm so glad she's doing well. Eliana, please put more water on for tea and use some of this wonderful milk in the porridge today. Tal, wait a few minutes while I gather some herbs for your mother."

All three—Eliana, Alethia, and Tal—just stood there for a moment, Tal smiling at Alethia, Alethia smiling at Tal, and Eliana looking from one to the other, wondering why they were both smiling so much.

"I have to get going," said Alethia, breaking their tableau. "Bedwyr . . ."

"Yes," said Tal. "I need to go, too." He turned to Glenna. "Would it be all right if I come back this evening to get the herbs? Gregor is expecting me, and clockmakers are especially fond of punctuality."

"Of course. I'll have some packets ready for you."

"Thank you!" said Tal. "Alethia, may I walk you to Bedwyr's?"

"Yes," answered Alethia, putting the handle of Bedwyr's basket over her arm. "Goodbye, Mother. I'll see you tonight."

Tal pulled the door open for her and winked at Eliana as Alethia pulled a soft shawl around her shoulders.

Eliana watched as her sister and Tal headed down the path, walking side by side, Tal smiling down at Alethia.

"Such a nice young man," said Glenna. "He takes good

care of his mother, who struggles with breathing problems."

"Sage said he's the King's Head Steward's son," said Eliana.

"Yes, which is why he has to tend to his mother and their household. His father—Brogan is his name—lives at the castle."

Eliana put the porridge on the stove to heat, wondering how it was everyone else seemed to know Tal.

Sage and Rowan emerged, mostly dressed, from the sleeping room.

"Where's Tal?" asked Rowan. "I wanted to say hello to him."

Yes, thought Eliana, stirring the porridge, *everyone knows him except for me.*

After breakfast, Eliana slipped back into the sleeping room and took Winston's feather from under her sweater. Even in the dim light, the colors seemed alive, and she ran her fingers along the length of it. Instantly, emerald and turquoise wisps appeared, swirling to form the shape of a dragon. Startled, she reached out to touch the image, only to have it dissipate like the colors that had streamed between her hand and Winston's scales.

"Eliana! Come help me gather herbs!" Her mother's call seemed to chase the last of the image away.

"I'll be right there, Mother!" Eliana took off her sweater, hung it on her clothes hook, and tucked Winston's feather under her pillow.

Chapter 21: King Halwyn

A MONTH EARLIER

A sliver of mid-spring light sneaked in around the heavy drapes covering the castle window and found its way directly into King Halwyn's right eye. Halwyn moaned and rolled over in his bed, pulling the blankets up to his ears.

He'd stayed up later than usual the night before, pacing and waiting for Brogan to return with Margred. Once she'd finally come to the Audience Hall—without Brogan—she'd given only vague answers to his questions about where and how to house a beast the size of the dragon Doryu had described. Then she'd apologized and asked to be excused to ensure that all was ready. She was sure Valo would be returning with the dragon before sunrise. Halwyn had been too tired to object and had released her to do whatever it was she needed to do.

And now, in the dim light of morning, the King's bedchamber was colder than he'd ever remembered it being. Turning over again, careful to keep his covers around him, he realized that the fire in the fireplace had gone out completely. No wonder it was so cold! Where was Brogan? His Head Steward usually tiptoed in during the night to add wood to the fire and to make sure there were no slits in the drapes.

"Brogan!"

When there was no reply after several moments, the King decided he would get himself up and dressed. There were his pants and silk shirt on the floor right where he'd left them the night before. Just as he swung his scrawny legs off the side of the bed and was scratching his hairy belly, his bedchamber door creaked open, and a young woman peered around it. Halwyn shrieked—in a most un-kingly manner—and pulled his blankets up to his chest.

"Oh, Your Most Royal of Royal Highnesses, I am sincerely sorry. But Brogan's mother has taken ill, and he's gone to Tibbet Mill to see about her. I'm his assistant, Linette, at your service."

"Brogan's mother ill? I didn't even know he had a mother. And he didn't tell me he was leaving." Halwyn glanced down at his pants on the stone floor, trying to decide if he should make a grab for them.

"Margred gave him leave, sire," said Linette. "When she woke me just now, she said it was all quite sudden and that Brogan left in the middle of the night."

No wonder he didn't come check on me last night, thought Halwyn.

"Well, come then, Linette. Give me my pants and shirt. And go fetch my breakfast. I'll eat in the Audience Hall. And be sure the fire is blazing in there!"

It was only after the King was dressed and eating his breakfast by the roaring fire that he turned his attention once more to the missing treasure and the dragon who was to find it. Had Valo come back last night? Why was no one reporting to him?

"Brogan!" he called but then remembered Brogan was gone. "Linette!"

The young woman scurried to his side. "Yes, my King?"

"Summon Valo! And Margred . . . and that Dragon Speaker, Doryu. Summon all of them!"

Linette curtsied, her forehead almost touching the floor, and scuttled out the side door to do his bidding.

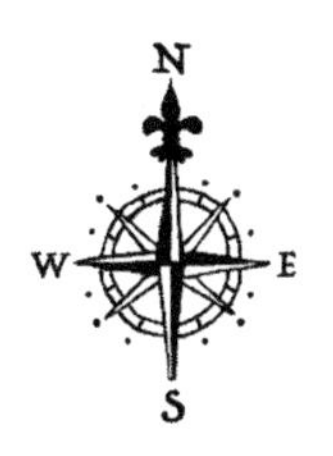

Chapter 22: Doryu

While Halwyn waited for Linette to bring his breakfast, the long line of soldiers on horseback made their way through Morganshire and up through the castle gates.

"Wake up, old man," said Valo, his hand once again on Doryu's knee. "We're here."

Doryu tried to open his eyes, but even the pale early morning light hurt, and he squeezed them closed again. The steady hoof beats of the horses slowed and came to a stop. A rooster crowed. A goat bleated. Destre snorted and tossed her head.

"Margred," muttered Valo.

Doryu's eyes flew open, and he saw the King's Counselor coming toward them. Her lustrous hair shone in the sunlight, and Doryu realized that many would find her beautiful. In fact, several of the soldiers were staring at Margred with what looked like admiration. She stopped a few feet away from where the riders waited.

"I see you've brought Raiden to us," she said, gesturing with a tilt of her chin to the sky to the east of the courtyard walls.

Squinting against the sun, Doryu could see the silhouette of Raiden soaring in the cold onshore winds coming from the Seething Sea.

Today will be clear, he thought, though a dark heaviness pressed on his chest.

Valo turned and started to lift Doryu to the ground.

"Not here," Margred said, then added, "I'll need a horse." She smiled up at Valo and waited, her hands tucked inside a heavy blue cloak.

A moment passed while the Captain of the Guard and the King's Counselor stared at each other. Then Valo turned to one of the guardsmen, motioning for him to hand over his short, white mare. As the soldier started to dismount, Margred reached to grasp the halter of the black stallion ridden by Angus.

"This one will do," she said.

The horse's eyes widened until the whites showed, and he started to pull against her hold. Margred put her other hand on his nose, murmuring to him as she did, and the horse quieted.

At a signal from Valo, Angus dismounted and handed the reins to Margred. He held out his hand to assist her, but she ignored him and easily fitted her foot in the stirrup. She rose gracefully to sit side-saddle, her right leg hooked around the pommel. She held the reins loosely in one hand and rode toward the courtyard gate.

Shaking his head, Valo turned Destre to follow Margred. Angus pulled himself up behind one of the other soldiers as they all rode back through the courtyard gate, then made a sharp right turn to follow a rocky trail around the outer castle wall. As they made their way, continuously curving to the right and slightly downward, the cold sea breeze blew from the south and whipped around the castle wall.

Doryu saw now that the wall itself was circular, not square as he'd thought. Had he never been on this path before? Coming up the village road, the walls flanking the front courtyard entrance were at least somewhat straight, but the rest—as was now plain—was rounded, with gigantic stones at its base.

The trek grew rocky and windy as they followed Margred. By Doryu's estimation, they were approaching the southernmost point of the castle wall. The smell of the ocean and the rasping cries of gulls filled the air.

All at once, Destre stopped walking. Valo reached to pat her neck, but she nodded her head up and down and snorted. Valo talked to her, trying to soothe her, but she refused to move any further. Ahead, Margred on the stallion was moving farther away, curving continually to the right.

Where is she taking us? thought Doryu, as Valo jumped down to the path to lead Destre forward.

Now that Doryu's view was no longer blocked by the Captain of the Guard, he could see the path begin to widen as it turned. To their left, the remnants of a cloud bank obscured the horizon. Just as he pulled his cloak tighter against the bitter wind, Destre stopped again.

"Halt!" shouted Valo. "Halt!"

At the base of the castle wall was an arched opening so wide that twelve horses could have ridden through it side by side. Standing in front was Margred, hair streaming in the wind, holding the reins of the stallion. Behind her stood eight or nine soldiers—men and women. They were dressed completely in midnight blue and had swords in scabbards at their sides. Some had war hammers hanging from their belts.

"Valo!" called Margred. "Tell Destre there's nothing to fear! See how calm this stallion is? Bring the Dragon Speaker; we have need of him."

Valo stood for a few moments, unmoving, then handed Destre's reins up to Doryu.

"Stay here, old man," said Valo, and he began walking toward Margred. By now, several of the King's guardsmen had ridden up alongside Destre.

"He told me to stay here . . ." said Doryu.

"Yes," said Angus. "He'll signal when he wants us to advance."

They watched as Valo spoke with Margred. The wind prevented them from hearing what they said, but Margred leaned forward, her mouth moving. Valo vigorously shook his head while reaching for a rolled parchment that Margred took from within the folds of her robe. Valo unrolled and read the parchment, then thrust it back. When he turned to stride back toward them, Doryu realized he'd not seen Valo truly angry before. His eyes were slits in his dark face, his jaw clenched so hard Doryu thought the Captain might break his teeth.

When Valo reached Destre, he stopped right in front of her and grabbed her halter on either side of her head. His hands were shaking as he gently laid his forehead against the white blaze on his horse's head.

Finally, Valo looked up and spoke to Angus, his voice shaking. "That witch has a parchment with the King's seal on the bottom that says she . . . that Margred is to take charge of you. I am relieved of my duty."

Angus and the others gasped and began to speak all at once, but Valo raised his hand to stop them. "We are to do her bidding. King Halwyn has commanded it. We are all sworn to follow his command, and so we shall."

Valo continued to stare at Angus until Angus and the others answered: "Yes, Captain."

"I am no longer your captain," Valo said. He reached inside his cloak and, in one fierce movement, ripped the faded captain's emblem from his shirt and dropped it on the rocky path. As he led Destre, carrying Doryu, toward the dark opening in the castle wall, the emblem was trampled into the dirt by the horses that followed. High overhead, Raiden flew in loops, casting his dark shadow on the sandy soil of the immense clearing in front of the cavern.

Doryu had never felt this old, this exhausted, this sick before. For many years, he'd been comfortable, warm, and well-fed in his dungeon cell. He'd thought he'd live out the rest of his days there with his stove, chair, and teacups. If he felt lonely now and then, he had his books and fascinating conversations with Cook. Now, as Valo led them closer to Margred and the black cavern, Doryu was certain death awaited him here. He closed his eyes, tilted his head to the warmth of the sun, and took a deep breath of the sea air.

So be it, he thought. *But somehow, I must save Raiden. One last time.*

Valo, leading Destre, came to a stop in front of Margred, whose eyes were lifted, following the dragon flying above them. The old Dragon Speaker raised his hand, thinking to call to Raiden, to warn him. But just then, behind Margred, one of her soldiers stepped out into the morning light. Held firmly in front of him was a small, older woman. Her thin, brown dress and threadbare shawl did nothing to protect her from the cold. She shivered violently, and as she did, her fluffy gray hair shook like a dandelion in the wind. Although he hadn't seen her since he'd left the trapper's clearing over sixty years ago, he knew her. His baby sister.

Jade.

Doryu slowly lowered his hand, his eyes on Jade now instead of Raiden. Why had he believed Margred would leave his sister in peace? Now both she and this dragon were in danger. He'd hoped to warn Raiden, but now he knew if Raiden left, Margred would kill Jade.

"Doryu, why don't we get everyone inside where it's warmer?" said Margred. "Jade is an old woman now, and the cold is too much for her." Margred had moved to stand beside Destre, her hand on the Dragon Speaker's knee. Her voice was soft and gentle, contrasted by her terrifying smile.

In desperation, Doryu looked to Valo, but he was staring out toward the southern cliffs, his expression unreadable.

Margred put her hand on Destre's nose, murmuring to her as she did. She took the reins from Valo and led the horse toward the arched entrance of the cavern.

"Come, Valo. And bring the rest of the guardsmen. There's plenty of room for everyone." As Margred passed the soldier holding Jade, the Counselor nodded to him. Pulling Doryu's sister by the arm, he followed Margred into the gloom.

"We'll get everyone settled and then invite Raiden to meet with us," said Margred, as if she were hosting a high tea.

Outside, Raiden rode the ocean air currents as the evil woman with the flowing black hair led everyone into the cavern.

Once inside, torchlight revealed the horrors that Margred had in store for them. Doryu saw the massive iron collar meant for Raiden and dank cells lining the left side of the cavern. From the dimness in the back of the cavern emerged many more soldiers, men and women. The tunics they wore were finely stitched, the same deep blue as Margred's robes. The soldiers all looked well-fed and well-rested, as if they'd been on holiday. On each chest was sewn an emblem bearing a silver leaf.

Doryu watched, his stomach roiling, as Jade was thrown into one of the cells. The clang of the cell door echoed in his chest. Jade's hands grasped the bars, and her eyes found his. She smiled—a small, sad smile—and Doryu remembered again how she used to hold onto his thumb. He couldn't fathom why Margred had imprisoned her. Raiden had agreed to help, partially to ensure her safety. And even more baffling, how did Margred think Raiden could find anything if she managed to get the iron collar on him?

Margred's soldiers started gathering the reins of the horses. The King's men dismounted and gathered around Valo, eyes moving from their former Captain to the woman the King had put in charge. Valo stared at the ground.

As Doryu's eyes adjusted to the dimness in the cavern, he could see it was gigantic, more than twice the size of the castle above. It must have been carved out long ago, and now Margred had turned it into what looked like a small city, with supplies stacked next to tables and cots, iron stoves with plenty of wood for cooking, and—off to the far right side of the cavern—stalls and piles of feed.

As Valo and his men led their horses to the stalls, Doryu thought he heard—faintly—someone calling his name from the left side of the cavern.

"Doryu."

At first, he thought it might be Jade, but then he realized it was a man's voice. There, in the cell to the right of Jade's. Hands grasping the bars. Moving closer, Doryu could make out a shadowy form. Closer still and . . . Brogan! It was Brogan, shivering, with dark circles under his eyes.

"Doryu! You'll join us over here now!" Margred called. "We have much to do before things can return to normal."

One of her soldiers, eyes like black granite, came to escort him to the entrance of the cavern.

At that moment, the fear that had filled Doryu turned to a burning anger. Yes, Margred had manipulated him, had put him in a seemingly impossible position, but she needed him. The fact that he was standing here and not in a cell proved it. He would stop acting like a foolish old man. He would use her need of his ability to understand the speech of dragons to his advantage. He would figure out how to save Jade, Brogan, and Raiden if it were the last thing he did.

Doryu turned on his heel and walked back to where Margred waited, her usual half-smile on her face. The Dragon Speaker stood directly in front of her and spoke in a low voice.

"Have your soldiers bring blankets, warm clothes, and food for everyone. And I mean *everyone*, Margred." He pointed to the occupied cells on the east side of the cavern. "And don't even think about putting that thing around Raiden's neck."

Margred's smile dropped from her face, and her eyes

narrowed to mere slits. "I will honor your requests, Dragon Speaker. At least the ones I can. But if it is necessary to confine the dragon for our own—and its own—safety, I will be forced to use the collar."

"He won't harm anyone," said Doryu.

"Let's all hope that's true," said Margred, as she gestured to one of the soldiers. "Much of it depends on you."

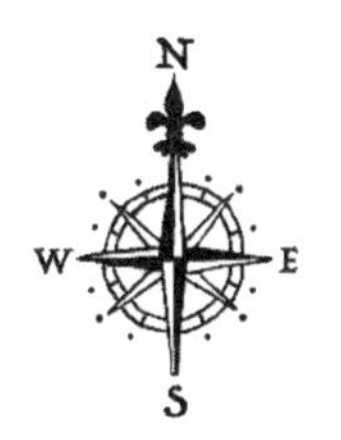

Chapter 23: King Halwyn

"Linette!" shouted King Halwyn, still sitting by the fire in the Audience Hall. The remains of his breakfast were on the table, leftover remnants of egg congealing on the plate.

"Linette!"

Finally, his stand-in Steward scurried into the room, a tray dangling from one hand.

"Yes, your most regal sire?"

"Where have you been? Take these away at once!" Halwyn indicated with a swoop of his hand the leftovers by the fire.

"Yes, Your Highness! Right away!" She began piling plates, saucers, and cups on the tray, dropping crumbs on the floor as she did.

"And where is everyone? I commanded you to summon

them all! Valo, Margred, the Dragon Speaker . . ."

"I—I can't find anyone, Your Lordship."

"Have you checked their chambers?" bellowed the King. "The soldiers' quarters?"

"No . . . I will, though, sire. Right away." Linette began to curtsy but jerked to a stop as all the King's breakfast dishes began to slide. She half-curtsied instead and hurried out of the room.

King Halwyn sat, chin resting on his hand, pondering all that had led to this . . . this upsetting time. Things had been going along just fine before the first of the year. The Christmas celebrations had been filled with dining and drinking and dancing with various unmarried women who hoped to catch his eye. Halwyn had enjoyed their flattery as they'd waltzed around the Banquet Hall, but he enjoyed the solitude of his bachelorhood too much to make one of them his queen. He'd known he must marry one day and have an heir who would become ruler when he was gone, but he'd figured he had plenty of time for that. But now it seemed that he had been wrong in that assumption . . .

Halwyn must have dozed off there in front of the fire, chin on his hand, for he was jolted from a misty dream by Margred's voice in his left ear.

"Halwyn, wake up. You wanted to see me?"

Halwyn struggled to shake the fog from his head,

realizing Margred was finally back, hands as usual tucked into her robes.

"Where were you this time, Margred? I summoned you hours ago!" *Had it been hours?* he wondered. It seemed like it, but he'd completely lost track of time.

"Your Grace, I've been busy carrying out your wishes. Valo and Doryu have delivered the dragon to me, and I've been occupied with getting him settled in his quarters."

"The dragon? The dragon is here? Where?" asked the King.

"In the lower chambers. Don't you remember I told you last night I prepared a comfortable place for him there?"

"No, I don't remember! I wouldn't have asked you if I had remembered. *You* will do well to *remember* to whom you are speaking, Counselor!" King Halwyn was on his feet, his hands in fists at his sides.

"Please forgive me, sire," said Margred, taking a step back. "I didn't mean to be disrespectful. It's just that I haven't slept in two days, making preparations to procure a dragon for you. To find your missing treasure . . ." Margred's voice had dropped to a whisper.

"Well . . ." said Halwyn. "Well, that's behind us now. But where are Valo and Doryu? I sent for them, as well. I want a full report."

"They are with the dragon, Your Highness. Valo is there to ensure its safety, and Doryu must stay to communicate with it. Neither will be available for some time, I'm afraid."

The King sniffed and lowered himself into the comfort

of his chair. "Well then, *you* can give me a complete report, Margred," he said.

"Using the torches I provided, Captain Valo and the Dragon Speaker were easily able to call the dragon to them. Doryu convinced it to assist us in finding your missing treasure. The Dragon Speaker and the dragon are together in their special quarters."

"When will the dragon find the treasure? How soon will it all be back?"

"Soon, Your Majesty. I will begin working with the Dragon Speaker regarding how to instruct the dragon. It may not happen right away, but soon."

"I want to see it. The dragon. Take me to it," said Halwyn.

"Oh, if only that were possible, sire. Unfortunately, it cannot be disturbed at the moment. The process of using dragons to locate treasure is a delicate one, one that could fail should too many interruptions take place. Surely you can understand how distracting it would be if the King of Morganshire dropped by!" Margred laughed, tossing her hair back over her shoulder.

"Well, yes, I can see how that would be distracting," said Halwyn, straightening up in his chair. "But you'll report to me every day! Twice a day! I want to be kept informed every step of the way."

"Certainly, Your Highness. You deserve nothing less. And now, I must get back to the task at hand! You'll have your treasure back before you know it, and all will be as it was."

Margred inclined her head to the King in her version of

a bow and left Halwyn, sitting as always by his fire with his fingers entwined on his rounded stomach.

Chapter 24: Doryu

ONE WEEK AGO

As pale, spring sunlight began to fill the sky, Doryu lay on his sleeping mat outside Jade's cell. He'd been awake for several minutes but didn't want to wake his sister, whose hand he held through the bars. For many nights now, as the cave began to darken, they had lain side by side, separated by bars, and whispered tales of their lives.

Doryu shared about his life as a Dragon Speaker; Jade told him about growing up in the trappers' compound. They both cried as she related the deaths of their parents. Jade smiled as she told her brother about meeting the boy who grew up to become her husband. She told Doryu all about her three children, their marriages, and her four grandchildren. Watching the emotions written on her face as she spoke, Doryu grew to love his baby sister for who she was now—a kind, gentle woman who deserved to live out the rest of her life in her snug cabin.

Doryu sighed. At least now she had blankets, warm boots, and a fur-lined cloak to keep her comfortable while they waited for this ordeal to be over. Margred had kept her word about the warm clothing and even slightly better food, but everything else had gone from bad to worse.

At first, Raiden had stayed in a nearby grove of birch trees, returning to the cavern at sunrise and again at dusk. Each time, Raiden would repeat what he'd told Doryu before: he didn't have the ability to find hidden treasure. And to his knowledge, neither did any other dragon.

"But why did you come, Raiden? Why did you agree to help?" asked Doryu, purposefully keeping his back turned to the cavern entrance. Margred was there, standing away from the dragon but keeping watch nonetheless.

"I agreed to help *you*, Doryu. You. When you touched me, I saw the danger you and your sister were in. And I haven't forgotten how you saved my life when I was a child. That is a debt I'm glad to repay. We just need to figure out a way to get everyone to safety so I can go back to my family."

Every morning and every evening, the two met, the majestic black, silver, and white dragon lowering his head so Doryu could place his hand on his shining scales. After the first day, Doryu no longer spoke aloud. They'd learned all he had to do was think the words while he touched Raiden as he had the night at the base of the Granite Hills. Even as

Margred grew bolder and came closer to them while they spoke, she had no way to know what they were saying. Thus, they were able to mislead her while they planned an escape. The days passed with Raiden flying out every day, pretending to look for treasure.

What about your family? asked Doryu—communicating just by touch—on the second day. *Did you go back to tell them what happened?*

No, I can't risk leading any of her soldiers to my cave. They still think I live alone. If they knew about Nerys and Winston, they might try to go back with their poisonous torches and capture them, too.

Won't they be worried about you?

Yes, but they know, no matter what happens, I will find a way back to them.

But it had only taken Margred a week to suspect she was being deceived. On the morning of the eighth day, as Raiden landed in front of the cavern, she walked up to the dragon and spoke directly to him.

"Dragon, you should have been able to find the treasure by now. Especially the one I seek. It is substantial, much more substantial than Halwyn's meager pile of gold. You will find it today, or the consequences will be severe." She turned to place her hand on Doryu's chest, pushing him back when he moved to speak to Raiden.

"No, none of your secret conversations this morning, old man. I know it heard me perfectly well. It will find the treasure I seek today, or else." She gestured to a soldier who came and took Doryu by the arm.

"I'm watching you, old man. There's a cell for you, too, if you don't cooperate."

As the soldier pulled him away, Doryu wondered once again what treasure it was that Margred sought. Substantial, she'd said. She was wrong about what the dragon could and couldn't do; could she be wrong about the other treasure, as well?

That evening, Margred waited with Doryu for the dragon's return. In part, Doryu hoped the sky would remain empty, but he feared for those kept captive in the cavern behind him. Valo and his soldiers were just as much prisoners as Jade and Brogan, and the food and water they were given seemed to make them weaker. Valo's face was ashy, his eyes dull. All the men and even their horses grew more listless by the day, sleeping most of the time.

Just as Doryu was sure Raiden wouldn't return that night, there was a change in the wind, and the massive dragon dropped before them, causing Margred to take a few steps back.

"Well? What did you find?" Margred asked. "Doryu, ask him what he found and where it is." She shoved him forward; he stumbled to his knees, scraping them on the rocky ground.

Raiden lowered his head to him, and Doryu could feel the warmth of the dragon's breath on his face. He reached to put his hand on Raiden's neck. Once again, they spoke without words.

I'm still trying to make a plan, Raiden. I know you didn't find anything today, either, but did you see anything that might help us?

No, nothing, said Raiden. *Doryu, do you think she will let you and the others go if we help her find what she seeks?*

I don't know. We can only hope if she gets the treasure she seeks, she'll take her soldiers and leave Morgan Castle, leave Morganshire. If I could only figure out a way to talk to Valo. I'm sure she deceived him when she showed him that parchment. He needs to know that Halwyn would never strip him of his rank . . .

Out of the corner of his eye, Doryu could see Margred shifting from side to side; she took one step forward.

Raiden spoke again. *Today I flew to a kingdom far to the east. Circling high above, I saw a place where the ocean enters between two rocky points to become a round lake. On the other side of this lake was a river that flowed into it as well.*

Cantington Bay! You flew to Cantington? Did you see Canting Castle? A castle many times the size of Morgan?

Yes, there was a castle. But the most important thing I saw was a man-made thing, like a bird, floating atop the river. It had tall tree trunks pointing to the sky, and on them were the same symbols that Margred's men wear on their chests, but larger.

A ship . . . a ship with banners. Banners with a silver leaf?

Yes.

Doryu paused, then asked, *Did the ship ride high on the water? Or was a large part below the water?*

It was on top of the water.

Waiting for Margred's treasure. But why Cantington? Did it come down the Pearl River? From lands beyond the Black Mountains?"

Raiden shook his massive head from side to side. *I don't know, Doryu. And I don't know where the treasure is, either. Because she thinks I have the ability to find it for her, she won't tell us anything. I fear we're running out of time. I'm sorry, my friend.*

You need to leave now, Raiden. Leave us here. We're doomed anyway. Go back to the Granite Hills, get your family, and find a new place to live. Go west, to the hills of Dragon Fell. No one will know how to find—

Doryu! Raiden said, raising his massive wing blades.

Doryu's hand slipped from the silver and black scales.

Someone—one of the soldiers—gripped his arm. He was being dragged back into the cavern.

"Raiden! Fly!" shouted the old Dragon Speaker.

But Raiden was already surrounded by Margred's soldiers, each of them holding one of the horrible smelling torches. The blue and white lights lit the darkening sky.

Raiden's wings moved up and then down again and finally lay spread out in the dirt. A breeze from the ocean brought the poisonous fumes to where Doryu watched, held by the soldier, as Raiden's head slowly fell to the ground.

"No!" cried Doryu, gagging. "You gave me your word!"

"No one seems to be upholding his end of the bargain, old man," said Margred. "Get back in the cave."

Doryu watched in horror as Margred's soldiers—there were many more of them than he had realized—took ropes and tied them to Raiden's legs, tail, and neck. It took a very long time to drag the immense dragon through the entrance to the cavern, across the stone floor, and over to the iron collar. It took six soldiers to open the collar and wrestle one side of it under Raiden's neck. They closed and locked it with two iron padlocks.

Just as he had that night in the woods, Doryu fell to the ground and vomited. The nausea and weakness were from more than just the poisonous air. He knew that a plan to free them all was farther away than ever.

And just when it seemed things couldn't get much worse, a terrible sound filled the cavern. It was a cry the old Dragon Speaker felt clear to his bones. A cry that brought back memories of slashing swords and death.

Now, three weeks after Raiden had been chained, the dragon lay barely breathing, never moving, in the center of the cavern.

"Is he dying?" Jade whispered.

"I don't know," said Doryu.

The Dragon Speaker hadn't been able to get close enough to Raiden to even speak aloud to him in many days. One of Margred's soldiers, a woman with a scar from her left eye to her chin, stood watch over Doryu day and night. Whenever he moved or tried to speak to her, she jabbed her spear at him.

As daylight began once more to lighten the cavern, Margred stood in front of the chained dragon as she did every morning now. Today, she prodded him with a long, gnarled staff that she'd begun carrying. Did she somehow think that putting an iron collar around his neck would convince him to agree to find her treasure? She jabbed the unconscious dragon, but she was too far away to hear what she said. As Jade squeezed his hand, the old Dragon Speaker turned his head away and cried in frustration.

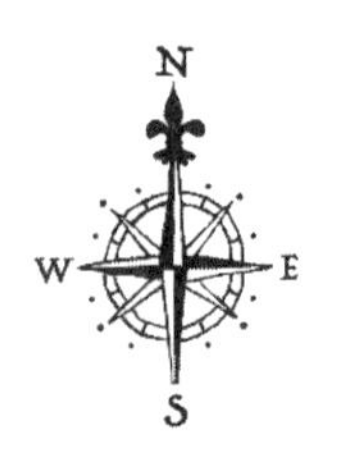

Chapter 25: Winston

DAY THREE

While his father lay chained beneath a castle, Winston was finishing the last of the benesaunus he'd steamed for breakfast. He looked around at the cool rocky walls of his home. Even with all the stores of food piled in the cave, it seemed vast and empty without his mother and father there. He pushed away a sliver of fear by focusing on the decisions he'd made the night before.

He was even more convinced that enlisting Eliana's help was the right thing to do. His parents had told him little about humans, only that they were dangerous and lived in the forests, by the rivers, and even in lands more than two days' flight away. But now that he'd met Eliana and knew *she* wasn't dangerous, he believed she could get help from other humans. Maybe one of them had seen his father and could tell Eliana where he was.

Winston swept the sleeping moss into a neat pile with his tail; his mother would be pleased to see how well he was doing on his own. *Mother*... she'd told him to stay at the cave in case Raiden returned, but he hadn't told her about Eliana. If he had, his mother surely would have agreed she might be able to help. With one final swish of his tail, Winston swept the thought of his promise to his mother to the back of his mind.

The sun was warm on the cave's ledge. Below in the forest, small birds were atwitter as they swooped from treetop to treetop. Winston got a long drink from the rivulet of cool water by the cave entrance and turned to launch himself once more into the sky beyond. As he dipped his left wing to begin the slow turn toward the south, he could see his shadow clearly moving across the surface of the trees. But today he had no fear of faceless humans below. Perhaps his parents were wrong; perhaps the humans who lived in the forest were kind and gentle, too.

The miles to the edge of the forest flowed below the young dragon. It seemed to take no time at all before he could see the open place in the trees that he now thought of as his landing meadow. *His.* He'd discovered it by himself. One last slight turn and he landed without a sound on the grassy ground.

I'm getting good at this, he thought and began the awkward maneuvering that would take him to the cramped space where he'd met Eliana. *Their* clearing.

By his calculations, Winston would be there at about the same time of morning as when he'd met Eliana two days before. His heart beat faster at the thought she might already be there. That he might find her with his feather in her hand, waiting for him. But then he realized he was moving too fast and was making too much noise. The gray and white bird in Eliana's yard would be frightened again.

Winston stopped, his hind end partially stuck between two tree trunks, his head peering around another. Quiet. Now that he was still, he could hear the sound of water moving over rocks, the cackling and clucking of the flock of birds in Eliana's yard, the brushing sound of a slight breeze high in the trees overhead. Winston started moving again, this time more slowly, carefully pulling his rear end free.

Finally, after several moments, there it was: the clearing with its layers of moss, greens and grays in gentle mounds. His eyes quickly sought and found the particular mound where he'd left his feather for Eliana to find. *Gone! It was gone!* He pushed himself fully into the clearing, pulling his wings closer to better fit. Eliana had been there and found his feather!

Almost camouflaged by the greens of the moss, a green object lay just where the feather had been. He crept close enough to smell it. Eliana! This soft thing smelled just like his new friend. Whatever it was, she must've left it for him.

Winston peered through the trees and brush at the edge of the forest. He could see glimpses of the stream, glimpses of Eliana's home. But other than the flock of birds scratching in the dirt yard, nothing moved. After several minutes of waiting and peering, Winston crouched down and rested his head on the soft, green thing Eliana had left for him. The sun warmed his scales, his breathing slowed, and try as he might to stay awake, he once again fell asleep.

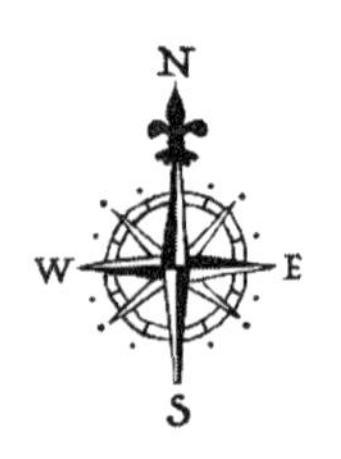

Chapter 26: Eliana

DAY THREE

While Winston was making his way to the clearing, Eliana and her mother finished gathering herbs from the garden and began tying them into small bundles. These, they would hang to dry to preserve them for use all year long. The scents of the freshly snipped stems and leaves filled the kitchen, mingling with the yeasty smell of bread baking in the oven.

"Eliana, set aside a bundle each of angelica, hyssop, and thyme for Tal's mother. They'll help with her breathing."

At Glenna's mention of Tal, Eliana thought of her sister and how oddly she'd acted around him. So much smiling. She wondered, too, when he might come back to get the herbs for his mother. She put them in a bowl on a shelf above the counter.

Mother and daughter worked quickly and efficiently

together; piles of tied herb bundles grew on the kitchen table while the twins built little twig and stick fortresses underneath.

"I'll finish tying the bundles," said Glenna. "Eliana, start hanging them on the drying wall. Boys, stop kicking!"

Cadoc had tied lengths of string horizontally from wooden pegs driven into chinks in the west wall of the kitchen. As Eliana began to hang the bundles on the top string, it fell uselessly into her hand; one of the pegs had split. Reaching to pull it loose, she felt a tap on her shoulder.

"I can make you a new one." It was Rowan, grinning his lopsided grin, holding his knife up for her to see.

Cadoc had given each boy a knife of his own on their last birthday. Sage had wrapped his in a cloth and put it in his prize box. *So it would be safe*, he'd said. Rowan kept his either in his pocket or in his hand, always at the ready for one of his many projects. Now, he held out his hand for the cracked peg. Within minutes, he'd carved a new one out of one of the sticks from his fortress project.

Eliana inserted the new peg and tied the string to it. She smiled to see that her brother had carved a little "R" on the end of the peg. Rowan was so much like their father, nimble fingers always busy. Maybe someday he would become a stone thacker, too. Or even a master stone carver like Cadoc had been in Cantington before he'd come to Morganshire and stayed to marry Glenna.

Once the herbs were tied and hung to dry, Glenna stood with her hands on her hips and surveyed the kitchen. Bits of herb leaves and buds were strewn across the table and floor.

"Eliana, please clean up in here. Boys, go get a bucket of water so your sister can scrub the floor after she sweeps. And take these sticks outside, too!"

The twins had already scrambled from under the table and were tussling over the water bucket.

"I'm going to town to see if Mr. Dodd was able to get the kelp I need for the sheep. I'll take Owen and the cart, so I can be back by dinner time. Children, listen."

The boys, who were trying to push their way out the back door with the bucket, turned to Glenna.

"Rowan and Sage, do what your sister says. Once all the chores are done, you may play in the yard, but don't go past the stream. Eliana, after you clean the kitchen, get some potatoes out of the root cellar to start for dinner."

"Yes, mother," the three replied in unison.

Glenna grabbed her shawl and market basket and headed out the front door. Their mule Owen would come running for the bit of carrot Glenna took with her.

Eliana sighed. With the boys either following her like newborn chicks or else getting into mischief, she'd wouldn't be able to go to the forest clearing again today. At least Winston—if he came—would find her scarf and know she'd been there.

After wiping off the table, Eliana swept the floor, bits of herbs mingling with the remaining twigs of the boys' project. Of course, they'd left the back door open when they went to get water, so it was easy to sweep it all outside into the yard.

The chickens came running, knowing they would find bits of herbs they liked.

Where're the boys? Eliana wondered. *They should be heading back from the stream by now.* Shading her eyes from the bright June sun, she scanned the yard. There was the bucket, lying on its side by the stream.

"Sage! Rowan!"

No reply. Eliana hurried toward the toppled bucket, wondering if they had waded upstream to hunt for crawdads. Or had they crossed the stream?

"Sage! Rowan!"

And then, there they were, bursting from the edge of the forest on the other side of the stream.

"Eliana! Eliana!" They were both yelling and waving their arms.

Eliana scanned their faces. They were smiling! Smiling and calling her name and waving their arms. In their excitement, they looked exactly the same.

"A dragon! It's a dragon, Eliana!" shouted Rowan.

"He's green and turquoise! And he's friendly!" called Sage.

"Come see!" Rowan grabbed his brother's hand. Sage was pointing toward the place in the forest where Eliana had first met Winston.

By this time, Eliana had splashed across the stream and up onto the strip of land on the other side. Her thoughts were so jumbled that she didn't know what to think first:

Oh no, the boys found Winston!

Winston is here! He came back!

Is he afraid? Will he leave again before I get there?

Will the boys tell our parents about him?

Winston! Winston!

Pushing her way past the last few trees, Eliana stumbled into the clearing, the clearing that was still very full of dragon. Winston was crouched with his front legs crossed on a mound of moss, his tail stretched out behind him. It was so long she couldn't see the end of it as it curved back into the forest. The ridge of feathers on Winston's arched neck riffled in a slight breeze. Sunlight hit them such that they looked like emerald green and turquoise flames dancing for joy. Hanging from his smiling mouth was the bright green of her scarf! This time, his teeth—each the size of her father's hand—didn't seem at all frightening.

"Winston!"

"Um-m-mh-m!" mumbled Winston.

The twins bumped up against her as they too pushed their way into the clearing. Sage grabbed her right hand. Rowan started to grab her left, but she gently pulled away so that she could reach out to touch Winston.

"Eliana! You came!" said Winston.

"I'm sorry I couldn't come yesterday. I found your feather!"

"And I found your . . . what is this? It smells like you, but I don't know what it is."

Eliana laughed and gently took her scarf from his mouth. Once again, the amazing colors streamed from her hand.

"Ohhhhhh!" breathed Sage and Rowan in unison.

Eliana put her hand back on Winston's neck. "It's a scarf. A scarf . . . well, let me show you." Eliana shook out the scarf and draped it around her neck. "It keeps my neck warm."

"And these other humans? They're so small. Are they your children?" asked Winston.

"No! These're my brothers. Rowan and Sage. Boys, this is Winston." As Eliana turned to make the introductions, she saw Sage's furrowed brow and Rowan's questioning frown.

"I met Winston a few days ago. And when I touch him like this, I can understand what he's saying. He just asked me if you're my children."

"Let me try," said Rowan, stepping forward to lay his hand beside hers.

"Me, too," said Sage. "Nice to meet you, Winston."

"I'm glad to meet you, too, brothers of Eliana," said Winston.

"Um um um muh mmmm," is what the boys heard.

"Why's he mumbling like that?" asked Rowan.

"I can't understand him, either," said Sage.

The four spent several minutes experimenting: just Rowan touching Winston, just Sage, both boys without Eliana, Winston gently putting one of his front feet on Rowan's bare foot. Nothing worked, except when Eliana put her hand on Winston.

Finally, their experiment concluded, Winston's smile

evaporated. "Eliana, I have to talk to you about something. I need your help."

"Boys, Winston needs help with something. Please sit down and stop throwing acorns. I'll listen and tell you what he says."

It took some time for Winston to tell Eliana about the strange lights in the forest that appeared a moon ago, about how Raiden had gone to investigate and how he'd never come back. As Eliana translated for her brothers, they sat, leaning against her, silent. Winston told them that yesterday his mother—Nerys was her name—had left, too, to search for his father.

"He never would've been gone this long unless something were terribly wrong. He's hurt or something . . ."

"Oh, Winston, I'm so sorry this happened," said Eliana, wrapping her arms around his neck. "How can I help?"

"I'll help, too," said Rowan.

Sage stood and wrapped his slender arms around what he could reach of Winston's neck. "Me, too," he said.

Winston said, "Are there other humans we could ask if they've seen my father? It seems like someone must've seen him by now. He's much bigger than I am, bigger than your cave." Winston tilted his head toward their house, which they could barely see if they peered around one of the trees at the edge of the clearing.

"Bigger than our house?" asked Eliana, her eyes widening.

"Yes, and he has the same coloring as the bird that guards the other birds in your yard."

"Ah, he means Henry the Fifth," said Sage, after Eliana relayed what Winston had said. "Silver, black, and white . . . wait! I know who we can ask! Bedwyr! I saw pictures of dragons on his maps! They weren't as beautiful as you, Winston, but they were dragons!"

"He might help us," said Eliana. "But we have to be very careful who we tell. Trappers, soldiers . . . well, I've heard stories . . ."

Winston nodded. "Yes, my parents told me humans are dangerous, that we have to stay hidden. But you're not dangerous, Eliana, Sage, and Rowan; you're my friends. And I have to find a way to help my mother find my father."

"Bedwyr is kind and gentle," said Sage. "He loves cats and children and beautiful colors. He'd love you, too, Winston. And he'd help us."

Eliana sat with her hand on Winston's neck, thinking about what Sage had said. Would it be dangerous to tell an adult—a gigantic mapmaker with a loud voice—about her new friend? Bedwyr had only lived in Morganshire for a short while; not much was known about him, except that he'd come from far away, some said from beyond the Black Mountains. That he'd made some maps for King Halwyn before coming to the countryside. The fact that he had knowledge—of the area, the castle, and the King—would make him a formidable ally. But would he be willing to help three children and a dragon?

Eliana looked at Sage, sitting quietly with his hand on

Winston's foot. Her brother was smiling, waiting patiently for Eliana to speak again.

"Sage, are you sure Bedwyr would help us?" She realized at that moment, she completely trusted his judgment about people, that whatever he said now would determine what they'd do next.

"Yes, Eliana. Yes, I'm sure."

Eliana spent the next several minutes telling Winston about Bedwyr, who he was, his stature in the community, and his ties to the castle and the King. Sage told Winston about how the mapmaker pretended he didn't let his cat Cow into the house, but the orange paw prints on the floor told another story. Sage explained about the maps with magnificent drawings of dragons on them, even one of a dragon with a boy standing beside him.

"Bedwyr speaks softly to me," Sage said. "And when he speaks loudly, it's because he's a big man, not because he's angry."

After a moment, Winston nodded.

"Winston agrees," said Eliana. "He says this is what we must do."

Sage nodded, too, and patted Winston's foot. "I think it's the best decision."

As he spoke, there was a strange gurgling coming from the vicinity of Winston's belly. The boys laughed.

Rowan said, "I'm hungry."

"Yes," said Eliana. "We should all eat before we go to Bedwyr's . . . What do you eat, Winston? Not . . . not meat, right?"

"No, I eat benesaunus." A few more minutes were spent during which Winston explained about benesaunus, what it was, how it was gathered. "I ate before I left my cave. I can eat some plants if I get hungry. I can last a long time without benesaunus if I need to." He shook his head. "My father . . . he's been gone too long. If he doesn't have benesaunus . . ."

Eliana jumped to her feet and shook out her skirt. "We're going to find him, Winston. I'll give the boys their lunch, and then you and I'll go . . ."

"We're coming, too, Eliana," said Rowan, standing and pulling his brother to his side. Sage nodded.

Determination was written all over their two freckled faces, and Eliana knew it was useless to try to dissuade them. Besides, their mother wouldn't want them left alone.

"We'll all go. But we have to hurry if we're going to get to Bedwyr's and back before Mother passes his place on the way back from the village. We can only hope she met up with acquaintances in Morganshire and is taking her time."

"Uh . . ." said Sage, as Eliana and Rowan turned to leave the clearing. "What about Winston? He can't just walk down the middle of the road."

After more discussion, it was decided Winston would fly just above the treetops at the edge of the forest, following along Kings Road. When he reached the path to Bedwyr's, he would make sure there were no other humans on the road before he crossed to land in Bedwyr's yard.

Eliana had just a moment to smile at the thought of her sister's face when Winston landed right in front of her mentor's home. *Large bird,* indeed!

After quickly making tomato sandwiches for their lunch, Eliana wrote a note for Glenna telling her they were going to Bedwyr's, in case she returned earlier than Eliana hoped. She knew her mother would think they were merely paying a visit to the Cartographer. Better to leave out some details than frighten her, Eliana decided as she and the boys set off toward Bedwyr's. As they hurried down Kings Road, they could see, off to their left, the breathtaking emerald and turquoise immensity that was Winston in flight.

Chapter 27: Winston

DAY THREE

After Eliana and her brothers left the clearing, Winston once again began to work his way back to his meadow. He tried not to think too much about the other human he would soon meet, the human who may or may not be able to help find Raiden. Winston had been able to feel the concerns Eliana had when she and Sage had been discussing Bedwyr.

Bedwyr. That was his name. Winston hadn't been able to understand much of what Eliana and Sage had said about him. He didn't know what *cat, map, drawing,* or *paint* were. But he had understood that maybe Bedwyr had come from beyond the Black Mountains. That he had worked for a human—King, they called him—who was powerful. That Bedwyr might be able to get help from this King.

Airborne once more, Winston could see the three—Eliana had said they were called *children*—walking along Kings Road. They were so small. Their heads were thrust forward, their slender legs moved back and forth, and their arms were bent like they were pulling themselves forward. But still, they moved so slowly! As slowly as he moved when he was maneuvering along the forest floor. If only they could fly!

Winston dipped his right wing and swooped away from the forest edge. After circling a few times, he flared his wing tips to slow himself and check on Eliana's progress. Had they moved at all? Even with all the circling, he was much faster than she and her brothers. With a downward thrust of his wings, he soared upward until he could see much more of the forest and land below him.

To the north, he could see a place cut into the earth, like a dark cave turned upside down and inside out. In its depths, he could see movement, humans moving among the rocky ledges. Winston hoped he was high enough that if they saw him, he would look like a hawk or eagle.

To the south, Winston saw a glimmer of what looked like sunlight on water. Checking to see that the children were the only humans in sight, he turned to the right, crossed high over the road, and then over fields of grasses. Here, the smell of salt filled the moisture-laden winds. Now he could see the water! Like a vast forest, only blue and gray, not green. And there was no end to it as far as Winston could see.

Abruptly the land stopped. Like a mountain that had broken off, with boulders being pushed by the water against the bottom. Winston rode the rising air currents up and out over the water that ran to the base of the cliffs and then back out again with sounds like the roaring of winter winds. White birds with compact bodies and orange beaks flew below him, sweeping across the surface of the water, calling to each other.

This place! It was so much better than the canyons beyond the Granite Hills, better than flyouts over the forest. Why had his parents never brought him here? Was it because of humans? To get here meant flying over the road . . . abruptly Winston's thoughts were brought back to the urgent task of finding his father. The children!

Heading north again, the offshore ocean winds carried him back across the grasslands to the road, where he could see Eliana and her brothers turning off the road. As they made their way down a dirt path, Winston began a slow, banking turn to hover and land in the open area in front of Bedwyr's home. Just as he was pulling his wings against his body, the children emerged from the path, and the door to the house opened with a crash. A human—twice as tall as the children and as big around as a sturdy oak tree—stood frozen in the doorway, reminding Winston in a strange way of the squirrel he'd frightened when he'd landed in the clearing that morning.

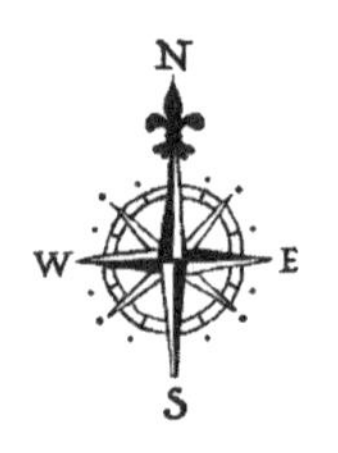

Chapter 28: Eliana

DAY THREE

Bedwyr's mouth opened, closed, and opened again, but no sound came out. His hands gripped the doorframe on either side of him. Under his left arm, Eliana could see Alethia peering out, her eyes so wide they seemed to take up her entire face. Winston's smile faded. Eliana hurried to his side and placed her hand on his neck. He shifted his back legs and crouched in the dust.

"It's all right, Winston. This is Bedwyr and my sister Alethia. Bedwyr, this is my friend Winston. He's a dragon."

"A dragon," said Bedwyr softly. "A real dragon. I thought . . . I didn't know . . . his colors! Look at his colors!" He took a step forward. Alethia stayed just inside the door, her hand over her mouth.

"Alethia, this is Winston! See? It was his feather you

found in the clearing," said Eliana.

Rowan and Sage moved to stand on the other side of Winston.

"He needs help, Bedwyr," said Sage. "Will you help us?"

"Winston asked me to ask you if you will help him find his father," said Eliana. "Please, will you help him?"

It took a while to explain everything to Bedwyr and Alethia. They brought chairs from the house to the yard as well as a little table with cheese, bread, and Bedwyr's eggs. Alethia was persuaded to make tea. Bedwyr listened, asking only a few questions, nodding, and stroking Cow, who had come to sit on his lap. The cat—clearly unconcerned about the dragon in the yard—licked her front paws, yawned, and fell asleep.

"There were tales in . . . in the place I was raised . . . of those who could speak to dragons," said Bedwyr, once all was explained. "I always thought they were . . . well, just tales. May I touch you, Winston?"

"He says yes," said Eliana after a moment and a mumble from Winston.

Gently setting Cow on the ground, the man stood and moved to place his ink-stained hand on Winston's wing. The sunlight shone on the dragon's feathers, the brilliant green and blue again looking like jewels.

"So beautiful . . ." said Bedwyr. "Yes, I think I can help you, Winston. I will go to Morgan Castle and ask for an audience with King Halwyn. I was of service to him not so long ago."

Just then, they heard the sound of boots crunching on the gravel-strewn path.

"What is this?" Tal came to an abrupt stop just inside the clearing. His upturned eyes flicked from Winston to Bedwyr to Alethia, then back to the dragon again.

Alethia took a step toward Tal.

"Seriously, what is this?" Tal said, a jerky movement of his hand indicating the whole of the green and turquoise dragon.

And so more introductions were made, another chair brought outside for the young man, and Eliana started at the beginning again. When she finished, Eliana saw that he was frowning and shaking his head.

"What's wrong, Tal?" asked Alethia.

"It's just . . . it's just that my father is missing, too."

"Oh no," said Alethia and Eliana.

Sage went to stand beside Tal, putting his hand on his arm.

"Tell us," said Bedwyr.

"As you know, my father—Brogan—is the King's Head Steward. He of course lives at the castle most of the time, so my mother and I rarely see him. Except for every other Sunday. He usually comes late the night before and has breakfast with us in the morning. Mother always has something special . . . Well, four weeks ago, a messenger came to tell us my father had to stay at the castle due to an urgent situation and wouldn't be coming the next morning.

"Two weeks later, the same thing happened. My mother wasn't worried the first time. Just last year, Father couldn't come home for several weeks because of a special ball the King was hosting. But the second time, when the same messenger said it was an 'urgent situation,' Mother asked for more details. *What situation? When would Brogan be able to return home?* The messenger just shrugged and said that was all the King's Counselor had told him. But then, right before the messenger left, he said, 'It is strange, madam. No one has seen your husband in many weeks.'"

Bedwyr made a sound deep in his chest, like the growl of a big cat; the little cat—back on his lap again—raised her head.

"Several weeks, you say?" asked Bedwyr.

Alethia's face turned pale, and the boys moved to stand next to each other. Rowan took Sage's hand in his.

Tal nodded. "The morning after the messenger came, mother packed a basket with Father's favorite biscuits and lemon preserves and went to the castle. It's a long walk for her, but I . . ."

"You had to go to your apprenticeship," said Bedwyr. "Continue."

"When she got to the courtyard gate, a guard stopped her. Except she wasn't one of the King's guards. Mother said she was dressed in dark blue except for a silver emblem on her chest. A leaf of some sort. When Mother asked to see my father, the guard told her he was busy with important

Morgan Castle business and couldn't be bothered at that time. When she tried to speak again, the woman took the basket from her hands and told her to take her leave. She stood with her hand on the grip of her sword until my mother turned to go."

Bedwyr spoke again. "The last time Brogan didn't come home, last year because of the ball, how were you notified?"

"His assistant, a young woman, brought a note from him, written in his own hand. Along with a bottle of cider vinegar from Cook."

"The messenger that came this time, did he bring a handwritten note? A gift?"

"No."

Bedwyr rose from his chair, dumping Cow onto the ground and startling Winston, who crouched closer to the ground and closed his eyes. Eliana wondered if he thought no one could see him when he closed his eyes.

"I must go to the castle at once," said Bedwyr. "Two missing fathers is two too many." He turned and strode into his house, leaving five children and one dragon looking after him.

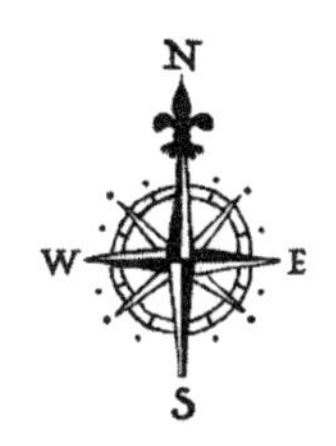

Chapter 29: Winston

DAY THREE

"You can come out now, Winston. Bedwyr's gone inside," Eliana's soft voice informed the dragon.

Winston's eyelids lowered, and Cow came into focus. The cat had come to sit in front of him and was making a low rumbling sound as she blinked up at him.

The tall, black-haired one—*Tal*—stood looking down the path. "I'm going to Morgan Castle, too," he said.

"So am I," said Eliana's brothers. They were so small, but their eyes reminded Winston of a hawk in pursuit of its prey.

"I guess that means I'm going, too," said Alethia.

"I don't think . . ." said Tal, but Eliana spoke before he finished.

"We're *all* going. Winston has to go so he can tell the King about his father. I have to go so I can tell everyone what

Winston is saying. I don't think we can stop Rowan or Sage. They will just follow behind if we say no. And our mother would want Alethia to make sure the boys are safe."

Tal nodded. To Winston, he seemed like another hawk but one whose prey had gotten away and wasn't sure if he could find another before dark.

Bedwyr emerged from his house, banging the door closed behind him. He had a reddish pouch slung over his shoulder and something furry on his head. It reminded Winston of an animal, one without a head or legs.

"Well, I assume we're all going?" said Bedwyr. He turned to walk with long powerful strides up the path to the road.

Winston asked, "Eliana, where are we going exactly? I will fly, but which way are you going?"

"We'll continue east on the road. It's almost two miles from here to Morganshire. We'll walk through the town and up the road to Morgan Castle, which is south of Morganshire. We should be able to get to the castle in less than an hour."

Eliana talks a lot about miles and hours, thought Winston. All he really needed to know was east. They were going east again. And then south. He wondered if the castle—whatever that was—was close to the raging waters he had seen. Thinking about the endless water was much easier than thinking about castle, King, and missing fathers, so as the five children followed the Cartographer out of the yard, Winston headed south to the sea. He flew in looping circles out over the waters and then back to the road so he could keep track of the agonizingly slow progress of Eliana and the others.

Winston was completing yet another loop from the waters back across the land when he saw a huge stone building thrusting toward the sky. It looked like it had clawed its way from inside a rock-strewn mountain perched high above the place where the land dropped off to the waters below. Winston could tell humans had made this thing. The stones that formed it were rounded and fitted together like the much smaller stones of Eliana's home. Crouched at the feet of what must be the castle were buildings of varying colors, looking to Winston like fall leaves laid out in neat rows.

Eliana and the others walked between these buildings. As they moved closer to the castle, Winston slowed and descended until he was flying just above them. What had seemed like slow progress before now seemed to Winston to be much too fast. Soon, his friends would be at the castle. The hope he had felt before now turned to fear. He could feel his heart pounding, and a strange buzzing sound seemed to fill his head.

The humans came to a towering stone wall in front of the castle. They walked through an opening in the wall and came to a stop in a dusty clearing. Eliana looked so small beside the humans who immediately confronted her and the others. They wore coverings the color of near night and some carried long sticks, which they pointed at the newcomers.

"It's because of me that Eliana is in danger," he thought. Winston flared his wing tips, lowered his powerful back legs, and landed between Eliana and the soldiers. Gusts of scalding steam billowed from his mouth—much hotter than his breath had ever been—surprising Winston and terrifying the men and women who stumbled backward.

Chapter 30: Doryu

DAY THREE

Deep in the cavern far below the castle, Doryu heard a whisper from the darkness of the cell next to Jade's.

"Doryu." It was Brogan. Doryu had almost forgotten the King's Head Steward was imprisoned there; it had been so long since he'd seen or heard him. Even when the guards brought their meals on battered tin plates, Brogan remained in the back of his cell.

Nearly a month ago, when Doryu had first discovered Brogan was in the cell next to Jade's, he tried to communicate with him. But their whispered conversations were always interrupted by Margred's soldiers who pulled Doryu away from the rusty bars of Brogan's cell.

During those first days, Doryu learned only bits and pieces of Brogan's story. That he'd been sent to summon

Margred, that Cook had told him about a secret staircase leading to a battered door on the far side of the cavern, that in the library was an ancient book Margred had been reading despite the fact that it was written in some indecipherable language.

"Poison," Brogan had said. "I know Margred has been poisoning the King. Just like she poisoned the dragon. And Valo and his men. Even their horses."

After Raiden was first chained to the cavern floor, Brogan had stopped trying to talk to Doryu. The Head Steward had watched silently from his cell day after day when Doryu was taken by Margred's men to stand next to the dragon who was growing weaker by the day.

One morning, after yet another fruitless conversation with Raiden, Doryu had managed to tell Brogan that the dragon would never be able to find what Margred wanted.

"Raiden doesn't have that ability," Doryu told him when the guards were distracted. "None of us can fathom why Margred thinks he can. And it seems she isn't even looking for the King's missing treasure. She is looking for a treasure that was lost centuries ago when there was only one king south of the Black Mountains. Now, Margred is so angry she isn't even considering that Raiden can't do what she is demanding. She thinks if she keeps him chained long enough, he will surrender to her wishes."

Seeing a guard coming to pull him away, Doryu hurried to say, "Brogan, we have to come up with a plan. Raiden won't last much longer without the special dragon food from the mountains. I am afraid of what Margred might do if . . ."

Brogan had said nothing; he'd turned to go back to his sleeping mat. His once shiny black hair had grown long and dull and lay on his shoulders like defeat.

That morning, Brogan finally spoke again. "Doryu, I have an idea," he whispered.

Doryu slipped his hand out of Jade's and edged his way closer to Brogan's cell. It wasn't quite full-morning and much of the cavern was still in shadow. The scar-faced guard had fallen asleep and was slumped over with her chin on her chest. Doryu slid closer to Brogan's cell. Brogan was half sitting, half lying with his left hand gripping one of the cell bars, but Doryu could see a light burning in the man's eyes, a light that hadn't been there the last time he'd seen him. Here was the King's Head Steward wielding what remained of his strength and determination.

"Doryu, you must go to the King. Thank God Margred didn't lock you in a cell, too. I'll create a distraction when they bring the midday meal, and you can use the secret staircase to get to the kitchen. Cook will help you." Brogan smothered a cough with his hand and continued, "First, you must go to the library. I hid Margred's book on the top shelf behind a row of books to the left of the fireplace. Take the book to the King. I'm sure she's been using the information in it. Help him understand what's happening—that Margred is poisoning him, too. That she's killing the dragon."

"Get away from there, old man!" It was the guard, awake now and on her feet.

Doryu grabbed Brogan's hand as the guard strode toward them. He nodded once and Brogan nodded back. The plan was full of potential pitfalls, but at least it was a plan. And if Doryu could get Margred's book, maybe he could reason with the King. But how was he to get past Margred once he reached the King's Audience Hall? He shook his head. One thing at a time. It was his fault Raiden was here; Doryu knew if he did nothing, the dragon would die. And he had no doubt that if that happened, Margred wouldn't hesitate to do away with Jade, Brogan, Valo, and all the other captives as well.

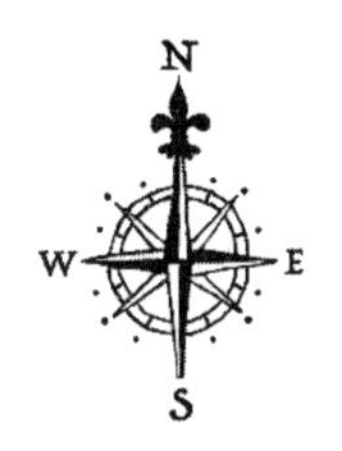

Chapter 31: Eliana

DAY THREE

In the castle courtyard, with Winston standing in front of Eliana and the others, it took the soldiers a minute or two to stagger to their feet and raise their iron-tipped spears. But even with his wings fully extended and clouds of searing steam billowing from his mouth, the young dragon wasn't enough to stop the soldiers from marching toward them across the dusty courtyard.

Sage and Rowan grabbed Eliana's arms and tried to pull her back toward the gate. Tal stepped in front of Alethia and told her to run. Bedwyr strode to Winston's side and held up both hands.

"Stop! Stop!" he shouted, but even his powerful voice couldn't be heard above the guards who were all yelling at the same time.

"Halt! Halt!"

"Get back!"

"Stop them!"

Many more guards emerged from inside the castle, some carrying battle axes. Others had crossbows, already loaded with arrows. They were all moving toward Winston and Bedwyr, who stood their ground.

Eliana wanted so badly to run, but her feet felt as though they were sunk in wet clay. Why weren't the guards listening to Bedwyr? Surely, they knew who he was.

The soldiers seemed to be moving slowly now as if in a strange soundless nightmare.

Sunlight threw flashes of silver. Eliana blinked. The advancing soldiers all had badges sewn to their tunics. Silver leaves. They looked familiar. The shape of them. Where had she seen them? It came to her then: a page in her mother's plant journal. *Nightshade.* And her mother's precise handwriting. *Poison.*

All at once, Eliana could hear again. And she ran. Toward Bedwyr and Winston. She grabbed Bedwyr's hand and tugged.

"Who are you?" Bedwyr continued to shout at the guards. "You aren't the King's guards. Where is Valo? I demand to speak to him at once."

Eliana tried to tell him about the poison. About the nightshade leaf these soldiers wore. But it was too late. It was all too late.

Eliana looked back over her shoulder and saw Tal, still

standing in front of Alethia. Her sister had her arms wrapped around the twins. Eliana had a moment to think how brave they were despite the terror written all over their faces. They could've run, but they hadn't.

Nothing had gone the way they'd planned. And now they were all in terrible danger. Her throat tightened and her eyes burned. She tried to smile at them, but her mouth wouldn't obey. She turned back to see the soldiers moving closer; one jabbed the tip of his spear against Bedwyr's chest. Another raised his axe.

A dark shadow fell on the courtyard, and a rush of air above them drew all eyes to flashes of gold and amethyst. A high-pitched cry like a hundred eagles protecting their young drove the soldiers back again, clawing at each other to get away as a great dragon, easily three times the size of Winston, dropped to the ground in front of them. It beat its wings against the air, filling the courtyard with a swirling wind. And the steam from the dragon's wide-open mouth was so hot that the men and women held their leather-clad arms in front of their faces.

Winston moved forward to stand beside the golden dragon. He lay his head against its shoulder, and he smiled. A massive wing arched over Winston and pulled him close.

Nerys! Winston's mother! thought Eliana.

"Those colors," Bedwyr murmured as he strode forward to stand beside Winston, half-hidden by Nerys's beautiful wing. The mapmaker reached as if to touch her but pulled back his hand and bellowed at the now subdued guards.

"I am Bedwyr, the Cartographer. I am well-known at Morgan Castle by King Halwyn, as well as by the Captain of the Guard and the Head Steward. I demand to speak to Brogan at once to seek an audience with the King."

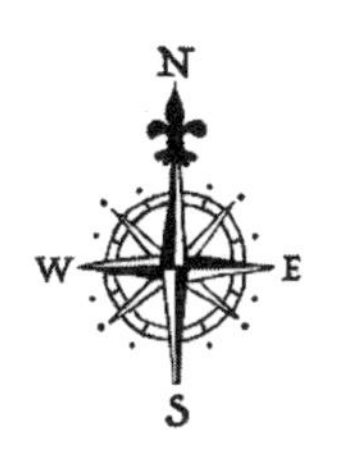

Chapter 32: Doryu

DAY THREE

Doryu rose to his knees and used the bars of Jade's cell to pull himself to a stand. The pain in his knees and hands was nothing new. He'd been feeling the effects of his age for a few years now. But the cold of the dark cavern seemed to be seeping into his bones these past weeks despite the warm clothes and blankets. He looked toward the arched entrance to try and judge the time. Brogan had said he would create a diversion when the guards brought the midday meal. Was it midday? And even if it were, the guards seemed to bring their tin plates and cups when they got around to it, not at any specific time.

Doryu knew they weren't getting the food from Cook. Although now it had some vegetables and scraps of meat, it was thin and runny, and tasted like dishwater. Brogan was right; poison was the only explanation for the lethargy of Valo and his men. And how else would Margred be able to convince the King to put her in charge if she weren't poisoning him, too?

In the cell to Doryu's right, Brogan was still half-lying by the bars. The Head Steward was gesturing toward the far side of the cavern, where the door to the secret stairway waited. Doryu nodded one last time at the man he now considered a friend. He began walking slowly toward Raiden, who lay in a deep sleep in the center of the circular cavern. A guard saw Doryu but said nothing. The dragon was dying and would be of no help.

When he reached Raiden, Doryu gently put his hand on his neck just below where the heavy metal collar had worn through the scales, revealing red, weeping flesh. In the first hours and days, when Raiden had recovered from the effects of the poisoned torches, he'd fought mightily against the chains. His cries had filled the cavern, and Doryu was sure even the King could hear them high above in his chambers. The dragon had struggled until he bled, but he hadn't been able to break the chains or pull them loose. Now the scales under Doryu's hand were crusted with dried blood. The metallic smell jolted Doryu back to the day he'd brought the dead King's sword to the castle.

Raiden, I hope you can hear me, Doryu spoke without words, praying Raiden could still hear him like he had before, just by touch. *Brogan and I have a plan.*

When Doryu finished his explanation, at first there was

no response. But then he felt a whisper, like the vibration of a leaf in a spring breeze.

Yes . . .

Doryu laid his head against Raiden's scales, and with what felt like hope, the old Dragon Speaker turned and made his way toward the wooden door at the back of the cavern. Slowly at first, then a little faster. His heart thudding against his ribs, he prayed for strength. Even in the gloom at the back of the cavern, he felt exposed, like a deer in the middle of a sunlit meadow.

Just when he was sure the guards would see him and call for him to stop, a loud metallic clanging reverberated throughout the cavern. It seemed to come from everywhere at once. Along with the cacophony of tin cups on bars, Doryu could also hear yelling—first one voice and then two—as Jade joined Brogan in his part of the plan. The guards began yelling, too, and running toward the cells. Realizing what he must do now, Doryu ran as fast as his old legs would allow away from the uproar.

When Doryu finally reached the back of the cavern and pulled on the door handle, the door was stuck. Or maybe even locked on the other side. As he pulled and pulled, he realized the noises from across the cavern were dying down. Brogan and Jade had done all they could, but it wasn't going to be enough. Any minute, a guard would notice him.

The air in the cavern swirled against the walls. A sound like a fierce wind in high forest trees filled the air and was joined a moment later by a deafening shriek. Raiden! His wings filled the center of the cavern, and his head was lifted with a cry that filled Doryu with a strength he hadn't felt in years. He braced his feet, and—with one last pull—the door opened and thudded against the rocky cavern wall.

Only Doryu heard it open.

Only Doryu heard the slight whoosh as it closed behind him, and he began climbing the dark, winding staircase.

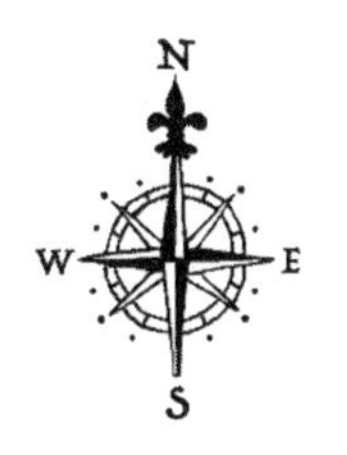

Chapter 33: Eliana

DAY THREE

“Are you deaf, man?” Bedwyr shouted at the taller of the soldiers standing before them in the front castle courtyard. “Where is Brogan?”

Eliana felt a movement at her side and turned to see Tal beside her, his dark eyes on the leader of the guards. Nerys beat her great left wing and opened her mouth to release more searing steam. Under her right wing, Winston lifted his head to add his own steam to hers. Most of the guards backed away.

“Ah, Bedwyr! How nice to see you again!” The voice seemed to slice through the guards, opening a path for a tall, slender woman with hair the color of wet slate. Her smile reminded Eliana of a bad apple, red and glistening on the outside but rotten inside.

"Margred." Bedwyr crossed his arms, and his eyes narrowed as the woman glided to a stop in front of the mapmaker. The leader of the guards took a step forward but stopped at a slight gesture of Margred's pale hand.

"There seems to be a misunderstanding here, old friend," said Margred, gesturing to indicate the guards, children, and the two dragons. "Let's go inside and have some wine. There is a warm and comfortable chamber where the dragons—"

"Margred, we didn't come for wine, and the dragons are staying here with us," said Bedwyr. "Where is Valo? And Brogan? We will speak with the King at once."

Margred shook her head, a sad smile pasted on her face. "Brogan has gone to Tibbet Mill to care for his mother who has taken ill. Valo . . ."

"No! She's lying!" Tal shouted, striding forward to stand beside Bedwyr. His hands curled into shaking fists at his sides. "My grandmother died when I was five. And my father would never leave without getting word to us. You're lying! Where is my father?"

Without taking his eyes off Margred, Bedwyr placed his hand on Tal's shoulder. "We'll get to the bottom of this, my boy. Margred has never been overly fond of the truth. We'll see what King Halwyn has to say. I'm sure there's a reasonable explanation."

While Bedwyr spoke to Tal, Margred's face changed from something resembling beauty to something else entirely. Her eyes became narrow slits, her skin mottled with red blotches. When she spoke, her voice was tight with anger.

"As you wish, Bedwyr. I will go to the King myself to request an audience." She turned abruptly, her midnight blue robes swirling around her. "Gunter, prepare some torches. It will be dark soon."

Margred disappeared through an archway at the back of the courtyard. The smile on Gunter's face reminded Eliana of the rabid dog she'd seen on the road when she was a little girl. Not really a smile at all.

"Prepare the torches!" Gunter called, and he and several of the soldiers turned on their heels to follow Margred back into the castle.

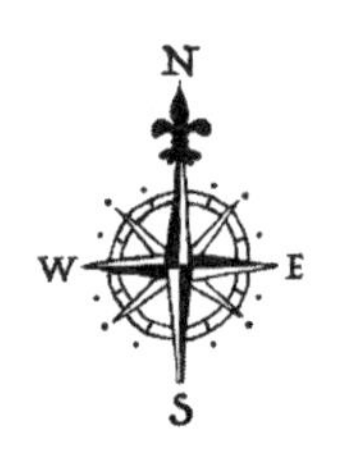

Chapter 34: Doryu

DAY THREE

Feeling his way up the secret stairway, the old Dragon Speaker climbed. The cold, damp walls and the complete darkness pressed against Doryu like a shroud. He could hear his heartbeat pounding in his ears. And as much as he wanted to be free of the darkness, he realized he was even more afraid of what he would find when he emerged into the light. Would Margred be waiting for him with poison and chains?

Up and up he climbed, until he feared his legs would give out once and for all. But just then his outstretched hand encountered what seemed to be another wooden door. He pushed on it, and it swung open into the castle kitchen. As he stepped into warmth and golden light, he was met with the incredible smells of good, healthy food.

"Hello, Doryu," said Cook. "You must be hungry. Here. I saved a bun for you."

Doryu took the bun—still hot from the blazing oven—and lowered himself to sit on a bench at the table that ran almost the length of the kitchen. Fatigue wrapped him in its grip from his feet to the top of his head. How could it be that even his hair was exhausted?

Cook handed him a cup of tea and turned back to continue stirring whatever was simmering over the fire. As he ate and drank, he realized he'd forgotten about good food and fire that was truly fire and not a sickening blue. Cook continued to stir, and the sound of her wooden spoon moving against the sides of the iron pot soothed him, easing the tension in his thin shoulders. He thought he would lie down on the bench and sleep for just a little while . . .

"Doryu, drink this."

Doryu's eyes snapped open. Cook stood in front of him with a bowl of something that smelled delicious. He realized at that moment he hadn't ever really seen Cook's eyes. She'd always been looking at the ingredients her assistants chopped, or into the pot, as she added some of this and some of that. Doryu had seen her kerchief-covered head bent over a mound of dough as she worked it with her strong hands. But never her eyes, until now. They were a deep gold surrounded by velvety brown.

"Drink," Cook said again. She watched him with her wonderful eyes while he sipped the rich broth. As he ate, Doryu felt strength flowing through him. His legs stopped trembling. He sat up straighter on the bench.

"Cook . . ." he began.

"Take the west service stairs to the upper level," she said. "There's no one staying in the guest rooms on the west corridor, so you'll have no problem getting to the library unseen. I made sure the fire is lit there to aid in your search."

She took the empty soup bowl from his hands and reached to pull him to a stand. "When you leave the library, take the east service stairs down to the Audience Hall and you will be safe." She tied a cloth bundle over his shoulder. "Hurry now. Be sure to give these to the King as soon as you see him. Tea and a bun. They'll help revive him. And there's a teacup he'll need as well. I've wrapped it in a kerchief for protection."

Cook gently turned Doryu toward the service stairs. As he started up, he heard her say, "There's another bun in there for you, too, Dragon Speaker. And I'll need the teacup back when this is all over."

The service stairs were wide and smooth compared to the rough spiral stairs Doryu had climbed from the cavern deep below the castle. Here, two narrow windows admitted outside light, pale late afternoon light.

It will be growing dark soon, he thought. Cook had told him to hurry, and now he was filled with an urgency even stronger than before. How much time had passed since he'd left Raiden, Brogan, Jade, and the others in the cavern? Had he dozed off on Cook's bench?

Hurry now. And so he did, quickly reaching the uppermost level of the castle. He made his way down the dim west corridor, passing the closed doors to the guest rooms. Cold air from the open colonnade chilled the corridors even as it provided freshness. Doryu was glad to push open the library door and find a fire blazing mightily on the east wall to his left.

"Thank you, Cook," he whispered. Pulling the door closed behind him, Doryu stood for a moment. Hearing only the crackling of the fire, he moved quickly to the shelves to the left of the fireplace. Brogan had told him to look on the top shelf behind some other books.

Fortunately, there was a three-legged footstool by a fireside chair. Doryu moved it in front of the bookcase and gingerly stepped up. His feet wobbled at first, but he was able to grab onto a shelf in front of him. He reached up and felt around behind the books on the top shelf.

Something warm brushed his fingertips. He jerked his hand back, knocking a few of the books to the floor. In the gap where they'd been, he saw it. Just as Brogan had said. A black leather book with gold lettering. Doryu reached up again and grabbed it, wondering if the book itself was the source of the warmth he'd felt.

Hurry. He must hurry. He turned to step down from his precarious perch on the footstool and lost his balance, dropping the black book as he caught himself just before he fell to the floor.

Hurry, yes, but be careful, he thought. A little shaken, he bent to retrieve the book. As he was putting it safely in Cook's cloth bundle, he saw that one of the other books that had fallen was splayed open on the worn carpet. And on the floor beside it was a creased, yellowed parchment.

Competing with the need for haste, Doryu felt an almost physical pull toward the parchment, and he bent to pick it up. In the flickering firelight, he saw several drawings surrounded by words so small his aging eyes couldn't read them. But his eyes were still strong enough to see that some of the drawings were of teacups. Delicate teacups with strange designs on the sides.

"My teacups!" he said, his voice much too loud in his excitement. He glanced back at the door, thrust the parchment in the cloth bag, and began making his way as quietly as possible to the door on the east side of the library.

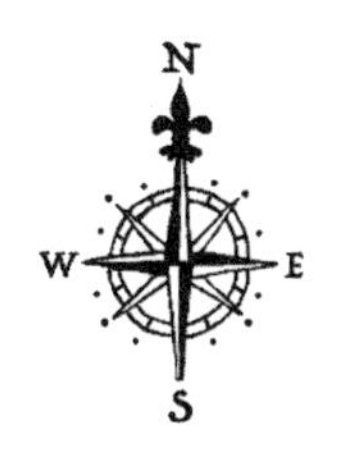

Chapter 35: Winston

DAY THREE

Still protected by his mother's wing, Winston watched as the woman they called Margred walked back into the castle. She'd said she was going to ask the King to meet with them, but Winston didn't believe her. She'd lied about Tal's father, and now he was sure she was lying about the King. How could Bedwyr persuade the King to help them find his father if they couldn't talk to him? Winston felt a hollowness deep in his chest along with terrible fear. Eliana, her brothers, and all the rest were here because of him, to help him find Raiden. And now his mother was in danger, too.

"Mother, I'm sorry," he said. "I shouldn't have left the cave. I wanted to help you. I . . ."

"I know, Winston. I know. What's important now is that

we finish this. Finish what we set out to do. I found him, son. I found your father."

"What!?" Winston pulled back and stared up at his mother. "Where?"

"He's *her* prisoner," she said. "She commands the soldiers dressed in the same color she wears and controls her captives with poison."

Winston gasped. Eliana, who couldn't understand their dragon language unless she was touching him, whirled to look at him.

Nerys continued, "I don't know for sure, but it's likely the boy's father—Brogan—is her prisoner, too. Why else would she lie about where he is?"

Winston nodded.

"And Winston, your father will be very weak. He's been without benesaunus for far too long. I've hidden some nearby, but we'll need to get it to him before he can even hope to fly." Nerys paused. "I wish we could tell your friends what's happening. It's going to take all of us," she said with a sweep of her wing, "to defeat that evil woman."

"But I can tell Eliana. She puts her hand on my neck and she can understand . . ."

"She's a Dragon Speaker?" Nerys lowered her head so that her huge amethyst eye was level with Eliana's face.

Eliana stood completely still as she was bathed in the warm breath emerging from her gigantic nostrils.

"I thought the last one had died when . . ." said Nerys. "In the days when we had to go into hiding. This one is so young." Nerys paused, then with a slight nod of her massive head, said, "Tell her."

Winston turned to face Eliana, who had moved to stand with her sister, brothers, and Tal while Winston and his mother spoke. Winston lowered his head so his friend could place her hand on his neck.

While Winston told Eliana everything his mother had said, the guards who remained in the courtyard talked and gestured toward them. Several looked back toward the archway through which Margred had gone.

Bedwyr frowned and moved closer to Eliana and Winston. "What's Winston saying, Eliana? Tell us quickly. Something's happening." He gestured toward the soldiers who remained, spears still in hand.

"I heard him say 'Dragon Speaker,'" said Sage, pointing to one of the guards. They all watched as the man turned and ran toward the archway.

"How do they know about Dragon Speakers?" Bedwyr muttered under his breath. "He whirled to face Eliana and Winston. "Tell us what Winston told you so we can make a plan. We don't have much time."

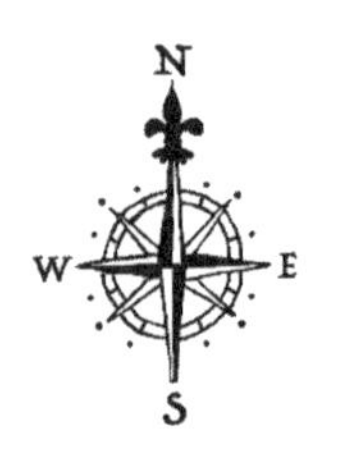

Chapter 36: Doryu

DAY THREE

Doryu pulled open the door at the far end of the library just enough to peer around the edge. The corridor beyond was empty, and he could see the east service stairway that led down to the King's bedchamber and Audience Hall. He opened the door a bit more so he could slip through, thankful for well-oiled door hinges. Just a little farther now. On his right he could see the iron door of the treasury.

It all started here, he thought. *Who could've gotten past the locked door and taken all the treasure? And where is it?*

Things seemed to have gone way beyond a search for the kingdom's modest treasure. A dragon lay dying in a cavern Doryu hadn't known existed. Iron bars imprisoned his own sister and the King's Head Steward. Valo seemed to have shrunk in size, and his face was lined with fatigue and illness.

Now Doryu prayed he could get to the King's quarters unseen and convince him to stop Margred, who still believed Raiden could find hidden treasure.

What if the King wasn't in his quarters? Doryu's heart fluttered at the thought but steadied as he remembered Cook's certainty that he was.

The east service stairs were only dimly illuminated. It must have been later than he'd thought when the guards brought their midday meal. Much later. And maybe he *had* dozed on Cook's bench. This time of year, full dark wasn't until after dinner. His heart stuttered again at the thought the guards might even now be bringing the evening meal to the prisoners. Would they realize he was gone and sound the alarm?

Doryu made his way as quickly as his old legs could carry him down the service stairs to the long corridor that ran alongside the King's bedchamber. Straight ahead, he could see the heavy wooden door leading to the Audience Hall. The King would be in his Audience Hall, where he took his meals, wouldn't he?

Hurrying toward the door, Doryu recalled the last time he'd stood before King Halwyn. Had it really only been four weeks? Valo had been there, strong and fierce, with firelight dancing on his dark skin. Brogan, too, had been there, ever ready to serve his king. Doryu shuddered to remember Margred's breath in his ear as she'd threatened Jade's life. King Halwyn hadn't been able to see how evil she was. She'd convinced him to approve all that happened after that.

Doryu placed his hands on the door to the Audience Hall and pushed. At first, it didn't budge, but then, with a slight squeal, it opened. A fire blazed ferociously in its place on the eastern wall; it was so bright that at first Doryu didn't see the figure hunched in a chair before it.

That smell. The air in the Audience Hall smelled of the blue and white torches used to capture Raiden. Doryu gagged and shoved the door open as far as it would go. He nudged an iron doorstop in place to keep it open and allow fresh air in.

"Your Highness! King Halwyn," Doryu called as he ran toward the figure slumped in front of the fireplace. Here the poisonous smell was much stronger.

Using one arm to cover his mouth and nose, Doryu turned to the windows on either side of the fireplace and tugged the heavy drapes aside. Within seconds, fresh, salty ocean air poured into the room, pulled by the cross-draft created by the open corridor door. Gulping breaths of the cool air, Doryu ran back to the King and gently shook his arm. Halwyn's face was the color of day-old porridge, but he was still breathing.

"Your Majesty! King Halwyn!"

Chapter 37: King Halwyn

DAY THREE

Halwyn's dream of missing treasure and captured dragons faded as someone shook his arm and called to him. He was so tired. Despite the recurring nightmares, all he wanted was for this person to leave him alone and let him sleep.

"King Halwyn, please. You must wake up," the voice insisted.

"Mmmmmmmm," mumbled the King, opening one eye to see who was bothering him. "Brogan? Is that you?"

"No, sire. It's Doryu."

"Dor-who? What?" Halwyn struggled to remember who Dor-who was.

"Doryu," said the voice. "The Dragon Speaker."

A gray wrinkled face with a scraggly beard hovered in the air in front of him. Halwyn pushed himself up in his chair, knocking over a goblet of soured wine. He took a deep breath. The air was cool but didn't feel harshly cold anymore. It smelled like kelp floating on ocean waves. Halwyn took another deep breath.

"Where's Brogan . . . I mean, Linette?" he asked the face. He was hungry all of a sudden. And thirsty. He looked down at the spilled wine and then back to the face. Doryu? Was that his name?

The old man took a cloth bundle off his shoulder—which was now in focus, too—and laid it on the ornate table beside them. From it he took a wine skin and two buns, and something wrapped in one of Cook's kerchiefs.

"It's tea, Your Highness. To go with your bun. Cook sent them," said the Dragon Speaker.

Yes, thought the King. *That's who he is: the Dragon Speaker.* Who he'd sent to help capture the dragon. Shaking that thought aside, he said, "Tea?" and realized it sounded like just the right thing.

Doryu unwrapped the kerchief, saying, "She sent a teacup, too . . . Oh!"

At the old man's gasp of surprise, the King looked to see what he was holding. It was a white porcelain teacup with abstract blue designs swirling around the sides.

"It's like mine, Your Majesty," said Doryu. "I have two just like it down in my . . ." The Dragon Speaker stopped. "I have much I need to tell you, King Halwyn. Margred has been poisoning you. Brogan's locked in a cell in a cavern below the lower dungeon, and Valo's been replaced by Margred's own soldiers."

"Wha . . . what?" stammered the King, starting to rise.

Doryu gently pushed him back into his chair.

"Yes, we'll need to hurry, but first you need to hear the whole story. And we'll need to figure out how to stop Margred." Doryu paused and added under his breath, "and determine what that parchment means."

As the King ate his bun and sipped tea from the porcelain cup, Doryu sat on a stool beside him and told him all that had happened since the night he went with Valo to capture the dragon.

"So Brogan isn't in Tibbet Mill? Margred said . . ."

"She lied, Your Highness," said Doryu.

"And Valo? He thinks I dismissed him as my Captain of the Guard?"

"The scroll Margred gave him was very convincing, sire. It had your seal on it."

The King put his chin in his hand and stared into the fire. After a few minutes, he spoke again. "She's been throwing something into the fire. I thought I saw it once. The flames turned blue for only a moment, but then they looked normal again."

After another pause, the King resumed. "Did she lie about the dragon, too? It can't find the missing treasure?"

Doryu sighed. "Although dragons can't find hidden treasure, Margred *believes* they can. She's taken extreme measures to capture Raiden to force him to do her bidding based on that belief." Doryu poured more tea into the blue and white teacup. "Things have changed, Your Highness. I know he's telling the truth about not being able to find treasure. We've tried to keep this fact from Margred, because right now that's the only thing keeping any of her captives alive."

The King sat straighter in his chair and rubbed his head with both hands so that his wispy hair once again formed a halo around his head.

I'll need a bath once this is all over, he thought, as the Dragon Speaker reached once again into his cloth bag.

"Another bun?" the King asked, smacking his lips.

"No, sire. Something more important."

Wondering what could be more important than another of Cook's buns, Halwyn waited as Doryu pulled out a black leather book and an old parchment. As the old man put the book in his hands, the King grunted with surprise at its warmth. The gold lettering on the front seemed to be in another language.

Doryu said, "Before he was captured, Brogan found this in the library, beside the chair where Margred often sits. He said it was open to a page with drawings of leaves, the same leaves Margred's guards now wear on their tunics."

The King looked up from the book, his eyes narrowing.

Doryu continued, "Brogan hid the book in the library and told me where to find it. He said you would know what to do with it."

Chapter 38: Eliana

DAY THREE

Down in the courtyard, with only a few of Margred's soldiers left to guard them, Eliana hurriedly told Bedwyr, Tal, and her siblings what Nerys had said about Margred and the captives in the cavern; Bedwyr's eyes narrowed until his wiry eyebrows almost obscured them.

"I knew that woman was wicked the first time I met her," he said, his voice rumbling with anger.

Tal's face was as white and hard as the piece of marble Eliana had found in their creek last winter. "We need to find them right now," he said. "Are they in the dungeon?"

Eliana moved to put her hand on Winston, but when she did, Winston said, "It'll be faster if my mother speaks directly to you, Eliana."

Eliana's eyes widened in surprise; she hadn't considered

she might be able to understand a dragon other than Winston. She lay her hand on Nerys's scales, iridescent in the fading western light in the courtyard.

"Hello, Eliana," said Winston's mother.

Eliana smiled at the sound of her voice, lower and richer than that of her son. While Nerys told Eliana about the cavern deep below the castle, Bedwyr paced, keeping one eye on the remaining guards. Alethia, Rowan, and Sage stood close to Tal.

"Why's it taking so long?" said Tal between clenched teeth. "Where are they, Eliana?"

"Raiden is in a cavern under the castle. Nerys thinks he is chained, but she wasn't able to tell. She couldn't tell who else was there. She's had to fly at night and stay out over the ocean. There are strange lights—maybe torches?—in the cavern."

"Are Margred's soldiers there, too?" asked Bedwyr.

Nerys nodded.

Eliana continued, "Nerys says the entrance is down a trail that goes around the castle. Guards are posted outside, as well as inside the cavern. There isn't a way to get into the cavern without them seeing us."

In the silence that followed, Eliana heard the shuffling sounds of boots. The guards in the courtyard had once again lifted spears, crossbows, and battle axes. Beyond them, blue lights moved toward them from inside the castle. The man whom Margred had called Gunter emerged first, holding a torch high above his head. He was followed by more and more soldiers, some carrying torches, all wearing the silver leaf badge on their chests. They filled the courtyard, and as they did, smoke from the strange torches filled the air.

Nerys, Winston, Bedwyr, and the children all backed toward the outer courtyard gate.

"We're too late!" Bedwyr called. "Run!"

But as the children turned to obey his command, the enormous castle gates began to close, pushed by several more of Margred's guards who had come from the front of the castle.

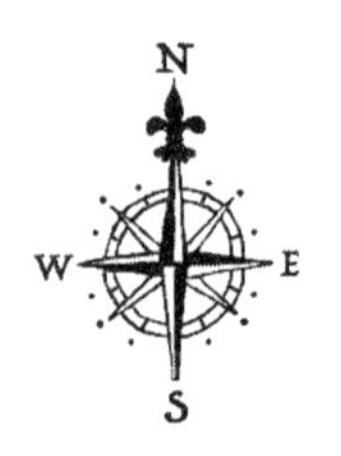

Chapter 39: Winston

DAY THREE

Moving Winston behind her, Nerys lifted her massive head and spread her wings to beat against the noxious fumes from the torches.

"Now, Winston! Take her and go now! We need you to get your father!" she called back to him.

Winston hadn't told Eliana this part of the plan. There hadn't been time, and he'd hoped it wouldn't come to this, that there would be another way. But now, with even more soldiers emerging from the castle and the air reeking of what must be poison, he knew there was no choice.

Thrusting his head under Eliana's arm so that her hand was on him, he said, "Eliana, get on my back and hold on! We have to go now!"

Winston crouched as close to the ground as he could

and lowered his right wing. He stared into Eliana's eyes. "Trust me, Eliana," he said.

Looking into the young dragon's blue-green eyes, Eliana realized *he* had trusted *her* from the first time they'd met. He'd trusted her enough to come back to the forest clearing, to go with her to Bedwyr's, to come here to this courtyard.

"We have to go get my father. He can help us," said Winston. "Trust me, Eliana."

And she did. Hidden by his mother's body and wings, Eliana stepped onto Winston's emerald and turquoise wing. Grabbing onto a ruffle of feathers at the base of his neck, she swung her leg up and over to sit on his back.

"We'll be back!" she called to the others but wasn't sure they heard her.

"Stop them!" It was Margred, followed by the guard who had called Eliana *Dragon Speaker.*

Winston pushed with all his strength against the ground with his back legs and rose above Nerys and the guards as Margred shouted and pointed at them. He could feel Eliana squeeze her legs and adjust her hold on his neck feathers.

Several of the guards began releasing spears into the air; Winston saw one pass close by his head and banked to the right to protect Eliana.

"Higher, Winston!" his mother called.

Winston pulled his wing blades in and then down, flight feathers pushing mightily against the air in the courtyard. Eliana tightened her grip even more. He beat his wings, again and again. When he finally looked below, the guards were mere specks in the courtyard. Even his mother had shrunk to the size of a songbird.

Winston continued banking to the right until the castle was just a small pile of rocks. He began a slow turn to the left to take them out over the wind-tossed sea.

"Oh, Winston," Eliana called. "The ocean!"

Winston turned toward the steep cliffs that fell from the southern edge of Morganshire.

"We have to get benesaunus for my father," said Winston. "He's been without it for too long. My mother hid some in a crevice on the cliffs above the water, not too far from the cavern."

As he explained how they would find and gather the food, Winston worried that he wouldn't have the strength to carry both the benesaunus and Eliana. He remembered the downward plunge when he'd gathered his first clump at the Black Mountains. He could only hope the updraft here would be strong enough to keep them aloft.

"We can do it, Winston," said Eliana. She leaned forward and laid her head against his neck. He hadn't even voiced his fears aloud, but somehow Eliana knew what he was thinking.

Yes, we can do it, he answered, and he beat his wings to fly faster toward the cliffs.

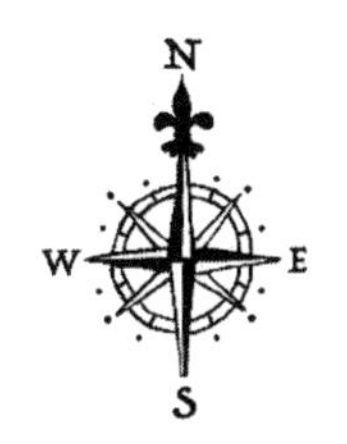

Chapter 40: Doryu

DAY THREE

In the Audience Hall, Doryu watched as King Halwyn flipped through the pages of the black leather book. The Dragon Speaker shifted on his stool, wondering if the King understood the urgency of the situation.

Halwyn seemed much revived now, his eyes bright in the flickering firelight. Doryu rubbed his fingers across the creases in the old parchment he held in his lap. While he waited for the King, he examined the drawings of the teacups, drawings that looked exactly like the teacups in his cell and the one Cook had sent to the King. Below the crease, there was a beautifully drawn compass rose.

As he was trying once again to bring the writing into focus, the King shouted, "Ah ha," and jabbed at a page in the black leather book.

"Here it is! It's sleeping nightshade. See? This page has smudges on it, like someone spent a lot of time looking at it. Nightshade would explain how Margred is making us all sleepy without actually killing us."

"How do you know . . . ?" began Doryu.

"I had a nursemaid when I was young who knew all about using plants for treating illness. She had a book, too, with drawings of leaves, flowers, berries . . . I remember nightshade because of the shape of the leaves and the flowers like little cups. It can be deadly in large concentrations, but in small, diluted amounts it can be used for inducing sleep."

The King turned to the next page in the book. He tapped his finger on a drawing there and said, "It can be used to make poison-tipped spears, too. Do Margred's guards have . . . ?"

"Yes," said Doryu. He remembered the sharp metal end of the spear carried by the guard who'd dragged Jade to her cell. Jade. He leaned forward and put his hand on the King's knee.

"Forgive my boldness, Your Highness, but I fear we're running out of time. The guards may have already discovered my absence. We can use the stairs in the kitchen to get down to the soldier's quarters. Maybe some of your own guards are still there . . ."

Just then, through the open windows on either side of the fireplace, Doryu heard shouting and the shrieking of a dragon, a sound he knew well. He hurried to the window to the left of the fireplace, followed closely by the King.

As he leaned out of the opening, the sounds became louder, but Doryu could see only the rocks and the tall grasses that grew at the base of the castle.

"Come with me, Dragon Speaker," called the King as he ran to the towering double doors on the north side of the Audience Hall.

"Help me open these things!" Halwyn tugged on the polished brass handle on the left door.

Doryu started toward the doors but turned back for the cloth bag Cook had given him. He grabbed the black book, the parchment, and the wineskin with the tea, and thrust them into the bag.

"Doryu, help me!" shouted Halwyn.

Doryu heard the frustration in the King's voice but still took a few more seconds to wrap the blue and white teacup in Cook's handkerchief and add it to the cloth bag. Slinging it over his shoulder, Doryu ran to grab the door handle on the right.

The two men braced their feet and leaned back to pull the weighty doors open. Hurrying through, Doryu saw they were on a broad exterior portico open to the main courtyard below. It was bordered by a low stone wall with spaces separated by toothlike sections.

The King had already run to one of the gaps in the wall and was peering through it. Here, the shouting they'd heard only dimly before was a tumult: men and women yelling, a high-pitched shriek, and what sounded like a thousand eagle wings beating the air. Doryu ran to stand beside the King. Despite the uproar, now punctuated by the sight of arrows and metal-tipped spears flying through the air, Doryu felt his aged heart leap. There, in the midst of a raging battle, was the most beautiful dragon he'd ever seen. Full-grown, gold and amethyst, wings beating, billows of steam pouring from her mouth.

"Is that Raiden?" the King shouted into Doryu's ear. His eyes were wide with wonder.

"No, that must be his mate. Nerys."

"We have to stop this, Doryu."

Maybe Margred's men will listen to the King, thought Doryu, struggling to hold on to the hope that was slipping away. But his heart faltered as Gunter, Margred's head guard, strode from the castle into the courtyard, carrying a blue-flamed torch. Right behind him was Margred, followed by at least a dozen of her soldiers carrying more of the poisonous torches. Doryu tried to grab the King's arm to pull him back, but Halwyn was much stronger than he looked and jerked out of his grasp.

"Margred!" bellowed the King, his voice thundering over the sounds of the battle. "I command you and your soldiers to stop at once!"

The yells and shrieks subsided, and Margred stopped and looked up and over her shoulder. Just before her violet eyes found the King, Doryu ducked behind one of the raised sections of the rampart. She mustn't find out he'd escaped the cavern.

"Ah, Your Highness! Just in time! We're about to capture another dragon. Perhaps this one will be able to find your missing treasure."

"She really does think dragons can find gold and jewels," muttered the King under his breath before commanding in a loud voice, "Stay there, Margred. I'm coming down."

Halwyn turned to Doryu, still hiding behind the rampart. "There are a lot of soldiers down there, Dragon Speaker. And a lot of torches. Maybe she left the cavern unguarded. You must get to Valo. We need him and his men to defeat Margred and her guards."

"But, sire, what about you?"

"I'm the King. Margred seems to still be aware of that fact. And besides," he said with the hint of a smile, "I see a good friend down there. Bedwyr and I—with the help of that beautiful dragon—should be able to hold her off for a while. Go now."

Doryu hesitated only a moment, then thrust the remaining wineskin of tea into the King's hands. The Dragon Speaker turned, and—still crouching below the rampart wall—ran through a door just beyond the guest stairway. He passed the storeroom and the laundry and ran into the kitchen. Of course, Cook was there, adding an armful of carrots to the soup pot.

"You'll need more tea, Doryu," said Cook, gesturing to three more bulging wineskins waiting on the table.

Doryu slung them over his shoulder along with the cloth bag, and Cook walked to the wooden rack of pots and pans.

Pulling the secret door open for him, she patted him gently on the back.

"Good luck," she said, and closed it behind him.

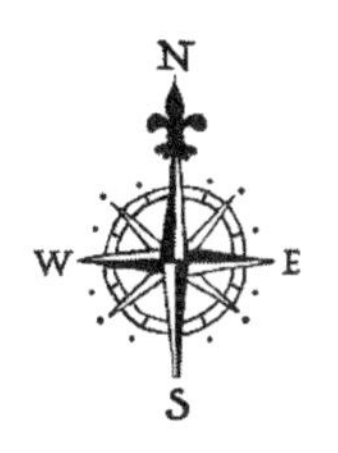

Chapter 41: Eliana

DAY THREE

Clinging to Winston with all her might, Eliana saw the Dead Rise Cliffs looming closer. Very few had ever seen this sheer rock face from the ocean and certainly not from high in the air above the waves. Only gulls, pelicans, peregrine falcons, and yes, dragons. The cliffs rose straight up at least a hundred feet from the sea, looking as if a giant had sliced off miles of moor with a broadsword. How had Nerys been able to hide benesaunus here?

What if it fell and was washed away by the sea? thought Eliana.

Don't worry, Eliana. There are ledges large enough to hold benesaunus.

Just as Eliana realized that Winston could hear her thoughts now and that she could feel his thoughts as she clung to his back, the dragon continued, *My mother said it's about fifty feet directly below a twisted tree growing at the cliff's edge.*

At that moment, Winston began to slow. His wings were fully stretched out from his body, tips flared upward. Eliana could feel a strong rush of air pushing them up from below.

Updraft! said Winston. *Look, there's the tree.*

As they hovered in the air, floating on the currents, Eliana could see a gnarled tree jutting from the clifftop, its branches and foliage reaching inland, permanently shaped by offshore winds.

Hold on, Eliana!

She clamped her legs as hard as she could, and Winston tilted back so his body was almost parallel to the cliff face. There was a pause, and then they were plunging downward. Eliana squeezed her eyes closed and tried not to think about the rocks piled below them.

They fell for what seemed an eternity to Eliana, but then there was a lifting sensation in her stomach as Winston leveled out, wings flared, to float once again on the glorious updraft.

"Updraft!" she called aloud to Winston, smiling with relief.

"Updraft!" answered Winston. "And benesaunus! I've got it. Now we just have to get it to my father."

As Winston rose higher, Eliana began to worry about how they were going to be able to take the special food to Raiden. Nerys had said he was chained in a cavern below the south side of the castle. She'd told them they must fly due north from the twisted tree to the large clearing in front of the cavern. And only if none of the King's Counselor's guards were there.

Eliana, I can do this alone if. . . began Winston.

No! thought Eliana. *I'm going with you. You'll need help to unlock your father. And besides, there are so many of that wicked woman's soldiers in the courtyard now that maybe none of them are still in the cavern.*

They rose above the cliffs, and Eliana could see the castle in the distance thrusting up from its rocky base. Its towers shimmered in the ocean air blowing inland across the grassland.

There aren't any guards in the clearing outside the cavern, said Winston, and Eliana realized then how sharp the dragon's eyesight was. She couldn't even see the cavern entrance yet.

Flying toward the castle, Eliana prayed they would be able to free Winston's father. And that Raiden would be strong enough to fly to the courtyard in time to prevent the capture—or even worse—of Alethia, the twins, Tal, Bedwyr, and Nerys.

Chapter 42: King Halwyn

DAY THREE

After Doryu was safely on his way, Halwyn walked to the broad opening in the rampart wall where the Grand Stairway led down to the courtyard. As he descended, a memory came of a time when he was a boy, holding his father's hand as Chares greeted visiting royalty. His father's hand had been so broad and strong, his robe a brilliant garnet red with white fur trim.

Now, so many years later, Halwyn lifted his chin, straightened his shoulders, and smoothed his own faded robe. His father was gone, his health and mind destroyed by his obsession with killing all dragons and exacting revenge for his own father's death. Halwyn could finally understand why Doryu had not continued to help Chares in his quest. How could anyone kill such a magnificent creature as the one now filling his courtyard?

Halwyn reached the end of the stairway and stepped down into the courtyard. Margred bowed her head and gestured with a flick of her hand for her guards to do the same.

"Your Majesty, I . . ." Margred began.

"Move aside, Counselor. I must greet my guests," said the King.

With another slight gesture of Margred's long fingers, the guards parted to make a path for the King.

"King Halwyn! Your Highness," said Bedwyr, bowing his head, his deep voice carrying across the courtyard. "We are so glad to see you."

The dragon lowered her head so it was on the same level as the King. Warm air wafted around Halwyn, and he was surprised to see it looked like the dragon was smiling. He was even more surprised to realize his hand was moving to touch the massive head. The scales were warm, not cold like he thought they'd be. So beautiful.

"King Halwyn, we must . . ." Bedwyr began but stopped at a slight shake of the King's head.

"We must all get acquainted," announced the King to the entire assembly. "Margred, we will need stools and refreshments. Since Linette is nowhere to be found, please see to it yourself."

"But, sire . . ."

"Now, Margred. I want our guests and your soldiers to be comfortable while we discuss how to enlist this dragon's help in finding the missing treasure. And tell your soldiers to extinguish those torches immediately. They stink!"

The King turned back to Bedwyr and winked. "Please, introduce your friends."

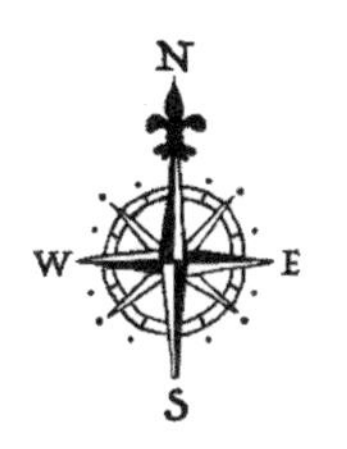

Chapter 43: Winston

DAY THREE

Nearing the cavern entrance, Winston could see a large, dark shape inside. It wasn't moving. Winston felt the words *we're too late, we're too late, we're too late* wheeling like frenzied bats in his mind. The benesaunus seemed heavier, and fatigue slowed the beating of his wings.

Winston, he's just weak. He's probably sleeping, thought Eliana, who had felt—and heard—his terror. *We have to hurry. Alethia and the others . . .*

Everyone's counting on us, thought Winston, lifting his wings as high as he could and back down again. And again. Then, they were there, and Winston pulled his wings back and thrust his back legs forward to let the benesaunus drop in front of the arched opening to the cavern. He landed and crouched down so Eliana could slide to the ground. Her legs trembled with fatigue from holding on for so long. She was so small, this brave human, his friend.

There was just enough light for Winston to see that the dark form in the cavern was a dragon. A huge dragon, a massive metal collar around his neck. Stepping closer, Winston couldn't see any guards or any of the horrible blue torches between them and the dragon. All the soldiers must've gone to the courtyard, taking their torches with them. Was this his father? He took another step and then another. Then Eliana was beside him, carrying as much benesaunus as her arms would hold.

"Is that your father?" she asked, dumping the benesaunus on the cavern floor. She reached to touch Winston's neck.

"I . . . I think so . . ."

"Winston." His name was a whisper from the captive dragon. It was Raiden! He was barely able to lift his head, but he was alive!

"It's my father!" Winston said as he scrambled to his father's side, with Eliana barely able to keep her hand on his neck. Now that she wasn't on his back, she had to touch his scales this way.

"He's so big," she whispered.

"Yes," said Winston. "But he won't hurt you." The young dragon put his head on Raiden's neck, just below the iron collar.

"Winston," said Raiden, "you shouldn't be here. There's an evil woman and guards . . ."

"They're all in the castle courtyard. And it looks like

they took all their poisonous torches with them. We—this is my friend Eliana—have come to rescue you."

Eliana moved some benesaunus in front of Raiden. Winston steamed it with his breath, and as his father ate, the young dragon told him all that had happened since Raiden disappeared.

When Winston got to the part about Eliana being able to understand him, Raiden turned so that his silver and black eye was only a few feet from her face. She looked like a mouse face to face with a falcon.

"Another Dragon Speaker? A young girl . . ." he said. "I thought Doryu was the last."

"Doryu? Who is Doryu?" asked Winston.

"It seems I am not the last Dragon Speaker," said a voice from the back of the cavern.

Winston and Eliana turned to see an old man coming toward them. An old man who had seen Eliana with her hand on Winston.

"Doryu! Thank goodness you're safe!" Another voice, thin and weak, came from the left side of the cavern.

But then, movement from the right caught their attention. Coming toward them was a riderless gray horse, head hanging low, on legs that looked unsteady. It stopped and nickered. Winston had only seen horses in the distance from high above. But even so, he could tell this one wasn't well.

The horse nickered again and blew air out its nostrils. It lifted its head and looked at Winston and Eliana, before turning to walk back into the gloom.

"Doryu, we have to hurry," spoke yet another voice from the left. Winston and Eliana turned to look at each other.

"There are a lot of people—and a horse—here," whispered Winston.

"Maybe one of them is Tal's father," said Eliana.

"Put your hand on my father, too. We have to make a plan."

"Yes, we should make a plan," said Raiden. "Doryu, we need you, too."

"Yes, we need to stop Margred," said the old man. He took a cloth bag from his bony shoulder and laid it on the ground. Smiling, he put one hand on Winston and one on Raiden.

"Did you find the King?" Raiden asked Doryu.

It took several minutes for the two dragons and the two Dragon Speakers to share what had happened.

"So that woman has been using sleeping nightshade all this time," said Eliana. "Winston, we have to get back to the courtyard! The torches . . . everyone's in danger."

"Father," said Winston. "Mother is there. In the courtyard."

Raiden's head jerked up, pulling against the giant chain.

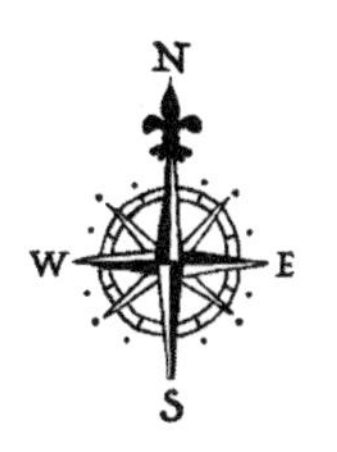

Chapter 44: Eliana

DAY THREE

Standing in the cavern deep below Morgan Castle, Eliana's thoughts and feelings flew around inside her like a murmuration of starlings. One hand was on Winston, and one was on Raiden who was so enormous she couldn't see all of him from where she stood. Across from her was an old man with a kind face—another Dragon Speaker. She remembered Bedwyr had said something about stories of Dragon Speakers in the place he'd come from. Was this one—*Doryu*—from there, too?

Hurry. Eliana kept hearing that word in her mind while the four made a plan. It hung in the air between them, and she knew the others could hear it, too.

It took only a few moments to confirm the King's Counselor had been poisoning not only Raiden but also the

King himself. That Margred had tricked and poisoned Valo, the Captain of the Guard. It was his horse Destre they'd seen, looking more like a ghost horse than a real one.

Doryu and Raiden told them Brogan and Jade were prisoners, as well. It was their voices they'd heard. Raiden, who continued to eat the benesaunus, said he was feeling much stronger.

"The air is clearer now that the torches are gone," said Raiden. "How is it that Margred's men aren't weakened by them?"

"Because she's been giving them the antidote," said Doryu, reaching for one of the wineskins. He held it up to show them.

"Cook gave this tea to me. And some to take to the King. As soon as we drank it, the awful sleepiness left us. All this time, Margred must've been giving me just enough of the antidote in my water cup to give me the strength to speak to you, Raiden." Doryu took the stopper out of the spout of the bag and poured a little of the tea onto the benesaunus.

"Winston, you should eat some of this, too," said Doryu.

Eliana realized Winston hadn't eaten anything since early that morning. Looking at him now, she could see he was exhausted. She ran back to the entrance of the cavern, grabbed more benesaunus, and brought it back to him.

"Here," said the old Dragon Speaker. He gestured for Eliana to open her mouth so that he could pour in a mouthful of tea. It was cool on her tongue and tasted faintly of citrus.

"Eliana, now that Raiden is recovering, there are others we need to help. Come with me," said Doryu.

Eliana followed him to the west side of the cavern. There, she saw iron bars and tin cups held by shaking hands. Doryu took the cups, poured in some of the tea, and handed them back through the bars. Doryu turned back to Eliana.

"Get the keys, Dragon Speaker. They're hanging over there next to the water barrels."

Protruding from a hook on the stone wall was a heavy ring of keys. Eliana took it to Doryu, who was grasping the hand of a small, older woman imprisoned in one of the cells. As he reached for the keys, Eliana smiled. *He called me Dragon Speaker*, she thought. *I am a Dragon Speaker*.

Chapter 45: Doryu

DAY THREE

Doryu tried one key after another until finally the lock on Jade's cell gave way. He pulled the iron door open and reached to pull his sister to him. Kissing her on the forehead, he realized how much he'd come to love her over the past weeks, beyond how he'd loved her as an infant.

"This is Eliana," he told his sister. "Eliana, please give her a little more of the tea. Here's another skin." Doryu turned to Brogan's cell and again tried key after key until he found the right one.

Brogan tried to pull himself to a stand, using the iron bars. Doryu hurried into the cell and put his hands under Brogan's arms to help him. The old Dragon Speaker could feel the Head Steward's ribs under his filthy tunic. He'd refused to wear the clothing brought to him by Margred's soldiers.

"Eliana, help me hold him up," he said. "Brogan, drink a little more tea. It'll help revive you. We have to get out of here before . . ."

"Leave me," said Brogan. "Take everyone else and leave me. I can't . . ."

"Yes, you can." Doryu held the wineskin spout to Brogan's mouth.

"Tal's here, sir. In the castle courtyard. He's been looking for you," said Eliana.

Doryu felt Brogan stiffen. The Head Steward opened his mouth to drink.

Turning to Eliana, Doryu said, "See if you can figure out how to free Raiden. It's got to be one of these keys."

Doryu watched as Eliana ran back to Raiden and Winston, the iron keys rattling in her hand. Jade followed.

"That tastes good," said Brogan. "What is it?"

"Tea. Cook gave it to me."

"Ah," said Brogan. "Did she give you a bun by any chance?"

Doryu smiled, realizing Brogan was reviving already. "Yes, she did. It's in my bag. We can share it. Here, put your arm around me."

Brogan said, "Doryu, we have to help my son."

"We will, my friend. With Raiden's help, we will."

The old Dragon Speaker and the King's Head Steward made their way slowly to the center of the cavern where Eliana and Winston stood looking up at the enormous metal collar around Raiden's neck. Even if Raiden laid his head on the ground, the two locks that held the collar together would be out of reach. Doryu remembered that two of Margred's men had stood on two others' shoulders to close the locks.

"I'll help with that, old man."

"Valo?" said Doryu.

They could all see the horse, Destre, coming back from the east side of the cavern, carrying the rightful Captain of the Guard. Valo was much thinner than before the ordeal began, but he was more alert than the last time Doryu saw him. Without any of the torches burning in the cavern, the winds from the sea continued to freshen the air.

"Drink this," said Doryu, tossing the wineskin to Valo.

"Wine?"

"No, tea from Cook. The antidote. Margred poisoned you."

"Do you have any more of that, Dragon Speaker?" It was Angus, one of Valo's men, leading his black stallion. "Oooooooo, I feel like I drank bad ale."

Behind Angus, Doryu could see more of Valo's men, some leading horses, some holding each other up. It was a ghost army led by a ghost horse, but at least they were upright and walking. Doryu handed another skin to Angus. He and the other men each had a mouthful and shared a little with the horses.

Within minutes, the soldiers and horses were stronger. Under Angus's command, three soldiers took the keys from Eliana, formed a human pyramid, and unlocked the collar imprisoning Raiden. With a clang that echoed throughout the cavern, it fell to the granite floor and cracked in two.

As the sound of iron on stone faded, Winston walked to where the collar lay and used his tail to shove it a little farther away from his father.

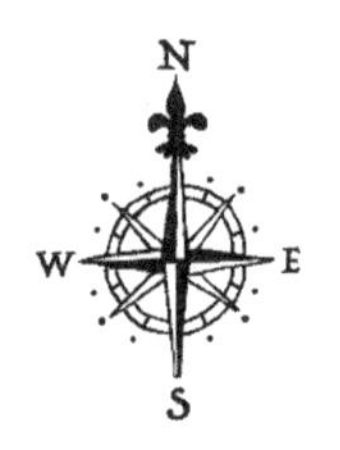

Chapter 46: King Halwyn

DAY THREE

In the courtyard, King Halwyn and his guests sipped tea—to which he'd added some of the antidote from the wineskin—and nibbled buns while Margred and Gunter stood off to the side. Nerys crouched on the other side of the tables and chairs, wings tucked, tail twitching from side to side. Her beautiful amethyst eyes remained fixed on Margred, whose sliver of a smile couldn't disguise her anger.

The King's command to extinguish the malodorous torches had been followed, and the air was filled with the smells of the Seething Sea, the citrus tang of the tea, and the yeasty aroma of Cook's buns. Even though the impromptu party was taking place in the dusty courtyard and not the Banquet Hall, the King was enjoying himself for the first time since the Spring Equinox Banquet in March. The terrible drowsiness was gone, and he felt like a king once more.

Keeping an eye on Margred, Halwyn chatted with Bedwyr, whom he hadn't seen in months. Where was he living now? How was his magnum opus coming along? Eggs for eyesight? How extraordinary!

Bedwyr introduced Alethia, Tal, and the twins. The King was delighted by the two boys who looked exactly alike. *How wonderful it would be to have a brother*, he thought.

"Tal," said Halwyn. "You remind me of my Head Steward, Brogan."

"Yes, sire. He's my father," said Tal. "He . . ."

"I hear he's in Tibbet Mill with his mother who is ill," the King asked, his smile benign.

Tal started to speak again but was drowned out by Bedwyr who began loudly coughing and clearing his throat. The Cartographer jumped to his feet, blocking Tal and the King from Margred's view. Between loud coughs, he whispered, "We think Brogan is her prisoner, sire."

"He is," whispered the King, between more of Bedwyr's coughs. "And so is Valo. Doryu, my Dragon Speaker, has gone to the cavern with the antidote for the poison. Without Valo and his men, we can't hope to defeat these imposters." He gestured at Margred's soldiers who stood in rows, weapons in hand. He smiled and waved at them in a friendly sort of way.

None waved back.

The tall girl—was her name Alethia?—smiled and said,

"Another bun, Your Majesty?" She curtsied, her hair a golden cascade around her face. She nudged Tal with her foot, and he too stood and began to cough and pound on his chest with his fist.

Alethia whispered, "My sister Eliana and Nerys's son Winston have also gone to the cavern. They'll free Winston's father. He'll help us, too."

The King jumped to his feet and pounded both Bedwyr and Tal on the back. "Sounds like a plan," he whispered. "We just have to stall long enough for them to get here."

Smiling broadly, Halwyn gestured for everyone to sit down again, hoping no one noticed the slight tremor in his hand. He knew he would only be able to stall so long before Margred saw the ploy for what it was. And as soon as she realized he no longer believed her lies, her fury—and her soldiers—would be unleashed. They were strong, well-trained, and armed with superior weapons that could severely injure even a dragon the size of Nerys. Unless help arrived from the cavern, all was lost.

Taking a deep breath, King Halwyn turned to his old friend and said, "Now, where were we? Bedwyr, I think you were telling us about your cat. You said her name is Cow?"

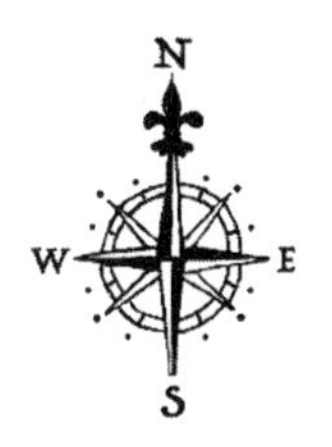

Chapter 47: Eliana

DAY THREE

In the cavern, once Raiden was free of the awful chains, plans were hurriedly made to deal with the situation in the courtyard above. Doryu, Brogan, and Angus would take half the soldiers back up the secret stairway. From the kitchen, they'd make their way down to the soldiers' quarters. Once armed, they'd enter the courtyard the same way Margred and her men had.

Raiden would fly from the cavern clearing to the courtyard, while Valo, Destre, and the rest of the soldiers and horses would ride back up around the castle. They'd enter the courtyard through the castle gates. When Eliana told them the gates were barred, Valo just smiled.

"Destre and the other horses will make short work of the gates. The wood is rotted, and the iron rusted," said the

Captain of the Guard. "The rest of you will stay here where it's safe." With a sweep of his arm, Valo indicated Winston, Eliana, and Jade.

Winston started to object, but Eliana put a firm hand on his neck. When he looked down at her, she shook her head.

Wait, she thought. *We have other responsibilities.*

He nodded.

Winston, Eliana, and the others watched as Valo and half the soldiers saddled their horses and left the cavern by the huge arched entrance. Silhouetted against the darkening sky, they looked like a formidable army. Raiden followed, momentarily blocking all light from the cavern. He spread his wings, crouched on his massive hind legs, and pushed. At first, he tilted to one side, his left wing dragging the ground. Eliana clasped her hands, praying that the weeks of captivity hadn't weakened Winston's father too much. But then, with two powerful wingbeats, he was airborne and flying toward the sea.

Surely, they'll be able to defeat Margred, thought Eliana.

Doryu bent to pick up the cloth bag and slung it over his shoulder. He hugged Jade and smiled at Eliana and Winston.

"Take care of my sister, please. I'd like to spend my remaining years with her."

"In your cozy cell, Doryu?" asked Jade, her arms tight around him.

Yes, thought Doryu. *In my cell.* He'd thought about going to live with Jade in the cabin in the forest. But now he realized he was meant to stay at the castle. To be of service to Halwyn. To atone for his part in the slaying of so many dragons.

"Yes, sister," said Doryu. "In my cell. We can find another cot for you."

The old man followed Angus and Brogan who, along with the rest of the soldiers, were heading toward the door in the back of the cavern. But after only a few steps, the Dragon Speaker stopped, turned back to Eliana, and took the bag off his shoulder.

"Keep this safe," he said, handing the bag to her. "There's a book inside that Margred will try to get her hands on. She wouldn't hesitate to use what's written on its pages to harm us all."

Doryu helped her put the bag on her shoulder.

"There's also an old parchment in there. I have a feeling it too is important. Perhaps even urgent. Maybe with your young eyes you can make out what it's trying to tell us."

Eliana and Winston looked at each other and then down at the cloth bag. Jade followed her brother a few steps, calling, "Be safe, Doryu. Please be safe."

Eliana moved to stand by the old woman. "Come sit down with us, Jade. I'm sure it will all be over soon." She saw that Jade was shivering. It was much colder in the cavern with evening approaching.

Eliana ran to gather several furs and blankets left behind by the soldiers. She spread them out to make a comfortable place to rest. Even Winston could get the front half of his body on the blankets. He sighed and laid his head beside

Doryu's sister. The breath from his nostrils soon warmed the air in their circle of furs.

Placing her hand on Winston's neck once more, Eliana wasn't surprised he too knew they should stay with Jade, however much they wanted to go back to the courtyard. They could protect her if Margred and her soldiers returned. A dragon, even a young one, who was unshackled and unpoisoned could help them all escape if need be.

Eliana reached into the bag. The first thing her hand encountered was another bun. She thought Doryu'd said Cook gave him one for Brogan. And Brogan had devoured it in a few bites.

Cook must have put more than one in the bag, she thought. It was soft and smelled wonderful. Eliana broke it in half to share with Jade. Reaching back into the bag, she found the book. When she pulled it out, her hand tingled. Despite the beautiful black leather cover and gold lettering, it somehow felt evil. Like the disgusting tomato worms that destroyed her mother's plants but worse. Much worse. She tossed the book on the furs a few feet away from them.

Doryu had said something about an old parchment, that it might be important. She once again reached into the cloth bag and pulled out a folded, yellowed parchment. Carefully opening it, she laid it on the ground so they could all see.

"Oh," said Eliana and Jade at the same time.

Winston looked from one to the other, puzzled by their surprise.

"My father has a teacup just like these," said Eliana

pointing to the drawings on the parchment.

"My mother had a drawing of teacups just like these," said Jade. "She told me she'd given Doryu her teacups when he left to take the King's sword to the castle. They had belonged to her great-grandmother. She knew the King would keep Doryu and wanted him to have something to pass on to his own children."

Eliana held the parchment close to her face. She shook her head.

"It's too dark in here now. I can't read the writing, but there's a compass rose here. Not as beautiful as the one on Bedwyr's map, though." Eliana folded the parchment and set it aside.

"Jade, please tell us about Doryu and the King's sword. And about how Doryu came to be the King's Dragon Speaker." Eliana put another fur around Jade's shoulders and pulled her close.

"I was only an infant when Doryu left, but I can tell you what my mother told me. It all started when the King—not Halwyn, but his grandfather—killed Raiden's father."

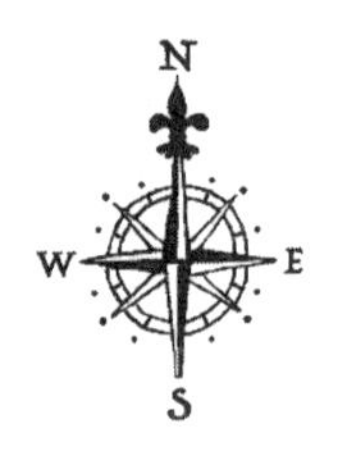

Chapter 48: Doryu

DAY THREE

By the time Doryu completed the climb back up the twisting secret stairs and into the kitchen, his legs were shaking with fatigue once more. He stumbled and would have fallen except for Angus, who caught him and helped him to the bench. The kitchen, although spacious, was filled with Valo's soldiers, all hurriedly eating buns and drinking tea.

Cook put a warm bun in the old Dragon Speaker's hand, and said, "Eat, Doryu. You need your strength. This is far from over."

Doryu, hearing the urgency in her voice, took a bite and pushed himself to his feet. He followed as Brogan and Angus led the way out of the kitchen and down the stairs leading to the soldiers' quarters. They filed past the stables, empty now, but smelling of hay and horses. To his right was the narrow corridor that led to the dungeon cells. It seemed so long ago that he had been in his cozy cell with its tapestries, warm fire, and teacups. Teacups like those drawn on the parchment he had given Eliana. Doryu hoped the young Dragon Speaker could figure out what the drawings meant.

In the soldiers' quarters, Angus and his men quickly armed themselves with swords and shields. Even Brogan grabbed a long knife, shorter and easier to handle than a sword. Doryu shook his head when Brogan offered one to him.

I'd probably just stab myself with it, he thought. He had no idea how he was going to help anyone, but Halwyn was in terrible danger. Doryu realized he had grown fond of the short, plump king and prayed he would be safe. The Dragon Speaker followed again as Brogan and Angus led the men out of the soldiers' quarters and into the corridor that would take them to the courtyard entrance.

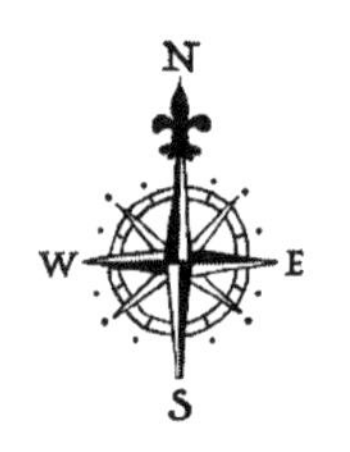

Chapter 49: King Halwyn

DAY THREE

In the courtyard, Margred began to pace. She paused by Gunter, and King Halwyn saw her whisper to him. Thinking his stall tactic had run its course, the King called loudly to Margred, "Come sit, Counselor. Join the party!"

Smiling a thin, tight smile, Margred spoke, "No, thank you, sire. We should make a plan to enlist this dragon's help at once. Your treasure—"

Hammering came from the outer courtyard gates. It sounded as if a hundred horses were beating against the wood with their hooves.

"Gunter, see to that!" Margred commanded.

As several of the guards started toward the gates, Nerys raised her wings and swung her head to block them with roiling clouds of steam. The King pulled Rowan and Sage into his arms. Bedwyr did the same with Tal and Alethia.

Margred whirled and began shouting at the remaining soldiers. "Light the torches. Take the King and the rest to the cavern. Lock them up with the others. Don't hurt the dragon! I need it to find the treasure now that the other one has refused!"

The soldiers surged forward, encircling them.

Under Bedwyr's arm, the King could see Alethia's face, eyes wide with terror.

"I'm sorry, Alethia," the boy—Brogan's son—said to her.

Halwyn had a brief moment to wish he'd gone to look for his Head Steward and Valo when they'd disappeared, instead of dozing by his fire. Sleepy or not, hadn't he sensed there had been something wrong? Especially when he'd seen Margred flick something into the fire?

An anger like he'd never felt before rose in the King's chest and turned into a bellow. "Stop! I command you to stop. I am the King of Morganshire. Stop!"

But Margred's soldiers only stopped for a beat before continuing to advance, some with spears lowered, iron tips only a few feet away.

Just then, there were shouts and the tromping of boots coming from the interior of the castle. Margred's soldiers turned away from the King and the others to face the new threat. Bedwyr stood as tall as he could on the toes of his boots to see over Margred's soldiers.

"Your own soldiers, Your Highness! Valo's men!"

The clanging of metal against metal, mixed with the

cries of wounded men, filled the back of the courtyard. Gunter and his soldiers, trying to avoid Nerys's steam, began making their way back to help the rest of Margred's soldiers. The front gates continued to shake from whatever was pounding against them.

The King could see Margred, her dark blue robes swirling like a storm, making her way to the Grand Stairway. He called to Bedwyr, "She's getting away!" He handed the twins off to Tal and Alethia. "Protect them. I'm going to stop her."

The King pushed and shoved his way through the battle, eyes locked on Margred who had now reached the top of the Grand Stairway. Halwyn didn't even pause when the tip of a spear nicked his arm and a trickle of blood ran down his arm.

The King reached the top of the stairs in time to see Margred running toward the guest stairway leading up to the library and her quarters.

"Where's she going?" he muttered as he followed her up the guest stairs. Out of breath and panting, he paused halfway up and leaned against the wall. His heart was pounding, and his right arm was beginning to ache where the spear had nicked it.

I'm only fifty. When this is over, I've got to get back to working out, he thought, right before he collapsed and fell down the stairs to sprawl—unconscious—on the walkway behind the rampart.

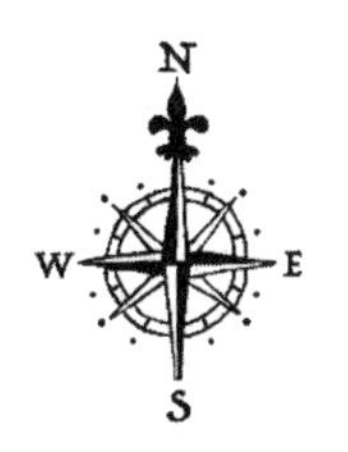

Chapter 50: Doryu

DAY THREE

By the time Doryu reached the courtyard entrance, the battle was underway. The sounds bombarded him clear to his bones: the clanging of swords, the thudding of spears against shields, the shouts of men, hammering sounds of horse hooves coming from the front gates, and above it all, the high-pitched shriek of a dragon. Nerys. After all those years helping Chares hunt dragons, Doryu could hear the differences in the sounds of male and female, young and old. Hurt? No, angry.

There she was. He could see her now. Head raised, wings beating, searing steam coming from her mouth. Had it been only Margred's soldiers, the dragon might have been able to beat them back with her wings and the steam. But now that the King's men were engaged in the fight, she had to hold back to prevent injury to them.

Where were Bedwyr and the children? Eliana had said the Cartographer and the children were in the courtyard, but he couldn't see them through the melee. Ducking his head as low as he could, he began to thread his way through the battle. Maybe he could help Bedwyr protect the children.

I should have taken the knife, he thought.

All at once, there was a tremendous crash as the old wooden gates gave way and fell into the courtyard. Valo was right; Destre and the other horses had been able to break down the gates.

Margred will have to surrender now, thought Doryu, but he gasped when Nerys swung her head around to face Valo and the other riders. Her shriek of anger filled the courtyard.

She thinks they are Margred's men! "Nerys!" he called, but she couldn't hear him. He could see Bedwyr just ahead. And Tal. Both encircling Eliana's siblings with their arms. Dodging swords and soldiers, Doryu ran to Nerys and ducked under her wing. He put his hand on her scales.

"They are the King's horses and riders! They are here to help!" he said.

"Where are Winston and Eliana? Where is Raiden?" Nerys's questions reverberated in the air above the pandemonium of the battle.

"They're all safe," shouted Doryu.

At that moment, what was left of the evening light was extinguished as if a cloak had been thrown over a candle. A shriek many times louder than that of Nerys filled the courtyard and the air began to swirl in dust-filled gusts.

"Raiden!"

Doryu could hear relief, happiness, and love in her voice as Nerys called to her mate. He could also hear the sounds of weapons being thrown to the ground as Margred's soldiers surrendered.

Dim light filled the courtyard again as Raiden flew in circles high above, calling to Nerys. Doryu stepped back and watched as the amethyst and gold dragon lifted off to soar with him. It looked like a dance. A dragon dance.

Looking around, Doryu could see many of Margred's soldiers sitting in the dust, heads hung in defeat. Most were injured. Here and there in the courtyard were mounds of dirt that had been used to extinguish torches. Valo, still mounted on Destre, was calling orders to King Halwyn's men.

"Tal!" It was Brogan running to throw his arms around a black-haired young man who must be his son.

Bedwyr stood with his arms encircling a girl and a boy with hair the color of summer berries. Eliana's siblings. But weren't there supposed to be *two* boys? Twins, Eliana had said. And the King? Where was Halwyn? Doryu turned in circles, scanning the courtyard.

"Bedwyr, where is the other boy? And King Halwyn? Where is the King?"

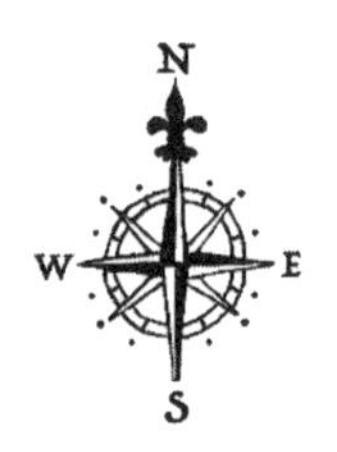

Chapter 51: King Halwyn

DAY THREE

"Your Highness? King Halwyn? Are you all right?"

For the second time that day, the King was being rudely shaken awake.

He moaned. The shaking continued. It came to him that he wasn't in his comfy chair or his royal bed. In fact, he was lying on what felt like rock, with one leg propped up by . . . something.

"Your Highness? Your arm . . ." said the voice again.

A young voice. Who was this? My arm? Halwyn realized that his right arm was throbbing from the tips of his fingers all the way to his shoulder. And it burned, too. Had he been injured?

King Halwyn opened his eyes just a slit to see a small, freckled face peering down at him. Who . . .? But then he remembered; it was one of the twins. One of the young Dragon Speaker's brothers. *Dragon . . .*

"Margred," said the King, trying to lift his head. "She's getting away!" His head felt like it weighed fifty pounds. And he was dizzy, so dizzy. "What happened?" he asked the boy.

"You were cut by a spear, one of the bad spears. I think it was poisoned. I'm Sage, by the way."

Poison. This time directly to his bloodstream. That would explain the pain and the headache and how sleepy he was again. And there were no sounds of battle. Was he going deaf, too? No, that didn't make sense because he could hear the boy. Sage. This one was Sage.

"The soldiers? What happened?" he asked.

"It's over, sire. More of your men came through the gate on horses and then a huge, *huge* dragon came and then the bad men were captured. See? The dragons are up there."

Halwyn's eyes followed Sage's finger, and he saw, high above, two dragons circling.

"Doryu?" asked the King. "Is he here? Bring him . . ."

Sage patted him gently on his shoulder and left.

Halwyn lay watching the beautiful dragons flying above as he grew more and more sleepy. Now the throbbing was moving across his chest. His heartbeat skipped once, then again. And he was dreaming again. Dreaming of holding his father's hand.

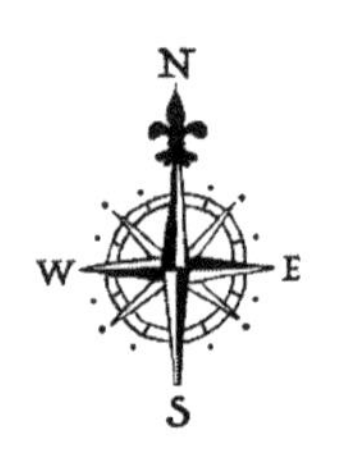

Chapter 52: Doryu

DAY THREE

In the courtyard, just as Doryu and Bedwyr called out that Sage and the King were missing, Rowan shouted, "There he is. Sage! Where were you?" Rowan ran toward the Grand Stairway just in time to keep Sage from stumbling down the last steep step in his haste.

"Doryu!" shouted Sage. "The King is hurt! He wants you." Sage pointed back up the stairs.

Doryu and Bedwyr started for the steps, closely followed by the others.

Sage said, "He was cut by a spear. One of the poison spears. I think he's dying."

Doryu gasped. But if the King were cut by a poisoned spear during the battle . . . Would the poison have done so much damage already? He remembered Halwyn had told him that nightshade in large doses can cause death.

"Everyone, grab whatever tea is left and bring it. It may be our only chance," said Doryu, following Bedwyr up the stairs.

Brogan, Tal, Alethia, and the boys ran to do as he asked and carried the cups up the stairs, trying not to spill a drop.

When Doryu reached the top of the stairs, he saw Bedwyr crouched beside the King who was lying on the rampart walkway. The way one of Halwyn's feet was lying on the bottom step of the Guest Stairs and the fact that he wasn't moving sent a chill through the old Dragon Speaker. Was he already dead? In addition to the fondness he felt for the diminutive King, Doryu knew the death of their monarch would be devastating for Morganshire. There was no heir. No son or daughter. No niece or nephew. Who would rule? Would some outsider be sent from Cantington?

His feet slowed, fearing what he would find when he reached the King. But Bedwyr looked up and said, "He's alive. Just barely, but he's alive."

"Thank God," said Brogan.

Doryu ran to join Bedwyr, calling to the children, who had arrived with the tea, "Bring the tea here! Quickly."

The King's arm was now swollen to twice its size. Something thick and yellow oozed out of the cut where the spear had nicked him. He was unconscious now and didn't respond to their voices or even to gentle shaking. Doryu used the edge of his robe to wipe away the pus and began drizzling tea directly onto the wound.

"You must get him to swallow some, Bedwyr," he said.

"I'll hold his head," said Brogan.

Sage and Rowan gently moved the King's foot off the step and began patting his leg. Bedwyr pried open Halwyn's mouth and poured in some tea. At first, it dribbled uselessly back out and down his chin. But then there was a choking sound, and the King began to swallow.

"Keep going," Doryu instructed Bedwyr, as he continued to pour tiny amounts of the antidote on the wound.

Finally, the King moaned, and his eyes fluttered.

"We must get him into his bedchamber," said Doryu. "We can send someone to Cook for more tea. And more buns," the Dragon Speaker added as his stomach rumbled.

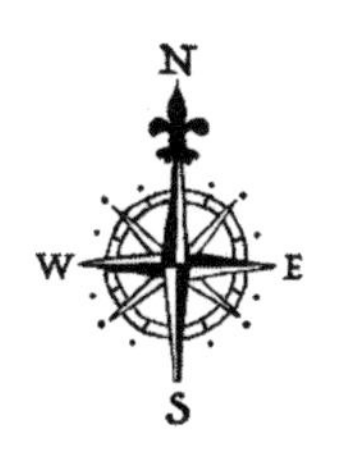

Chapter 53: Eliana

DAY FOUR

In the nest of furs on the cavern floor, Eliana woke to see that the cavern entrance was an arch of pale light. Jade was still asleep, her frail body almost hidden under the pile of furs and blankets. Winston's eye, a few feet away, was open. Eliana reached over and touched him, careful not to wake Jade.

"It's morning, Eliana," said Winston.

"And no one has returned," said Eliana.

"Now that I've heard Jade's story, I understand why we've stayed away from humans. My father saw his own father die at the hands of a king."

Eliana shook her head; she couldn't even imagine what it would be like to watch her own father die. By now, he and her mother would be sick with worry. After finding her note, they would have gone to Bedwyr's to see if they were all there but would have found only an empty cottage. What must they be thinking now?

Eliana sat up and looked around the cavern. In the early morning light, its vastness was revealed. *Who made this place*? she wondered. Her eyes found the broken iron collar and thought again of Raiden and all the others who had been captives here. Had Valo and his men been able to defeat Margred and her soldiers?

Just then, her hand brushed against something lying on the furs. The parchment. She had forgotten about the parchment Doryu had given her. Grabbing it, she jumped up and ran to the cavern entrance with Winston following close behind.

"Wait for me!" called Jade.

Eliana smiled to see Doryu's sister looking much better than she had when they first found her. Tea, a bun, and sleep.

In the clearing outside the cavern, the ocean breeze was crisp, but the sun felt warm. Eliana and Jade sat leaning against Winston, who blocked some of the wind. Now Eliana had no trouble seeing the drawings sketched on the parchment. In the center, arranged on the four sides of a square, were black line drawings of teacups. The fine detailing clearly showed the intricate designs on them.

"I've held my father's teacup so many times. . . I know these are the same designs," said Eliana.

"And whoever made this parchment made the drawing my mother had. The drawing style is the same," said Jade.

Within the square bordered by the teacups was a delicately drawn compass rose. And now, with the light provided by the sun, Eliana could read what was written on the parchment. Aloud, she read the words at the top of the parchment: "Using the Dragons to Find Treasure."

Eliana and Jade gasped. Winston huffed. This is what Margred had been claiming all along. That dragons could find treasure. But Raiden had said it wasn't true. And what did the teacups have to do with any of it?

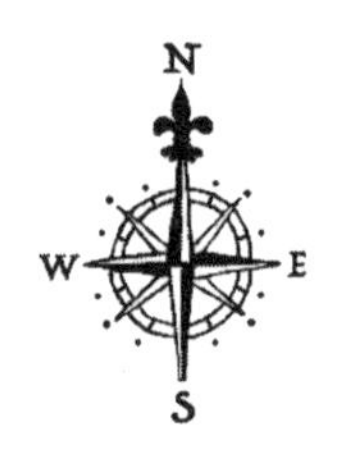

Chapter 54: King Halwyn

DAY FOUR

That same morning, King Halwyn woke to hear what sounded like a roomful of people murmuring in an annoying way. Someone had opened the curtains in his bedchamber, and light was prying into his tightly closed eyes. He tried to call for Brogan, but his mouth was so dry his tongue was stuck to the roof of his mouth.

"Mmmmmm," he managed. What he meant was "close those blasted curtains!"

"Your Majesty!" said Brogan. "You're awake!"

"Of course I'm awake," the King tried to say. "You left the curtains open."

But what Brogan and the others heard was more mumbling. The King tried to point at the curtains, hoping Brogan would get the idea, but found that his right arm was too heavy to lift, and it hurt to try. Brogan put one hand under the King's head and held a teacup to his lips.

"Drink some of this, sire," said the Head Steward. Whatever it was, it smelled good, like lemon blossoms. The King took a sip and then another.

Brogan is so good to me, thought the King.

Wait. Hadn't Brogan been away? In Tibbet Mill to take care of . . . ? No, that had been one of Margred's lies. Margred. The King opened his eyes and tried to sit up. There was Brogan, thin and pale but smiling at him.

It all came back to Halwyn: the missing treasure, Margred and her lies, the dragons, Brogan and Valo held captive, the battle, and falling down the stairs as he'd tried to stop Margred from getting away.

Halwyn reached out and pulled his Head Steward into a hug. Over Brogan's shoulder, the King could see the old Dragon Speaker, the Cartographer, and four children, all smiling at him.

"What happened?" asked the King. "The battle . . . Margred?"

"It's over, sire. Some of her soldiers were captured, but Margred has not yet been found," said Bedwyr. "Valo and his men are searching for her and the soldiers who escaped. They can't have gone far."

"I'm sure they'll find them," said Brogan, propping the King up on a mound of pillows. He continued to give Halwyn tea, as well as bites of one of Cook's buns, while the others explained what happened.

"You were so brave, Your Majesty," said one of the twins. "You ran right through the battle to try to stop Margred."

"That's when you were nicked by a poison spear," said the other twin.

"You almost died," added the first one.

"Now, now, boys," said Doryu. "Let's let the King rest." Turning to the King, he added, "I must check on Jade, Eliana, and the dragons. I'll report to you later . . ."

"We will *all* go check on them, Dragon Speaker," said Halwyn. "Help me up, Brogan."

Chapter 55: Winston

DAY FOUR

Using the dragons to find treasure? That's what Eliana said was written at the top of the parchment. Winston's tail began to twitch. Both the old Dragon Speaker and Raiden had said that Margred was wrong, and Winston had never known his father to lie.

"What else does it say, Eliana?" he asked. Both he and Jade waited while Eliana squinted at the miniscule script, turned the parchment to the left, right, and then upside down.

"Well, whoever wrote this wasn't worried about right side up. And the writing is so tiny . . . Wait! It's . . . well, it's kind of like a map. The writing is written around the four cardinal directions. Starting at the top, north. Then here . . . east." Eliana turned the map so the title was at the top and read, "*Using the Dragons to Find Treasure.*

"*Step 1: Hold a compass so the baseplate is level and the orienting needle is pointing away from you. The compass is now pointing due north or zero degrees.*

"*Step 2: Place a map and a compass on a flat surface, making sure the compass's orienting needle and north on the map are aligned.*

"*Step 3: . . .*"

Winston's eyelids began to drift in an upward direction. The sun felt good on his scaly head, and he hadn't slept much the night before. Eliana's voice faded as she continued to read about things he didn't understand. Of course he understood north, south, east, and west. His parents taught him at a young age to use the location of the sun in the sky. In the morning, the sun is in the east. The sun sets in the west. The Black Mountains are north. Beyond the forest is the south. And now Winston knew that south also meant the sea. But *compass, needle, map?* Just more strange human words that meant nothing to him.

"Winston! Listen to this!" Eliana shouted. "Are you awake?"

I am now, he thought a little grumpily. But the sight of his friend's face looking up at him made him smile. She bent her head to the parchment.

"Listen to this part, Winston:

"*Step 5: With the sun directly overhead, arrange the Dragon Cups so that one sits at each of the four cardinal directions.*"

Dragon Cups? What are Dragon Cups? Dragons don't use cups. They drink from cold mountain streams. Winston thought as he shook his head.

Eliana continued to read:

"*The Dance of the Dragons will find the treasure.*" She laughed.

"The Dance of the Dragons, Winston! Not real dragons. Dragon *Cups*. This is telling us that the teacups drawn on the parchment—the ones that match Doryu's cups and the one my father has—are called Dragon Cups. This says they can find the missing treasure!"

"But we need four of the special teacups, Eliana," said Jade. "Is it possible that Doryu still has the two my mother gave him?"

"We could get my father's," said Eliana.

"That's only three," said Jade. "And how will we get a map and a compass?"

"I have a compass and a map," rumbled a familiar voice. "What do we need them for?"

And there, coming down the rocky pathway to the clearing were Bedwyr, Tal, Brogan, the twins, and Alethia. They were closely followed by Destre, Doryu, and the man they called Valo. Perched on top of Destre was a short, plump man with hair like milkweed floss. The man raised his hand, and everyone came to a stop.

"Your Majesty," said Bedwyr to the man on the horse. "May I present Eliana, Jade, and Winston. Everyone, this is King Halwyn."

While both Eliana and Jade curtsied, Winston scanned the sky for Raiden and Nerys. Had they both been captured this time? Doryu had said Margred tricked and poisoned the King, too. Was that true? His scales rippled and his feathers shook. But just then two gigantic, dragon-shaped shadows moved across the clearing. Together again, his parents soared high above. Winston raised his head and called to them.

"Mother! Father!"

His parents flew, wingtips almost touching, out over the sea. They rose on the updraft, dropped their left wings, and began a looping turn to bring them back to the clearing.

"They are so beautiful, Winston," said Eliana, with her hand on his side.

"Yes, they are, aren't they," said Winston, realizing he'd never thought of them as anything other than his parents. All these years, he'd thought of himself first and how they would provide food, shelter, protection, and instruction. It had been all about him. But now, seeing them together high above the cliffs, he began to know them as dragons outside of himself, with lives of their own.

"Thank you, Eliana. Thank you for helping me find my father," said the young dragon.

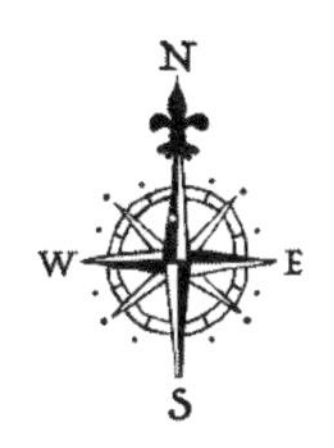

Chapter 56: Doryu

DAY FOUR

Doryu followed Destre's twitching tail down the path leading to the cavern. When the King called for a halt, he almost ran into Destre. Angus, who was behind him, reached out and stopped him just in time.

"I don't think Destre would appreciate your face in her rump," Angus said with a chuckle.

The soldiers behind him chuckled as well, but instead of feeling laughed at, Doryu felt like they were including him as one of their own. They were dirty and looked as tired as he felt; they—and Nerys and Raiden—had searched all night for Margred and her soldiers without any sign of them.

"Thank you, Sir Angus, for saving me—and Destre—from embarrassment," said Doryu. The soldiers all laughed again, and Angus patted him on the back.

By the time the old Dragon Speaker reached the vast open space in front of the cavern entrance, Bedwyr was introducing everyone to the King. And there was Jade, running to him, her happy smile making her look like a young girl. Doryu put his arm around her, and they watched the incredible sight of Raiden and Nerys landing on the far edge of the clearing. Winston hurried to his parents, who each put an enormous wing over their son.

"Ahhh," said Bedwyr and Sage at the same time.

The morning sunlight bouncing off gold, amethyst, emerald, turquoise, black, white, and silver scales threw brilliant shafts of color in all directions as the dragons embraced.

Doryu's eyes filled with tears. Seeing the three dragons together—parents and son—lifted some of the burden he'd carried all these years of having helped Chares kill dragons.

At least these are safe, he thought. *And this king will protect them.*

"Doryu! Doryu!" called Eliana, running to him, holding the creased parchment in her hand. "Jade, Winston, and I know how to find the missing treasure."

"Did I hear you say you needed a compass and a map?" asked Bedwyr.

"Yes, and four Dragon Teacups," said Eliana.

"The treasure? Dragon Teacups?" The King slid off Destre and dropped to the ground.

"Doryu, do you still have the blue and white teacups our

mother gave you when you left home?" asked Jade, looking up at Doryu.

"Yes, in my cell . . ." A sudden, horrible thought occurred to him. "Valo, you didn't . . ."

"No, old man," said the Captain of the Guard. "We didn't put any of Margred's soldiers in your cell."

"Thank you," said Doryu, letting out the breath he'd been holding. "I have two cups. And Cook gave me another just like it. It's in the bag I gave Eliana . . ."

Eliana was already running back into the cavern and soon came out carrying the cloth bag. She handed it to Doryu. As Doryu was pulling out the teacup Cook had given him, the King spoke.

"Will someone please tell me what that old parchment and teacups have to do with my treasure?" asked the King, brushing his wispy hair off his forehead.

"Eliana," said Jade. "You should read the parchment to everyone. After that, as soon as we gather all the teacups, this fine Cartographer can help us find the missing treasure."

Chapter 57: Eliana

DAY FOUR

Sitting with the King on one side and the twins on the other, Eliana read the parchment aloud, turning it as the words moved from north to east to south to west according to the compass rose in the middle. When she finished, she showed everyone the drawings. The King picked up the parchment.

"Doryu, two of these cups are in your cell?" he asked.

"Yes, sire."

"Brogan, you know where his cell is. Please get the cups." The King paused, then asked the question Eliana had been expecting.

"Where is the fourth cup?" Halwyn looked around, waiting for an answer.

Sage nudged Eliana.

"My father . . . it's . . . my father has the fourth cup," she said. *Where did the Dragon Cups come from and why does Father have one?* she wondered.

"The cup is at your home? Where's your home? I'll send Angus and some men for the cup," said the King.

Eliana didn't answer. Her legs felt hollow, and her mouth was dry. Glancing at her siblings showed her they felt the same. Their parents would be desperate with worry by now, imagining the worst had happened to their children. If they saw soldiers coming to the house, dusty boots stomping on the slate steppingstones her father had made... No, she herself must go. She must go and tell them what happened, and beg them to forgive her. Beyond that, she had no idea how she'd convince Father to give her the cup and leave again.

"I'll take you, Eliana." It was Winston, who'd come up behind her to nudge her with his nose.

"I'll go, Your Majesty," said Eliana. "Winston will take me. It'll be much faster."

"Take you? How will he... Oh, you'll fly!" said the King, who hadn't seen Winston escape the courtyard with Eliana clinging to his back.

After some discussion, it was decided that Winston, with Eliana on his back, would fly to the Fallonds' home. Raiden and Nerys would stay with the others to keep watch for Margred should she be so foolish as to return.

Doryu handed Eliana the cloth bag. "To carry the teacup," he said. "Put it over your shoulder."

"Here," said the King, and he handed her a silver ring with the insignia of Morgan Castle. "To show your parents you represent the King. I'll need that back, of course."

"I should go with you, Eliana," said Sage. "I can help explain . . ."

"No, Sage, stay here. You can help Bedwyr set up the map and the compass."

"I can help, too," said Rowan, putting his arm around his brother's shoulder.

"Be careful, sister," said Alethia, giving her a hug. "We'll get the map and compass set up while you're gone."

Once more in the air, this time flying high above Kings Road, Eliana felt both happiness and trepidation. The thought of facing her mother and father after their children had been gone for two days was terrifying.

When they see me, they'll understand, Eliana, said Winston.

Maybe they won't be home, she said.

They'll be so worried, said Winston. *It will be good for them to know you're safe.*

Eliana sighed. With the thought of her parents' frightened and disappointed faces in her mind, she tried to think of how to convince her father to let her take the cup to the King.

Below, the shadow of a dragon slid along the road, moving westward toward Eliana's home.

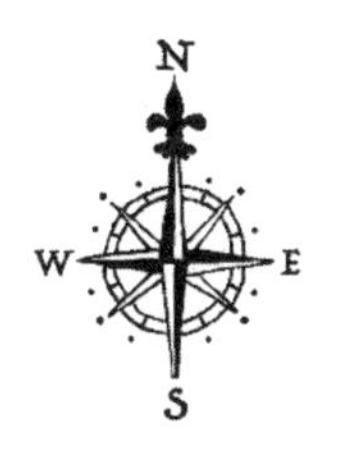

Chapter 58: Winston

DAY FOUR

Winston could feel Eliana's conflicting feelings racing down her legs and arms as she clung to his neck. He understood how she felt about disobeying her parents. He'd left the cave when Nerys told him to stay and wait in case Raiden came back. And it was because of him that Eliana went to Bedwyr's and to the castle, which nearly got her and her sister and brothers killed. What made him think he could help his friend explain everything to her parents? All the Fallond children had disappeared yesterday morning because of him.

We'll help them understand, said Eliana, trying to convince herself as well. *When they see you, they will understand.*

When Eliana spotted the sheep pasture, she told Winston to land. As he flared his wings to touch down, the sheep just moved a little farther away. They kept an eye on him after he landed but continued to graze.

On the other hand, Owen the mule was more than a little alarmed. He galloped to the far northwest corner of the pasture, kicking out with his hind legs and braying as if he were being attacked by a wild cat. Eliana dropped to the ground and ran to try to calm the creature, whose eyes were rolling in his head so only the whites were showing.

"Eliana!" A human that must have been her father burst from their home, leapt over the fence in one giant bound, and ran to grab his daughter in his arms, her feet dangling off the ground.

"Eliana!" There was her mother, yanking on the gate to the pasture. Not stopping to close it, she too ran to hug her daughter.

"Alethia? The boys?" her father asked, quickly scanning the pasture for the rest of his children.

"They're safe, too. They're with the King. See? Here's his ring."

But then Eliana's father caught sight of a dragon in the pasture. His face turned white, emphasizing the dark circles beneath his eyes. He slowly stepped backward toward the fence, pulling his wife and child with him.

"Glenna, get the hatchet," Winston heard him say under his breath.

Turning to see what had alarmed him, Eliana's mother gasped.

Winston didn't know what *hatchet* was, but it didn't sound like something good.

"No, Father. It's all right. That's my friend Winston," said Eliana. "He's a dragon," she added, as if they might not have noticed.

Chapter 59: Eliana

DAY FOUR

It took Eliana many minutes to convince her parents Winston wasn't dangerous and that they didn't need the hatchet. Glenna and Cadoc sat on a log while Eliana told them the rest of what had happened, starting with the King's missing treasure and ending with the teacups.

"You need my teacup?" said her father.

"To help find the missing treasure?" asked her mother.

Eliana nodded and saw that Glenna's face was pale and her hair had come loose from her kerchief. She looked so much like Alethia had when Margred's men attacked. Her father had new lines crisscrossing his forehead and was squeezing Glenna's hand so hard her fingers were turning white. Her mother didn't seem to notice. Eliana's heart ached at the pain she'd caused.

I shouldn't have . . . she thought but stopped herself. If she could go back in time, she knew she would still choose to help Winston. But now, she was faced with the reality of how that decision had affected her parents. They both seemed to have aged several years and looked smaller somehow. Vulnerable. Like Alethia and the twins had looked in the courtyard with Margred's terrible soldiers advancing on them. Yes, she had her own life to live, but she was part of a family whose lives were entwined with hers. *I'll have to be more careful,* she thought.

When Eliana's father had asked for a hatchet, Winston had crouched to the ground, wings and tail wrapped around him. And he had stayed like that—looking like he was trying to make himself invisible—the whole time Eliana explained the situation to her parents. Now Eliana said, "Winston, it's all right now. I want you to meet my parents."

The three humans watched as the wondrous emerald and turquoise dragon unfurled, smiled his big, square-toothed smile, and came to stand beside Eliana. She put her hand on his scales and then pulled it away, showing her parents how Winston's colors streamed from her hand. Her mother reached out to the wisps, and they twirled around her hand like ribbons in a breeze. Glenna's laughter filled Eliana's heart.

"I can talk to him this way," she said, reaching for her mother's hand. "I'm a Dragon Speaker."

"What?" said Cadoc. "What did you say?"

At Cadoc's tone, the wisps and the laughter faded.

"I'm a . . ."

"Dragon Speaker," he repeated. Cadoc sat staring at his hands, palm up in his lap. Eliana could see the scars and calluses that marked them.

"Your great-grandfather was a Dragon Speaker," he said.

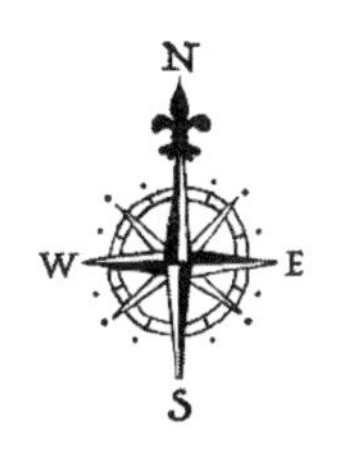

Chapter 60: King Halwyn

DAY FOUR

In the clearing outside the cavern, King Halwyn watched as Bedwyr, the twins, and Alethia studied the old parchment, turning it around and around. The Cartographer had already pulled a map from his pouch and spread it out on the ground. The King still had no idea how a map and teacups were going to help them find the kingdom's missing treasure.

And what about Margred? She'd been so determined to find the treasure that she'd done terrible things. Would she give up now and disappear? Halwyn decided that as soon as Valo and his men were rested, he would send them out again. He didn't like the idea of his former Counselor and some of her soldiers hiding somewhere nearby.

"See, boys," said Bedwyr, bending down to show the boys an object in his hand. "Here is the indicator arrow.

We'll turn the compass so the arrow is pointing due north. Now, we'll turn the map so north is aligned to the compass. When Eliana gets back . . ."

The King shook his head and wandered over to Doryu and Jade, who sat cradling three of the delicate teacups in their laps. When Brogan returned with the cups from Doryu's cell, Halwyn sent him off again, this time to fetch food and ale for everyone. It was almost noon, and his stomach was rumbling. At least now, both his Head Steward and his appetite were back.

If all this works out and the treasure is found, first I'll set aside the tribute to Canting and pay all the back wages. Then I will throw a banquet in my Banquet Hall, he decided. *With clams and mussels in a lemony dressing, dandelion greens with mushroom sauce, roasted chicken, fingerling potatoes, fig and caramel nut tart . . ."*

"Doryu, would you and Jade please bring the teacups?" called Alethia, interrupting Halwyn's food reverie.

The King watched as the old Dragon Speaker stood on wobbly legs, pulling Jade up beside him. Halwyn squinted, finding in Doryu's wrinkled face the memory of the young man who had argued with Chares so long ago.

It's a good thing my father let Doryu stay in the castle, thought the King. *And that Doryu didn't help him kill any more dragons.*

Chapter 61: Eliana

DAY FOUR

Eliana stared at her father. His words didn't make sense. Her great-grandfather was a Dragon Speaker? Why hadn't her father told her before?

"Your great-grandfather was a Dragon Speaker?" asked Winston.

"I . . . I didn't know," she said. "Father?"

Cadoc answered, his voice almost a whisper, "It was a story my father and uncle used to tell us late at night when we all sat around a dying fire. We lived . . . well, this was before I went to Cantington. By that time, all the dragons were dead . . ." Cadoc stopped, glancing at Winston. "Or gone somewhere else. When my father told us that his father—whom I had never met—had been able to talk to dragons, we thought it was just another story, like the ones about fairies and unicorns."

Cadoc paused. He held his hand up and studied his palm. Eliana felt her hand, the one resting on Winston's neck, tingle.

Her father continued, "But when I was ten, my father took me two days by cart to my dying grandfather's bedside, told me to say goodbye, and went to fetch water from the well. My grandfather was so old; he had outlived his wife, his siblings. I was afraid of him. His face was gray, his hair almost gone. His eyes were closed, and I thought maybe he was already dead. But as I turned to leave, he called to me.

"'Cadoc . . . you're Cadoc, right? Come here,' he said. His eyes were open and were murky gray, the color of rain clouds against the mountains. He reached for my hand, gave it a little squeeze, and said, 'I wish I had more time with you. To tell you about the dragons.'

"Startled, I pulled my hand from his. That's when I saw the colors running in the lines of his palm. His hand looked like a map, radiating with gold, blue . . . so many colors. His lifeline was the deepest and was scarlet. It looked like blood and scared me so much that I ran from him. When I told my father, he laughed at me. Said I should've listened to the old stories. I didn't understand then, but now I do. The stories were true; he was a Dragon Speaker, Eliana."

"But you . . .? You aren't . . ."

"I don't know. I've never seen a dragon until now." Cadoc stood, walked to Winston, and cautiously put his hand on the dragon's neck. "What do you think, Winston? Am I a Dragon Speaker?"

"Mmm mmmm mmmmm," is what Cadoc heard.

"It must skip generations," he said. Shaking his head, he reached for Eliana's hand. Holding it palm up in his roughened hand, he tilted it so that they could all see the remnants of emerald green and turquoise on her hand.

"The teacup was my grandfather's. It makes sense in a strange way that it's a Dragon Teacup. Although I still don't understand how it will help find Morganshire's missing treasure."

"So you will let us take it to Bedwyr and the King? The parchment will tell us how to use it." said Eliana. Beside her, Winston was shuffling his feet again. The sound of the dragon's feet moving in the grass startled Owen into more crazed kicking and braying.

"We have to go, Father. Winston and I will take the cup and . . ."

"I'm going, too," said Cadoc.

"We're *all* going," said Glenna, her determined face once more reminding Eliana of Alethia.

"I'll get the cart," said Cadoc. "Eliana, see if you can calm Owen down."

"Father, I . . ." said Eliana. "The King . . . I should fly back with Winston. It'll be much faster."

"What?" said Glenna.

"Fly?" said Cadoc.

Again, the minutes ticked by as Eliana explained how she was able to climb up Winston's wing and safely hold on. Her mother had her hand over her mouth again and kept shaking her head. Her father's arms were crossed over his chest.

"Winston won't let anything happen to me," said Eliana. "And the sooner I get back to the castle, the sooner the treasure can be found. Then we can all come home and get back to normal."

Glenna and Cadoc turned to each other.

"Normal?" said her father. "There's a dragon in our field and our daughter is a Dragon Speaker. And it seems that our other children are helping these two save Morgan Castle. I don't think we'll be going back to any sort of normal." He turned to Glenna, eyebrows and shoulders lifted; Glenna sighed and pointed at Eliana.

"You hang on with all your might, daughter," she said. "And you . . . Winston . . . I'm trusting you to keep her safe."

Winston smiled and nodded. Glenna pulled Eliana to her and hugged her so tightly she could barely breathe. Over her mother's arm, she watched as Cadoc hurried back to the house.

"Mother," said Eliana.

Glenna hugged her even tighter, kissed the top of her head, and finally released her as Cadoc came back into the paddock carrying a cloth-wrapped bundle.

"I know you will be careful with it," said her father as he handed it to her.

"I will," said Eliana. "Thank you."

When Eliana and Winston were airborne again, the dragon circled once over the sheep pasture.

They are so fragile, she thought, seeing her parents' upturned faces.

"Father!" she called down. "Take your hatchet! Be careful on the road." But her shouts were swallowed by the wind, and she knew they couldn't hear her.

Surely, Margred will be far from Morganshire by now, she thought.

My parents must be searching for her, said Winston. *What if they find her? And the soldiers with her? What if . . . I'm worried, Eliana.*

I am, too.

Finding Margred. Not finding Margred. Either way seemed dangerous. The dragon and the girl flew toward the castle, realizing the threat was far from over.

Hurry, Winston!

And the turquoise and emerald dragon flew faster than he ever had before.

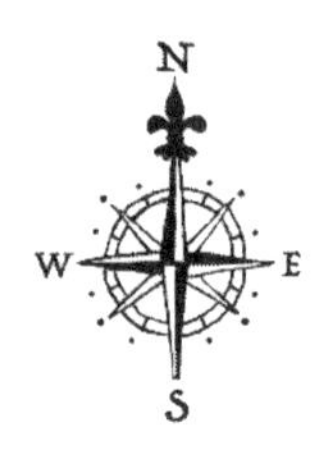

Chapter 62: Doryu

DAY FOUR

As Eliana and Winston were flying back to the castle, Doryu and Jade watched Bedwyr, Alethia, and the twins arrange and rearrange the map, the parchment, the compass, and the three teacups on the ground in front of the cavern. At one point, Bedwyr dragged the map, along with everything else, to a spot a few feet away from where it had been. Sage, Rowan, Alethia, and Bedwyr stood, looking down at the map, then out toward the sea. Sage pointed into the cavern. Alethia shook her head. Bedwyr ran his fingers through his beard. They talked and gestured some more. Bedwyr took hold of the edges of the map and dragged it back to the exact same spot it had been in before.

Jade chuckled.

"It doesn't seem like an exact science, does it?" said Doryu.

"No, but they are all enjoying the process," replied Jade.

Yes, she's right. They are, thought Doryu.

Alethia moved the map just an inch closer to the cavern.

Rowan turned the compass one way, tilted his head and squinted at it, and turned it back again. Finally, the four stood, all with hands on hips, over their handiwork.

"I think that does it, children," said Bedwyr. "Now all we need is the fourth cup." He turned to look to the west.

"I hope Eliana . . ." said Sage, going to stand beside the Cartographer. "My parents . . . I should have gone with her."

Bedwyr put a massive hand on the boy's shoulder, and they both continued to watch for Winston and Eliana.

After Valo, Angus, and the others had left—with Nerys and Raiden flying overhead—to search for Margred again, the clearing seemed empty and quiet. And now that Bedwyr and the children had finished setting up the map and other items, the only sounds were those of gulls who ventured from the cliffs to feed on insects in the tall grasses surrounding the castle.

The sun was warm, and Doryu saw that Brogan, Tal, and Alethia were leaning against a boulder at the edge of the clearing. Brogan was asleep, one arm around his son. Tal was quietly talking to Alethia, who nodded from time to time. The King paced from one side of the clearing to the other, hands clasped over his stomach, his tattered robe growing even more dusty.

Suddenly, Rowan called, "There they are!" as he pointed to what looked like an empty blue sky. But then Doryu could see a tiny green speck that grew into a dragon as it flew toward them. As they watched, Winston banked slightly to the left, dipping his right wing to begin slowing.

Will I ever get used to the sight of a dragon in flight? Doryu wondered. "I hope not," he whispered.

"Does she have the cup?" shouted the King. By now, they could all see that Eliana was indeed on Winston's back, the cloth bag slung over her shoulder.

"Does she have the cup?" Halwyn asked again, standing on tiptoe as if those few extra inches would help him see inside the cloth bag.

"I'm sure she does, Your Majesty," said Alethia, who went to stand beside the King. Patting him gently on his shoulder, she added, "She wouldn't have come back without it, sire. She is a very determined girl."

"She is indeed, Your Highness," said Tal. "From what I've seen so far, I can vouch for that." The young man smiled down at Alethia. He reached to brush a strand of hair out of her eyes, and Doryu saw that Brogan—now wide awake—was watching his son with raised eyebrows.

Winston, wingtips flaring, back legs reaching, landed with barely a sound. Doryu thought he would never get used to that either, the way dragons could control their immense bodies with such precision.

Eliana slid off Winston's back and down his wing, and she ran toward Bedwyr.

"I have it," she called. "My father's teacup."

Rowan and Sage were jumping up and down, both talking at the same time.

"We have it all set up!"

"The compass indicator is facing due north!"

"We just need the fourth teacup!"

Doryu laughed. *Maybe all of this is going to work out after all,* he thought.

Chapter 63: Winston

DAY FOUR

Winston crouched, tucked his wings against his body, and wrapped his tail around his legs. His parents and the King's soldiers were gone, searching for the horrible woman who had captured Raiden. It still made no sense to Winston. Why had Margred thought dragons could find treasure? And why was the treasure so important? Something about paying wages and tributes, but dragons had no need for any of that. And if they had no need for treasure, why would they want to find it?

Winston shook his head. The nonsensical thoughts circling in his mind, as well as the sun and the salty smell of the sea, made him drowsy.

I'll just sleep for a few minutes, he thought as his eyelids drifted up.

"It's not working! Why isn't it working?" The sound of Sage's frustration interrupted Winston's dream of flying with his parents over the vast ocean. Opening his eyes, he lifted his head to see all the humans standing in a circle, looking at the ground.

Bedwyr was shaking his head and yanking on his beard. The King was pulling at the fluff that grew on his head. Eliana bent down and picked up the thing—she had called it a parchment—and held it close to her face.

"We must have missed something," said Eliana. She read the words on the parchment aloud, turning it like she had the night before.

"Compass . . . map . . . four Dragon Cups. Due north. Yes, yes. We did all that!"

"Eliana," said Alethia. "I wonder . . ."

Everyone turned to look at Eliana's sister. "These are teacups. Maybe they need tea?"

"Brogan, get the tea!" shouted the King, even though the Head Steward was standing right next to him.

Tal's father walked quickly around the clearing, grabbing the wineskins Cook had given them. Carrying them back to the King, he said, "There is a little tea left in each of these."

"Give them to the boys," said the King. "Young men, let us see if Alethia is right."

Winston unwrapped his tail and moved closer. Sage and Rowan each took one of the skin bags and started to remove the wooden stoppers. But just as they did, Winston heard the rattling, clicking sounds of rocks skittering on a hill as well as the now- familiar braying of Owen the mule. Everyone turned to see Owen pulling the cart down the path with Cadoc and Glenna perched on the wooden seat.

Winston watched as the Fallond family hugged and laughed. Glenna wiped her face with a cloth she pulled from her sleeve. Winston felt happy for them, all of them together, but he felt afraid for his mother and father. He remembered the poisonous torches Margred's soldiers had used to capture Raiden.

What if . . . ?

Winston pushed that thought away as Bedwyr introduced Eliana's parents to the King, Brogan, Jade, and Doryu.

"Doryu is a Dragon Speaker, too, Father," said Eliana. "And my father's grandfather was a Dragon Speaker, Doryu."

Doryu nodded and started to speak, but King Halwyn held up his hand and said, "Speaking of dragons, let's get back to the task at hand. Rowan, Sage, I believe you were pouring tea."

The twins hurried back to the teacups and unstoppered the wineskins.

"Pouring tea?" said Cadoc.

"We did everything the parchment described," said Eliana. "But nothing happened. Alethia suggested that since they are teacups . . ."

"That perhaps tea is needed," said Cadoc. "Yes . . . she

may be right. Sometimes, in high summer when the sun is brighter early in the morning, something happens to my cup. In a sliver of sunlight coming in by the door, when I pour the hot water over the tea leaves, the pattern seems to change, to swirl. I always thought I was imagining it, but now . . ."

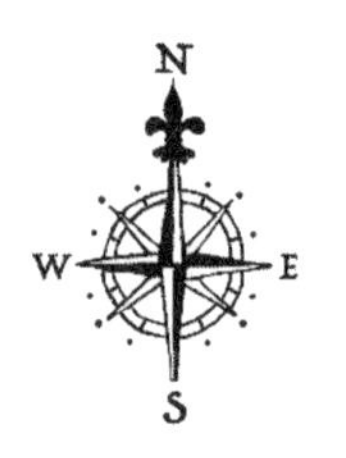

Chapter 64: Eliana

DAY FOUR

They all watched as Rowan and Sage slowly filled each of the Dragon Cups: north, south, east, and west. Eliana smiled to see how careful they were; they didn't spill even a drop or move the cups from their designated spots.

Her father had said the pattern in his cup seemed to change, to swirl, when the sunlight hit the cup. Like a dance? A dance of dragons, as the parchment said?

Winston nudged her from behind. "Do you think the dragons will dance, Eliana?" he asked.

Sunlight struck his scales, which launched emerald and turquoise beams into the air around him.

Like the first time I saw him, she thought. Only four days ago, but it seemed to Eliana that she had known Winston her whole life. She flung her arms as far as they would go around his neck, and with her ear pressed against his warm scales, she could hear his steady, solid heartbeat.

"Yes," she whispered. "I think the dragons will dance."

"Eliana, look," said Winston.

With one hand still pressed to Winston's scales, Eliana turned to see that everyone had moved closer to the map and the teacups. Alethia, without looking away from the map, held her hand out to her.

"Eliana, it's happening."

Eliana took her sister's hand and, with Winston still close beside her, moved so she and Winston's head were part of the circle. Shafts of light from the sun directly above them were filling the teacups so the tea looked like liquid sunlight. The liquid light shone through the thin porcelain sides of each cup, and they could all see that the designs on them were indeed swirling.

"They're dragons," said Sage.

And Eliana saw that the blue patterns on the teacups had transformed into elaborate dragons, tails swinging, wingtips spread, steam pouring from miniature nostrils. The light shone through the thin sides of the cups so that tiny dragon shadows began to leap and twirl across the map.

"Oh," breathed Alethia, squeezing Eliana's hand.

"Are they searching for the treasure?" whispered the King.

"Yes," said Eliana. "Winston says they are looking for something."

The tiny dragon shadows crossed and recrossed the map.

The south dragon went north and then east. The west dragon went south and then north.

"They're fading," said the King. "Why are they fading? They haven't found it yet!"

The King was right—the little dragons were now a very light gray, with indistinct edges. Their movements slowed as they flew over and under each other, seeming to grow tired from all their exertions.

"Do something, Bedwyr!" said King Halwyn, grabbing at his wispy hair again.

"Wait, sire," said Doryu. "Look."

The dragon shadows were flying closer and closer together, almost on top of each other. The needle on the compass spun around and around, no longer pointing due north.

"Bedwyr, the compass . . ." said Eliana.

"What . . .?" said the Cartographer, bending to reach for it.

"No, wait," said Doryu, grabbing his arm.

And all at once, the miniature dragons snapped together as if they had always been one, and the compass needle clicked back to due north. The newly formed dragon was no longer flying or cavorting; it was frozen with its neck outstretched.

And as they all watched, it grew tinier and tinier until it was a mere, dragon-shaped speck on the map, no longer a shadow but a mark as sure as if it had been drawn with ink.

Looking at the teacups, Eliana could see that the cups

were cups again, with blue patterns on their sides. The tea looked murky and tired, as if it had been brewed hours and hours before, which indeed it had.

Bedwyr and Alethia were on their hands and knees on either side of the map, drawing lines and measuring with a ruler that Bedwyr had taken from his pouch.

Finally, Bedwyr stood and brushed the dust from his knees. "The treasure is here, Your Highness," he said.

"What do you mean, 'here'?" said the King.

"It's here, in the castle."

"What? That can't be! Valo and his men searched the castle from top to bottom. They would have found it."

"Did they search your quarters, sire?" asked the Cartographer.

"No, of course not," said the King. "That's ridiculous."

"So, they didn't *actually* search the *entire* castle," said Bedwyr.

"Margred," said Doryu and Eliana at the same time.

"Her room is always locked," said Brogan. "Even when she's not there. And there is no keyhole on the outside of the door, sire. I checked when I was looking for her before . . ."

"You're sure the treasure is here? In the castle?" asked Halwyn.

"Yes, Your Majesty," said Bedwyr. "At least that's what this teacup dragon is indicating."

They all waited while the King stared down at the map.

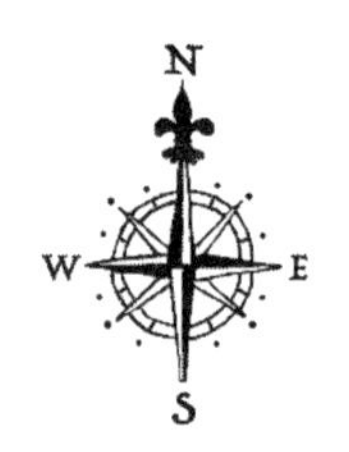

Chapter 65: King Halwyn

DAY FOUR

The sun beating down on his head grew more and more uncomfortable as the King stared at the map laid out in the clearing. Until just yesterday, he'd considered Margred to be his trusted advisor, his Counselor, who of course would have his—and the kingdom's—best interests in mind. When she'd first arrived in Morganshire almost a year ago, he'd believed her story without question. That she'd been a counselor to a powerful king far beyond the Black Mountains. That she'd been ill for a time and needed to settle down in a quieter but still important kingdom. She'd said she chose Morgan Castle because it was close to the Seething Sea, to the healthful ocean breezes.

At first, Margred *had* been useful. She advised on land disputes, helped him decide whom to invite to important banquets, and paid visits to barons, dukes, and wealthy merchants regarding daughters who might be willing to marry a king of a certain age. Even though Valo and Brogan had never warmed up to her, Halwyn had been glad to supply her with spacious quarters and a respectable salary.

Now, it seemed that Margred had never been trustworthy. That she had even gone so far as to poison him.

"If she stole the treasure and hid it in her chambers, why did she do all this?" asked the King, waving his arm to indicate the cavern, the castle, the dragon. "She said she was trying to find the treasure."

"Not Morgan Castle's treasure, sire," said Doryu. "She wasn't asking Raiden to find your treasure. She wanted him to find something more, a bigger treasure hidden long ago."

Halwyn rubbed the top of his head that was most certainly getting sunburned and said, "Well, let's search Margred's chambers. The tribute to Canting Castle is due soon. We can worry about the rest later. Bedwyr and Brogan, come with me."

"We're coming, too," said Rowan, grabbing Sage's hand. "We can search in small places."

The boys' father said, "I'll come, too. Owen can take us back up the hill."

Perched beside Cadoc, Halwyn clung to the rough wooden sides of the cart bench as they bounced and rattled up the hill. Brogan sat behind them, his long legs hanging out the back of the cart. Bedwyr and the boys followed on foot. Eliana and the others stayed with Winston.

Eliana's mother had given the King her slightly tear-dampened handkerchief to cover his sunburned scalp. So here he was, riding in a mule cart with a handkerchief on his head. Some might find it a comical, unkingly sight, but he found, to his surprise, he didn't care. He realized that up until this moment, he'd been way too concerned about decorum and what people might think. But now he was determined to be a better king, a king concerned with the kingdom and its people. And its dragons.

"Brogan," he said, turning around to call to his Head Steward. "If Margred's chambers are locked, how will we get in?"

"I can handle that," shouted Bedwyr, patting his leather pouch as he strode along behind the cart. "I've seen something like that before, in another castle, at another time . . ."

The Cartographer was true to his word. Gathered in front of the heavy wooden door to Margred's chambers, they all watched as Bedwyr knelt to push at a metal plate below the door latch. Halwyn gasped to see it swing to the side. Under the plate was a keyhole. Bedwyr pulled some long narrow tools out of his pouch. He poked one, then another into the lock just above the brass handle. *Click*, *click*, and the mechanism in the lock yielded. Halwyn started to reach for the handle, but Brogan stopped him.

"Allow me, Your Highness. I want to be sure it's safe," he said. As Brogan opened the door a crack, the King was surprised that the hinges made no sound.

"She's oiled the hinges," said Cadoc, holding both of his sons back from the door.

Brogan peered around the edge of the door, then pushed it open. The room was dark and cold and smelled like the tea Cook had given them. Brogan hurried to the windows and pulled back the heavy drapes. Sunlight and the smell of the ocean poured in as if they had been waiting for just that moment.

"There's no one here," said Brogan. "And there don't seem to be any traps or poison."

As they entered the room, the King was surprised at the size of it. Had he never been in this room before? It was almost as large as his own bedchamber and had massive pieces of furniture against all the walls.

"She picked these chambers for herself, Your Highness," said Brogan; as usual, he seemed to know exactly what Halwyn was thinking.

"Well, let's see if the treasure is here," commanded the King.

Within minutes, they discovered more locks: two metal-strapped trunks with padlocks, a gigantic wardrobe with a keylock similar to the one they'd found on the door, and a desk by the window with a drawer that wouldn't open no matter how hard Brogan pulled on it. Bedwyr easily opened all except the drawer.

"I can do it," said Rowan, crawling under the desk.

Halwyn watched as the boy lay on the floor under the

drawer and pushed at it with his feet. Then he sat up and poked at it with his fingers.

"Bedwyr, may I use your pick? I think I can figure out how to open this." Rowan called.

"I'll get it," said Halwyn. The King watched as the boy poked the tool here and there until the drawer slid silently open. Rowan scrambled out from under the desk.

"Let's see what she wanted no one to see, shall we, Rowan?" said Halwyn. They began pulling scraps of paper with scritchy writing and drawings of plants out of the drawer.

"She was making poison, right?" asked Rowan.

The King nodded, feeling yet again a sickening sense of betrayal.

"I should have known . . . somehow . . . realized," he muttered.

They heard a muffled shouting from across the room. Bedwyr was standing in front of the wardrobe, holding back several midnight blue robes and gowns from their hooks inside. The shouting seemed to be coming from deep within the wardrobe. Hurrying to join Bedwyr, the King realized it was Sage who was shouting and that he was indeed deep inside Margred's clothes closet.

"What's he saying?" asked the King.

"Treasure, sire. He's saying treasure," said the boy's father.

A thin piece of wood pried from the back of the wardrobe flew out, nearly hitting Cadoc. Then another. Rowan dove in to join Sage, and soon more pieces of wood joined the first to become a pile on the floor.

"What are they doing . . . oh!" gasped the King.

And there, emerging from between a cloak and a robe was a boy's hand, and on the palm of the hand was a stack of gold coins.

"It was clever of her to hide it here," said Bedwyr sometime later, sitting on one of Margred's trunks and stroking his beard. They were all tired from the events of the morning and the work of unearthing the kingdom's treasure from all of Margred's secret compartments. Most of the gold and silver coins had been found inside the wardrobe. The wooden trunks had false bottoms under which were more gold and silver, as well as pouches of jewels.

"It's all here, isn't it?" said Brogan. He and the King were sitting on one of the other trunks.

"Yes, I think so. The Royal Treasurer will need to do a full accounting . . ." The King paused. "Valo and his men. Do you think they are safe? Do you think they've found Margred?"

"Don't worry," said Sage, who was sitting on the floor with his father and brother. They'd moved the pile of wood and were leaning against the wardrobe door. "They have Raiden and Nerys with them. They'll keep your soldiers safe."

"I pray you are right, my brave little soldier. All of you," said Halwyn, looking around the room. "Once everything is settled, we'll have a banquet to honor you all."

"And Eliana?" said Sage.

"And Winston?" said Rowan.

"And . . ." began Sage.

"Yes, everyone who had a hand or wing in helping save the kingdom." The King's stomach rumbled a king-sized rumble.

"We'll have dinner now, in the courtyard so everyone can join. Brogan, let Cook know. Cadoc, will you and your sons please summon the others?"

Once everyone else had gone to do the King's bidding, he turned to look at Bedwyr.

"Well, old friend. You, most of all, deserve honor. If you hadn't believed the children and the dragon, well . . ." he paused, the unspoken words speaking volumes. "Thank you."

"You're welcome, Your Highness. But I have to say that I'll be glad to get back to my cottage, my cat, and my maps." Bedwyr stood, pulled the King to a stand, and put his arm around his shoulder. "Now, let's eat!"

At the sound of the Cartographer and the King laughing as they made their way down the corridor to the stairs, three gray rats with chocolate brown eyes scurried unseen into a chink in the rock wall.

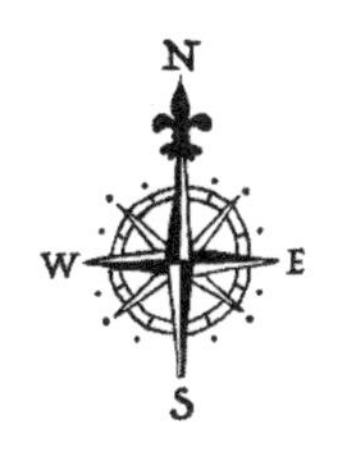

Chapter 66: Winston

DAY FOUR

While Eliana, her family, and everyone else ate dinner in the courtyard, Winston sat on the road just outside the open gates. Brogan and Tal had brought benesaunus from the cavern, but Winston could only manage to eat a few bites. He wished his mother and father were there to steam it for him. It tasted better when one of them steamed it for him than when he steamed it for himself.

Raiden and Nerys still had not returned from their search for Margred. Neither had Valo nor Destre nor the rest of the King's soldiers. Winston scanned the darkening sky.

I wish we were back in our cave, thought the young dragon. It had been so long since all three of them had been together, lying on the soft moss bed, Raiden snoring, Nerys's heart beating along with his.

Now that humans—both good and evil—knew dragons still lived in the Granite Hills, would they ever be truly safe again? Winston sighed. He thought about the moment he and Eliana had first found themselves eye to eye. About discovering she could understand him when she touched him. About the joy he felt when he was with her. If he'd stayed hidden in the Granite Hills, he never would have met her, and they never would have been able to help free Raiden.

Yes, good things had happened because he left the cave, but it could have easily been different. He could have been captured by Margred. Nerys could have been killed in the battle with Margred's soldiers while she was trying to save him.

Winston nudged the pile of benesaunus away. All the might-have-beens made his head and stomach hurt. He knew he still had much to learn about the world, and he would listen to what his parents had to teach him in the years to come.

A wink of silver blinked against the sky far to the east. A few evening stars shimmered there as the sun lowered itself into its western bed.

There it was again. Not a star. Something reflecting the last sunlight. Winston stood and stared where he'd seen the flash. Yes. Again, this time bigger. And he heard it, his father calling to him. Winston called back to him, and then Eliana was there with her hand on his neck.

"Winston?"

"It's my father!"

"Your mother? Is she . . . ?" asked Eliana.

"I don't . . . yes! There she is, right behind him."

Winston called again. Two dragons answered. And then the road in front of the courtyard was all dragon, with a girl dancing in the middle.

Chapter 67: Eliana

THE EVENING OF DAY FOUR

It was some time after Raiden and Nerys returned that Valo, his men, and their horses came up the road to the castle gate.

"More food, Brogan! And ale!" said the King. "And summon the stable boys to take the horses to their stalls."

Halwyn himself ran to Destre, took her reins, and helped Valo slide to the ground.

"Here, Valo. Lean on me," said the King. And the very short, plump King put his arm around his very tall, very tired Captain of the Guard, and walked him to one of the tables in the courtyard.

Eliana saw King Halwyn serve Valo an immense plate of food. Saw him pour him a cup of ale. Saw him sit and wait while Valo and his men ate and drank.

At first Eliana couldn't understand why the King wasn't

shouting questions at the men. Did they find Margred? Her soldiers? What had happened? But then she realized what the King was doing: he was caring for these loyal men first. In some ways, Halwyn now reminded her of her parents, the way they loved, nurtured, and protected her and her siblings.

After the men had eaten their first plate of food, including at least three buns each, Valo leaned forward with his arms on the table.

"We had some trouble finding their trail at first. Margred somehow got out of the castle after you followed her up the stairs, sire. Maybe another hidden stairway?" he glanced at Brogan, who shrugged and shook his head.

Valo continued, "That witch met up with her soldiers who'd gotten by us during the battle. They must've stuck to rocky paths at first because we found no sign of them until we'd searched clear to the White Pony Inn.

"Behind the inn, in some muddy ground by the creek, we found fresh boot prints and drag marks where boats had been pulled into the water. They'd hidden some canoes there, Your Highness. Must have covered them with branches, or the innkeeper would have seen them. Margred had been planning this for a long time."

Eliana could see the muscle in Valo's dark cheek bulging in and out. Not just anger, but also frustration, she realized. *He blames himself for what happened*, she thought.

The King reached over and awkwardly patted Valo's hand that was bunched into a fist.

"You never liked her," said the King. "I should've listened to you. Go on, Valo."

"We couldn't follow the creek on horseback. The water is too deep and the sides too steep where it winds through the forest and grasslands. But the dragons could follow from above." Valo smiled and chuckled a little to himself.

"They searched downstream while we headed east on Kings Road. The horses, sire. They were spent. We had to walk some of the way to Tibbet Mill. We stopped there to let them eat and drink. We owe the innkeeper there some silver, by the way. I hope . . ."

"Don't worry about that," said the King, waving away the concern. "We found the missing treasure."

"What?" said Valo, standing and nearly knocking the table over.

Eliana tapped her foot while the King and Brogan relayed everything having to do with finding the hidden gold, silver, and jewels.

"So, the innkeeper will be paid," said the King, at last. "Continue, Valo."

"The dragons met up with us there, at Tibbet Mill. Since we didn't have a Dragon Speaker with us, we had to rely on yes and no questions. It was a good thing I knew they could understand us." Valo looked over at Winston, who'd come into the courtyard to crouch beside Eliana. The dragon smiled his biggest, toothiest grin at the Captain of the Guard.

"Not sure I'll ever get used to that," said Valo. "Good

thing I know you only eat that disgusting green stuff."

Winston huffed a little steam from his nostrils. "Disgusting?" he said to Eliana. "Steamed, fresh benesaunus . . ."

"Valo, please," said the King.

"The dragons followed Margred and her soldiers downstream. They were moving fast, sire. They'd even passed The Wild Rose by the time the dragons spotted them. We figured all this out by asking questions about the landscape—where streams join the creek, where the creek widens, where the fen begins . . .

"Margred had a ship waiting, Your Highness. A ship with dark sails and that leaf emblem on them. It was just upriver from Cantington Bay. From high above, the dragons saw them boarding, using long oars to maneuver through the drawbridge and set sail up the Pearl.

"The dragons couldn't stop them without attacking the ship. And there were townspeople and Canting Castle guards everywhere. If they'd attacked . . ."

"The old stories about dragons being terrible, bloodthirsty creatures would have appeared to be true," said Halwyn.

The King and Valo sat staring at each other for what seemed to Eliana a long time. She saw what they saw in each other's eyes: defeat and relief.

"So, she is gone," said King Halwyn.

"Let's just hope she stays that way," said Valo.

After everyone had finished every morsel of food and every drop of ale, Brogan—with Tal's help—began directing the cleanup of the courtyard. He gave Doryu a warm robe to put over Jade's shoulders; she'd fallen asleep with her head on one of the tables. The old Dragon Speaker tucked it around her and laid his hand gently on her wispy hair. He crossed to where Eliana stood with Winston.

Doryu pulled Eliana to the side. "I need to take Cook's teacup back to her," he said, patting the cloth bag. "Will you accompany me?"

"Yes! But . . ." she looked over at her parents who were helping Brogan. "I need to ask first."

Doryu smiled and nodded. "I'll wait here," he said.

Weaving through the King's soldiers who were laughing and slapping each other on the back, Eliana finally caught up with Glenna.

"Mother . . ."

Glenna turned then, and a shaft of late western sun lit her face. She smiled, and Eliana saw her, really *saw* her, and how beautiful she was. She threw her arms around her mother, who smelled like bread, herbs, and woodsmoke.

"I'm sorry, Mother."

"I know you are," said Glenna, patting her on the back. "But we were so afraid . . . afraid we'd lost our passionate Eliana. Our amazing, funny, adventurous daughter."

Eliana's smiled, as her happy tears dampened Glenna's blouse. She knew now that she wasn't just the child in the middle, the invisible, nothing-special one. Her mother's words unlocked memories of her parents laughing at the stories she told about Owen, the sheep's "watch mule," listening in rapt attention to the poems and songs she made up, letting her take the cart into the village by herself. *I am not just one of their children,* she thought. *They really see me.*

"Did you want something, Eliana?"

Eliana smiled up at her mother, vowing once again to at least *try* to avoid adding more lines to her face. Remembering the old Dragon Speaker's invitation, she asked, "Doryu wants me to go with him to the castle kitchen. May I?"

"Just don't take too long," said Glenna, kissing her forehead.

Eliana and Doryu made their way up the Grand Staircase to the rampart on the main castle level and then into a corridor lit by a few torches. Eliana felt small. And cold.

I'm glad I live in our cozy home, she thought as they continued down the corridor to the kitchen.

The kitchen was more inviting than the rest of the castle, with its long wooden table, delicious smells, and blazing fire. The woman who must have been Cook was stirring something in an iron pot hung over the fire. On the table were more buns as well as three cloth-wrapped bundles. A walking stick leaned against one of the benches.

"Ah, Doryu. Eliana. The two Dragon Speakers. You've brought back my teacup. I knew you would, once all the hubbub over finding the treasure had died down." She took the cloth bag from Doryu and removed her teacup.

Eliana frowned; how did she know *she* was a Dragon Speaker?

"Oh, what's this?" asked Cook.

Eliana and Doryu leaned forward to see what she was looking at in the teacup.

"That must have dropped from the King's pocket. Or one of the boys," said Doryu. "Strange . . ."

Sitting in the bottom of the teacup was a single red jewel.

"That looks like the one that was in the King's sword," said Doryu.

"It looks like the stone woven in my father's leather bracelet," said Eliana.

Cook tipped the cup so that the jewel rolled from one side to the other. And when it did, the light from the fire filled the cup.

And then, the blue design on the side of the cup turned red.

And the design swirled and danced and . . .

Cook tipped the jewel into her hand. Smiling, she turned to set the cup on a narrow shelf jutting from the rock wall beside the fireplace. Eliana thought she saw Cook slip the red stone into her apron pocket.

"Are you going someplace?" asked Doryu, nodding to the bundles and walking stick. Eliana decided she must have imagined what had happened with the red stone and the fire, or surely he would have said something.

"Yes," Cook answered. "My daughter's having her baby tonight. A boy. My grandson!" Her golden eyes sparkled in the firelight. "And that teacup will be right here waiting for him, for when he's ready."

Cook turned, bent down, and looked directly into Eliana's eyes.

"They live at The Wild Rose, Eliana. My daughter is the innkeeper's wife. You'll want to visit my grandson someday, I'm sure."

"But . . ." said Eliana.

"Go along now, both of you," said Cook, with a little flick of her reddened hands. "And take these buns with you. Everything else will wait for another time."

Eliana and Doryu made their way out of the kitchen and into the corridor, which felt even colder than before after the warmth of the kitchen. Eliana glanced back. Cook stood just inside the kitchen, the light from the fire forming a red halo around her.

Had Eliana really seen the designs in the cup turn red and start to swirl? Why hadn't Cook said anything about it? There was something strange about her. Strange and powerful. How did she know her daughter was having a boy? Eliana's thoughts were interrupted just then when Doryu came alongside her and touched her elbow. She stopped and looked into his smiling, wrinkled face.

"Being a Dragon Speaker is a gift, Eliana," he said. "A gift that may bring adventures and even a comfortable life for you and your family. I was your age when I discovered what

I was. But I had no one to guide me. To warn me. In fact, I used my gift to participate in a great evil. Evil for which I can only try to atone."

"Evil? What . . . ?"

"I'll share with you all I have done and all I have learned if you'll allow me. I would like to offer you an apprenticeship, a Dragon Speaker apprenticeship."

"Yes, oh yes!" breathed Eliana. "But I'm only twelve. And the cost . . ."

"I believe King Halwyn will make an exception in this case. And the only cost will be your company."

"My parents . . ." *Was this really happening?* It was just a few days ago that she thought nothing exciting ever happened to her.

"I'll come speak with your parents soon. I'm sure Valo and Destre won't mind bringing me." Doryu paused, then spoke again. "Do you think you can find your way back to the courtyard? Cook and I have some things to discuss before she leaves."

"Yes, I think so," said Eliana. She watched the old Dragon Speaker as he went back into the kitchen. An apprenticeship! She made her way to the courtyard, her mind whirling with all that had happened since she'd met a dragon in the forest.

Eliana found her family and Winston waiting by the courtyard gate. The boys and Alethia were already asleep in the back of the cart. Cadoc held Owen's reins in his hands. Glenna was dozing with her head on her father's shoulder. Eliana decided tomorrow would be soon enough to talk with them about what Doryu had offered.

Winston nudged her, so she put her hand on his beautiful scales again. "He said I could take you back to your home, Eliana! A night flight!"

Eliana whirled to look at her father. "We can fly?" she asked.

"We'll see you at home," said Cadoc, smiling at her as he twitched the reins. Owen took off at a trot, seemingly glad to be as far away from Winston as possible.

"Home," she whispered, watching the cart grow smaller as it headed down the road through the village. "The best journey *sometimes* does lead home."

As Winston flew above the forest, the full moon hung like a silver platter in the dark sky. A few striated clouds hung below the moon, reminding Eliana of finely wrought lace. The tops of the trees rippled in a slight breeze, a vast ocean of blue-green leaves spreading as far as they could see. As before, when they flew together this way, they could communicate without words.

We found him, Eliana. We found my father, said Winston.

And we helped free Tal's father and Jade, said Eliana.

And we chased Margred and her soldiers away.

And the jewels, said Eliana. *The King got his jewels back.*

And Doryu asked me to be his apprentice. A Dragon Speaker apprentice. She leaned forward to lay her cheek on Winston's neck, wondering at all she might learn about dragons from the old Dragon Speaker.

I'll teach you about dragons, too, said Winston. Eliana laughed.

Yes, I know you will, she said. The air rushing past her face pushed happy tears into her ears, but she couldn't let go to wipe them away.

Eliana let the wind push her tangled curls out of her eyes. That was when she saw far in the distance, brushed by moonlight, the Black Mountains. Range after craggy range, a barrier between what she knew of the world and what lay beyond. Beyond the Black Mountains.

Maybe Winston and I will go there someday, she thought. *Maybe my true north lies there.*

What's true north, Eliana? Winston asked.

True north is finding our way without getting pulled off course by the wrong things. We just have to figure out the right course. For both of us, said Eliana.

Winston dipped his left wing and turned in a slow, gentle loop that took them away from Kings Road and out over the ocean. Eliana could feel him pondering all she'd said.

We'll do it together, Winston, she said. *We're friends now. Best friends.*

Forever? asked the dragon.

Forever, answered the girl.

END

Discussion Questions

1. Who is your favorite character? Why?
2. This story is seen through the eyes of four different characters: Eliana, Winston, King Halwyn, and Doryu. Did you like the fact that the book is written that way? Why or why not?
3. Which character is the most like you? In what ways?
4. In the first chapter, we learn that Eliana is forbidden to go into the forest alone. What would you do if you heard rustling and saw glints of emerald and turquoise in the woods?
5. Are the physical characteristics and behaviors of the dragons surprising to you? If so, in what ways?
6. Did you get a feeling early on that Margred is evil? What did the author do to give you that impression?
7. How did Margred use the humans' ignorance about dragons to further her own means?
8. Are the maps and castle diagrams useful? In what ways?
9. Why do you think the book is called *True North*?
10. The author says that whatever she writes must be *true*, whether it is *real* or not? What do you think she means by that?

Acknowledgments

Recipe for a Novel:

- Put all the author's life experiences in a (very) large bowl. Be sure to include all the people who influenced her, encouraged her, loved her.
- Mix in all the books and stories she's ever read, including books about writing.
- Add a measure of creative writing classes, writing coaches, and writing conferences.
- Sift in grandchildren (who are supposed to be asleep) saying, "Tell us a story!"
- Stir carefully, using an olivewood spoon, adding posts and DMs from social media friends as needed.
- Pour into an old, battered cake pan and bake for three or four years.
- Test for doneness using beta readers and a stellar editor.
- When cool, frost with an amazing cover.

My heartfelt thanks to:

- Eden and Kate, who asked, "Tell us a story" and then became consultants throughout the journey.
- Alexa and Mason, who promise to read the finished book.
- Lisa, who was my companion on writing retreats, who drew maps to orient me and my characters, who encouraged me and read multiple versions, and without whom this book never would have seen the light of day.
- Leslie, who has always said I had a novel in me and cheered me on along the way, and who can find those little annoying typos that remain even after multiple reads.

- William, who encouraged me to pursue hybrid publishing, even offering financial support.
- Christa, who identifies plot holes in everything I write and who encouraged me to slow down and take the time the story needed.
- Randy, who told me to go for it.
- Scott, for helping me zero in on how the characters grew and changed.
- Jerry and Nancy, who patiently listened to me talk about the book ad nauseam.
- Teachers and writing coaches, who encouraged and nudged me to be better.
- Holly and Jessica T. from Acorn, whom I met at a writing conference so long ago and who told me they would love to have me as one of their Acorn authors.
- Jessica H., who kept calm and carried on despite my multiple questions.
- My editor, Lindsey C., whose input on word level, sentence level, and big picture aspects was invaluable, and who sweetly pointed out how many words indicating size I used.
- My beta readers: Lisa, Leslie, William, Rod, Joe, Emily, Sally, Randy, Christa, Eden, Kate, and Betsy.
- Ruth Hunter, artist extraordinaire for the interior maps and art.
- My Launch Team—Leslie, Grace, Joe, and Jennifer—who keep saying I can do this.
- Riv and Leslie F., who helped with last minute fine tuning.
- Readers, teachers, librarians, bloggers, reviewers, and booksellers. You form the world in which this book will live. Thank you!
- Educators, librarians, parents, grandparents, and everyone else who encourages kids to read and who reads to them, takes them to the library, sets up little free libraries, and buys them books. And those who listen to and read (with rapt attention) the stories they create.
- And finally, to God, from whom all blessings flow.

Author Bio

At six years old, Laura Findley Evans wrote her first story about a man named Brill who flew to the moon. When her teacher asked her to stand up and read it to the class, she learned just how powerful a story can be. A creative writing major, she has written many more short stories. *The Dragon and the Girl: True North* is her first novel. It began when her grandchildren said one night (when they were supposed to be sleeping), "Tell us a story." And so she did. Laura would like you to know that whatever she writes must be true, whether it is real or not. She hopes you will discover truth in this story. You can visit her online at www.LauraFindleyEvans.com, where full-color versions of the maps are posted.

Susie Bakonis Photography